BACK CRACK BOY

This story is set in the rough, tough and destitute Merseyside of the 1930s. We see life as it was seen through the eyes of Liam, the child of a working-class family, whose guiding advice from his father was stark and simple: "Fight yer own bloody battles!"

Despite their appalling poverty, life was not all misery for Liam and his family; on the contrary, as we quickly learn, life with the gang was sometimes hilarious. We are introduced to the delicate art of pawn-shop economy; to grid fishing; to the horsemuck and pig's bladder trades and to winter warmers. And to key bombs, and other diversions that kept the gang amused. The characters include Dinny, the untouchable, at nine a better fiddler than Nero, and peaceful Uncle Mick, the trouble magnet. And we see the Means Test, and its disastrous effect on family and community life, and finally the vicious riots of 1932 that it caused. Life was never dull!

Joseph McKeown

Back Crack Boy

CORGI BOOKS

BACK CRACK BOY

A CORGI BOOK 0 552 11293 3

First published in Great Britain by Robert Hale Ltd.

PRINTING HISTORY
Robert Hale edition published 1978
Corgi edition published 1980
Corgi edition reissued 1986

Corgi Books are published by Transworld Publishers Ltd., Century House, 61-63 Uxbridge Road, Ealing, London W5 5SA, in Australia by Transworld Publishers (Aust.) Pty. Ltd., 26 Harley Crescent, Condell Park, NSW 2200, and in New Zealand by Transworld Publishers (N.Z.) Ltd., Cnr. Moselle and Waipareira Avenues, Henderson, Auckland.

Made and printed in Great Britain by
Hunt Barnard Printing Ltd., Aylesbury, Bucks.

Dedicated to the memory of
My Mother.

FOREWORD

My name is Liam, by circumstances a nobody, born on Merseyside in one of the roughest and most destitute periods of its history. An era in which comedy walked hand in hand with stark tragedy. When life revolved around the pawnshop, and when to work was millenium.

I

Lost and Found

I have no real memories of my first few years, just a series of fleeting impressions. The cold brick of the kitchen floor striking harshly against my bare backside. The glow of the kitchen fire in wintertime as it reflected from the glistening blackleaded grate. A sunbeam streaming through the narrow fanlight then shattering into a million coloured lights against the wall as it passed through the two ornamental 'glitters' on the sideboard.

These were years of faces and figures only. Flitting constantly in and out amid a Babylonian chatter. This is the lasting impression. *Noise.* Strident or subdued, depending on the time of day, but always a background of noise. High pitched laughter, jarring with startling suddenness. Horses dragging clanking carts down the cobbled streets. Ships' sirens, ranging from the fussy, irritating whoops of the tugs, to the sonorous bellow of huge liners as they navigated the turgid brown waters of the Mersey less than a quarter of a mile away.

The world was never still, and in the centre of it all, my linchpin, my mother. Small trim and ceaslessly active. Never far from my immediate orbit. My father is a shadow in these early years. He came and went, sometimes clean, sometimes coal-black from his work among the oil and grease of the shipyards. But his presence was always fleeting, a quick chuck under the chin, a few unintelligible words, perhaps a thorny hand affectionately rubbing the top of my head, and he was gone. My brother Con, far above my lowly state, wrapped up in his own mysterious world, ignored me completely. Only once do I remember him showing a direct interest, when my mother invited him to examine my newly acquired teeth. I bit him, and again his interest waned. On the other hand my sisters almost suffocated me with affection, especially Teresa, and I learned to look forward to the nightly bath on the kitchen table, or in the sink when they howled with laughter as they tried to hold my slippery body.

But my mother was the first person I fixed with certainty. She was the centre around which all else revolved, so long as I could see her, or hear her, nothing else mattered. Gradually from the continuous stream of relatives and friends, other shapes appeared frequently enough for me to identify. Aunt Aggie was the first. I dreaded her, and each time I recognised the familiar rustle of her long black dress, I dived for safety under the table, but there was no escape. I would be swept up in her powerful arms, and crushed unmercifully against the unyielding whalebone of her stays. Others come crowding in. Uncle Tom, her jovial husband. Short and round with a long curling moustache, he smoked his clay pipe interminably. Then of course there was Mrs. Taylor. I was never quite sure whether she was one of us or not, so often was she in the house. But though I liked her cheery face, I disliked intensely the full red lips that smacked incessantly against my cheek every time she entered the kitchen. But even when I got teeth I never bit her as I did most of the others.

Time passed swiftly; soon the dresses of babyhood, worn by both girls and boys alike, changed into knitted breeches and a short smock. My name, Liam, became familiar to me through constant repetition. Uttered short and sharp when I did wrong, which was often, soft and lilting when Mam was in a good mood. Admonishing wags of her finger when I did wrong swiftly developed into a sharp tap on the back of the hand, then all too soon, an even sharper slap on the bare backside.

I distinctly remember the day I was breeched, because within minutes of acquiring the new garments I headed for the stairs and came crashing down. I remember I felt resentful of the fuss and baby talk that greeted the mishap. From breeching it was a short step to exploring beyond the front door for which I headed at every opportunity. Soon I was on chatting terms with all sorts of people on both sides of the street. Women sandstoning their front steps especially intrigued me and I would stand for hours if allowed, just watching them scrubbing away, until both the step and the pavement immediately in front of the houses shone.

For the first time I came in free contact with the other small denizens that crowded the streets as their mothers worked indoors, and tentative friendships formed during our long, unintelligible conversations. More and more often I accompanied my mother and sisters on shopping expeditions without the push-chair to which, until now I had been condemned. I suppose I must have been about three when Teresa took me to an entirely new district on such an expedition. Mother's instructions to her were crystal clear as she lectured her in the hot sunshine outside the front door before we went.

"Now keep y' eye on 'im," she said as she replaced a straying hair. "Are y' listenin'?" Her voice sharpened, and I watched her face suddenly harden slightly as my sister's attention wandered momentarily.

"I 'eard y', Mam, honest I did!" Alarm sounded in Teresa's voice as she saw a glint in the grey eyes. "I'll watch 'im, don't worry."

"You'd berra," snapped Mam. "Now y' know what y' goin' for?"

Teresa nodded as I shifted uncomfortably in my breeks and smock. The heat had already begun to prickle.

"All right then," said Mam, wagging her finger at me as we prepared to go. "You be a good lad now, d'y' 'ear?" I pursed my lips and said nothing as Teresa jerked my arm and started off.

A vague uneasiness overtook me as we left the familiar streets, and I gazed suspiciously around me as I encountered the blaring noise of the main shopping centre. I felt hot and frightened, my legs were like lead, and my arm almost out of its socket as she dragged me more and more impatiently along.

"Come on, Liam, 'urry up, I've gorra lot t' do," she urged. My lip quivered; I began to howl. I wanted my

Mam. Teresa shook my arm irritably, "Now shurrup!" she snapped, "Y' can't go 'ome yet."

"I want me Mam! I want me Mam!" I chorused between yells as she hauled me along, her long plaits bobbing like two donkeys' tails down the straight back.

"I want. . . ." Slam!, her small hand connected sharply with my bottom.

"Now shurrup," she yelled, "or I'll give y' t' that man over there." She pointed to where a red-faced fishmonger was busily chopping the heads off some fish. I took one terrified look through the open window and howled even louder. People stopped momentarily on the crowded pavement to look sympathetically at her.

"What's the marrer, luv?" asked a thin, hawk-faced woman, bending down and peering suspiciously at me as I plonked myself on the pavement. " 'as 'e wet 'iself?"

Teresa shook my aching arm irritably as she almost snapped the woman's head off.

"No 'e 'asn't wet 'iself . . . 'e's cryin' that's all . . . 'e wants 'is Mam."

"All right luv," replied the woman testily, "I was only askin'. There's no need t' snap me bloody 'ead off." She tossed her head, "*Kids*!", she exclaimed as she hitched her bulging shopping bags more comfortably then stalked off muttering to herself.

"There," snapped Teresa, very much like my Mam as she bent down and glared at me, "see what you've done? People are lukin'."

I didn't care who looked, and I didn't care if they thought I had wet myself. I wanted my Mam.

By this time half the shopping centre were pausing to have a look at us as my sister stamped her small foot in exasperation. Suddenly a high-pitched squeaky voice sounded behind me, and I twisted round to see a thin, freckle-faced girl of about Teresa's age, staring at us as she sucked a huge toffee apple. I eyed it greedily.

"Hi, Teresa," she said, momentarily removing the toffee apple from her sticky lips.

"What's up with your Liam? . . . 'as 'e wet 'iself?"

Teresa missed my outstretched hand by a fraction as she stamped her foot.

"*No!*, 'e 'asn't wet 'iself," she exploded. "Everybody keeps askin' if 'e's wet 'iself ... why?" she asked the world at large.

The newcomer waved her toffee apple nonchalantly.

"Well," she said authoritatively, "kids allus 'owl when they wet theirselves. Our Michael does anyway, 'e's allus doin' it," she added by way of proof.

"I don't care what your Michael does, Annie Rogers," snapped Teresa indignantly, "Our Liam doesn't."

"Well, what's 'e cryin' for then?" asked Annie, gazing at me disgustedly.

" 'e wants t' go 'ome an' 'e can't," answered my sister as she bent down and gave me another shake.

"Well, why can't y' take 'im then?" persisted Annie between licks at the glistening apple.

" 'Cause I can't that's why," snapped Teresa. "I'm on a message for me Mam."

"What for?" asked Annie, rapidly losing interest in me as a point of conversation.

"Wool," answered Teresa laconically. "An' she'll skin me if I go back without it." Suddenly her face brightened.

"Hey, Annie," she said. "I'll tell y' what. You watch 'im for a minute while I go inter Barney's." She nodded to a large drapers immediately behind us. Annie remained silent and I watched her enviously as she licked the toffee apple reflectively. At last she shook her head slowly.

"Aw, I dunno, Teresa," she said, gazing at me with obvious dislike. " 'ow long'll y' be?"

"I won't be a minute, honest I won't," answered my sister pleadingly, then she bent down to gaze fixedly into my tear-dimmed eyes. "You'll be all right won't y', Li?" She gave my shoulder a sharp jolt to emphasise the point. I said nothing as the hot sun beat down unmercifully on me, but my lip quivered and the corners of my mouth turned down.

"Now don't start agin!" she snapped, recognising the danger signals. "You be a good lad now, d'y' 'ear? I won't be long." My hand was transferred to the reluctant Annie's.

"*Kids!*" said Annie venomously as Teresa departed towards the shop.

For a few minutes Annie and I maintained a dignified silence. I felt as though I were in an oven. Suddenly I wanted my Mam more than anything. I began to shriek at the top of my voice. Annie did her best. She offered to let me lick her toffee apple, but I had long passed this point. She took a different tack.

"Ah, there's a good lad then," she cooed, squatting on her haunches and ignoring the inconvenience to the passing crowds. "Luk at that funny man," she said pointing to a poor wretch limping past with a deformed shoulder and leg, in an effort to entertain me. The funny man left me cold.

"Come on," she suggested, a note of desperation in her voice, "Let's play 'Ring aring a roses!" and suiting the action to the words, her spindly legs began to gyrate as she yanked me unceremoniously to my feet, bumping from one irate shopper to the next as she swung me madly around. I felt terrible. Sweat vied with tears as they poured down my smock.

"Hey Annie!, what y' doin'?" The dance stopped as suddenly as it had begun and I went sprawling in the gutter as Annie let go and faced the squat, fat newcomer.

"Waddee yer think?" she snapped, wiping the perspiration from her forehead. I sat and stared dumbly at the newcomer as she chewed the end of her plait meditatively.

" 'oo's that anyway?" she asked, flicking her thumb at me. Annie looked first at me then the newcomer. She clucked disgustedly.

"It's Teresa's brother ... She's in there." She nodded towards the shop. "I'm mindin' 'im," she added to clarify the situation.

"Aw," said our new companion non-committally.

Thankful that the dance had stopped I plonked myself gratefully on the pavement while the two girls chatted.

All around me moved a forest of legs and swinging baskets. I fell into a semi-trance. Once or twice I glanced up but the girls seemed to have forgotten me, nor was there yet any sign of my sister. Thankfully I resumed my inspection of my surroundings.

How or when they moved I didn't know, but when I next glanced upward there was no sign of either Annie's spindly legs or the newcomer's fat ones. For a moment or two I just sat, not knowing quite what to do, then I spotted Annie a short distance away, looking in the window of a greengrocer's. Immediately I got to my feet and wobbled towards her. She turned. The legs were spindly, but the face had no freckles. It wasn't Annie. Curiously I peered among the moving crowd. Relief flooded through me. There she was, just going into the little bakery shop across the road. I stepped off the kerb. A sudden scream rent the hot air, as I cowered back from the hooves of a slithering carthouse as it skidded to a halt almost on top of me. I felt myself snatched high into the air.

"Holy Mother'f God!, I thought 'e was a goner," a harsh voice rasped in my ear. "Are y' all right, young feller?" I gazed in awe at the bearded face less than two inches from mine. "Where's y' Mam?" the face asked. Remembering Teresa's strict instructions I pointed dumbly to the corner shop where I thought Annie was.

"Some people don't care what 'appens to their kids!" A high-pitched female voice, not unlike Aunt Aggie's, broke in on the coversation, but it faded immediately as my bearded friend carried me swiftly across the road and dumped me in the shop doorway.

"Now you be careful, young feller". The soft friendly voice fell on my ear. I felt a sharp tap on the backside as he propelled me into the shop. "Go to y' mam now … go on". The voice and beard vanished. And so had Annie. I howled again, and this time I *was* wet.

For what seemed an age I wandered in and out of the shops, dodging feet, getting knocked down, picked up, and knocked down again. I was fed up. I gave up looking for both Annie and my sister; I was going home. Again I crossed a road, a quieter one this time, then another.

At last I recognised some houses and wandered down a narrow street. Again I was wrong. Suddenly blind panic overtook me. I realised I was lost and wanted to let the whole world know about it. I sat and howled as I had never howled before.

For some minutes nothing happened, not a person appeared on the street, not a door opened. I might as well have been in a different world to the shopping centre just a short distance away. I sat on the pavement and looked at the silent houses, tears trickling down my cheeks. Oh how I wanted my Mam. Even Aunt Aggie would have been welcome at that moment. But nothing moved.

I have no idea how long I sat petrified with fear but suddenly across the road and directly opposite, a curtain moved and a face pressed flat against the glass. As quickly as it appeared it vanished, but something of my misery must have conveyed itself to the owner. Seconds later the door opened and a short, heavily built woman appeared on the step and eyed me with quiet malevolence.

"Stop that bloody 'ollerin' there!" she roared suddenly. Her high-pitched screeching voice hit me like an icy blast, and although not sure of the words, the tone reminded me very much of my mother's when I was up to something I shouldn't be. I shut up like a clam, and sat there, bottom roasting on the pavement, not knowing what to expect.

For a long moment we stared at each other in silence. Me with my lip quivering. She with her arms folded across an ample chest. Without warning she began to lumber towards me, and the nearer she got the less I liked her. I opened my mouth again, but before the first shriek had properly formed, she wagged her podgy finger at me and her eyes glinted menacingly. I buttoned my lip and gave myself up to fate.

"What's y' name?" Her shadow was cast over me like an evil spell as she stood with her enormous feet splayed in front of me. I shook my head and pursed my lips.

"Hmn, can't y' talk?" she snapped irritably, her lank, greying hair falling across her face as she leaned with infinite menance towards me. I gave up.

"Li-am", I faltered.

"Liam what?" she asked, her face softening a little.

"Liam Sullivan", I blurted out in a rush. I was on safe

ground because I had repeated this scores of times for the entertainment of visiting relatives.

"Y' don' live 'ere do y'?"

Silly question, of course I didn't, I was lost. I ignored this and shook my head.

"Where d'y' live then eh? ... Where's y' Mam'"

If I knew that I wouldn't be sitting there talking to her. Again I shook my head. She blew through her full lips in exasperation as she straightened up. For a second or two her round fat face twisted in pain as she held her back with one hand.

"Cor!", she exclaimed, momentarily losing interest in me as she eased her aching back. I sat looking forlornly at her. At last she bent down and grasped me with her moist hand.

"Come on, young feller, you'd berra come with me." She began to tow me across the road. I didn't like the look of her but I was too terrified to object, and together we covered the short distance to her front door, then down a narrow hallway smelling strongly of onions and into a dimly lit back kitchen, where a tall thin man with a drooping moustache and melancholy face sat, braces hanging loosely down his trousers, sipping noisily from a mug of tea near the empty fire.

"Is that you, 'ild?" The rasping voice greeted us as we crossed the threshold.

" 'oo did y' think it was?" she snapped as she urged me into the room. "Ol' Nick?"

His watery blue eyes widened in astonishment as he spotted me for the first time.

"What y' got there, 'ild?" he asked, with the mug half way to his lips.

"What's it luk like?" she answered sarcastically as she pointed to me. "A duck!?"

I glanced apprehensively from one to the other. Their harsh voices made me uneasy. My lip began to quiver again as the man rose and come towards me, hands outstretched, lips drawn back over yellowing teeth in a ghastly smile. I couldn't stand it. Panic overwhelmed me as I shrank towards the door yelling for my mother at the top of my voice. The woman's face screwed in annoyance as she waved her husband back to his seat irritably.

"There", she snapped. "Now luk what you've done. Started 'im off agin. Honest, y' face'd stop a clock, let alone frighten a kid ... siddown f'God's sake ... Shush," she added more gently, turning to me. " 'e ain't gonna eat y' luv." I wish I had had her faith, but I quietened down and watched her hungrily as she waddled to the table and started cutting a slice of bread. Suddenly it seemed years since I had last eaten.

" 'oo is 'e?" asked her husband, seated once more but still scrutinising me.

" 'ow the 'ell should I know?" she replied, buttering, then dipping the bread in the sugar bowl. " 'e was sittin' out there 'ollerin' like a stuck pig. 'e must be lost."

Her husband's voice filled with sympathy as he sat, meditatively twirling the end of his moustache.

"Aaah!, y' poor little sod. Are y' lost then?" he said leaning towards me in concern. I just nodded miserably. He turned to his wife.

"Don't y' know 'im then?" She gave him a withering look.

"If I knew 'im 'e wouldn't be lost would 'e?" she replied.

He shrugged. "Suppose not," he answered lamely.

She looked at me for a moment or two in silence. The sugar butty dangled invitingly. My eyes glistened expectantly.

"Aah luk," she said, her voice filling with softness. " 'e's 'ungry."

She held out the butty. I took it gratefully and sank my teeth into it as she led me to a battered horsehair settee against the wall.

"You sit there luv an' get stuck inter that," she said, affectionately patting my head, "while I think what t' do with y'."

For a few minutes they sat quietly talking to each other whilst I munched contentedly at the bread. I felt much better for the unexpected meal, and I was still sucking the remains of the sugar from my fingers when they both came over to me. I caught the last few words as they crossed the room.

"You'll 'ave t' take 'im to the Bridewell," said the man as he came and sat down beside me. "Let the Scuffers luk after 'im ... Cor," he added, "I'll bet 'is Mam an' Dad's goin' mad lukin' for 'im."

His wife nodded.

"Per'aps 'es got 'is name an' address sewn in 'is smock?" she suggested, reaching towards me with her thick fingers. I recoiled instinctively, but relaxed at once as her podgy face crinkled into a smile. My smock was open and examined without result, but her fingers touched the chain I had worn round my neck as long as I could remember.

" 'ello, what's this?" she said, pulling the chain out and examining the holy medal at the end of it. For a moment or two she peered at it silently, screwing her eyes in an effort to read the inscription on the back. At last she looked up at her husband. She flicked her head at me. " 'e's one of *them*," she said laconically.

I looked at her puzzled.

"Y'know," she said nudging him on the arm confidentially. "One of them Romans."

Understanding dawned in his eyes. "Oh," he said meaningfully. "One 'a that lot eh ... a Catholic."

I looked first at one, then the other. I had no idea what they were talking about. I didn't look any different from them, but they said I was so I must have been. I felt vaguely uncomfortable. She was still fiddling with the medal trying to read it when her husband interrupted her.

" 'er, 'ild, give it me. Let's 'ave a decko at it ... Where's me glasses?"

She handed him his spectacles from the sideboard, and I twisted my neck obligingly as he turned the medal this way and that to get a better look.

"Hey, 'ild, listen t' this 'ere," he said as he caught the fading light. " 'I am a Catholic', it says. 'In case of accident or injury, send for the nearest Catholic priest'."

"Go on," she said disbelievingly, "fancy that. Still," she added darkly, "they're a funny lot arn't they?"

Her husband nodded agreement. That was two things I

had learned by getting lost. I was a Catholic, and we were a funny lot. I stored this up in my mind for future reference.

"Well that's that then, isn't it?" she said at last. "There's no need t' take 'im t' the Bridewell. You cin just take 'im t' that Father fella down the road. ..."

Instantly her husband bridled.

"I'm not goin' near that damn place!" he snapped, dropping the medal as though it had suddenly become red hot. "No thank *you!* ... You found 'im, you take 'im."

"What's up with you?" she asked in astonishment. "Any one'd think they were gonna eat y'. All y' gorra do is ring the bell an' bung 'im in, then they'll see to 'im."

He was adamant. "You take 'im," he said curtly, "I won't."

He did though. We approached the church as though it was an enemy outpost. Young as I was I could feel the tension in the hand that gripped mine. At last we arrived and he jabbed his finger on the bell-push. We were not kept waiting long. A motherly looking lady with almost pure white hair opened the door, and her eyes sparkled with recognition as soon as she saw my companion.

"Well, I'll go to our 'ouse," she exclaimed in a voice tinkling with humour, "Jimmy Driscoll! I never thought I'd live t' see the day when *you* came to the priest's house. What is it y' want?" she added as my companion shifted uneasily from one foot to the other. "Conversion, or the Pledge?"

"I want the Father," he answered edgily.

"Which one?" she asked lightly, "we've four of 'em 'ere."

"The red 'aired feller," he said truculently.

The housekeeper bridled.

"His reverence if y' please, Driscoll ... His Reverence!"

"You know damned well which one I mean, Hanagan," he snapped, "the Father, the proper one!"

"They're all proper 'ere, Driscoll, but I'll see if 'e's in."

She turned and vanished indoors, leaving us standing on the step. My companion gave me a look of intense dislike. Moments later relief flooded through me as I recognised the familiar broad-shouldered, sandy-haired figure of Father McCormack. His eyes twinkled as I flung myself at the hem of his cassock and was swept immediately into his arms.

" 'e's one of yours," said Driscoll, uneasiness in his voice as he found himself face to face with the priest.

A supressed titter came from the darkened hallway as Father replied archly, "One of *mine* Driscoll? You can't be serious?"

Driscoll looked puzzled for a moment then flushed.

"You know what I mean," he snapped, pointing to the medal still hanging out of my smock. "Anyway I'm off." He turned before the priest could thank him and vanished quickly through the churchyard.

The next hour was sheer joy. Mrs Hanagan fretted and fussed as she washed and tidied me up, then gave me a huge glass of milk. Almost before I knew what was happening my mother appeared as though by magic, nearly suffocating me as she hugged me in relief. It was all over, I had had my first real glimpse at the frightening world. I had learned a lot. So had Teresa, Mam had waled the daylights out of her. I also learned, years later, the reason for Mr Driscoll's reluctance to take me. He was a red-hot Orangeman from Northern Ireland which explained much that I didn't understand at the time.

2

Photo Finish

I wish it were possible for me to record some shattering experience to fill the void between meeting Mr Driscoll, and the photographic session that was to have such dire consequences for family relations, but I cannot.

Life hummed along with gentle monotony. At three, as the record shows, I got myself lost. From there onwards alas, I grew not in beauty but in perfidy. Nature refused to blossom along the desired lines, stubbornness clothed me like an armour, and repeated thumps failed to dislodge it. I was rechristened 'A Pig's Melt' by Aunt Aggie whatever that meant. I was not a lovable child. At three and a half I was bitten by a dog of obvious good judgement. At four I vented my growing frustrations by swatting flies, an occupation I pursued with fanatical zest all through the summer with the aid of a small Indian club given to me by my Uncle Matt. Unfortunately the files landed on window panes as well as window sills, and Dad had to replace three before he upended me and taught me the difference.

At five and a bit, the moment arrived that I had dreaded for months. I was hauled before the flint-eyed headmaster of 'Our Lady and the English Martyrs', our appropriately named school, and sentenced to nine years hard. There was no appeal. Prompt at nine on the Monday morning following the Easter Holidays in 1925, I was marched, no dragged to the grim grey walls and the gates clanged behind me as I joined the ranks of the condemned.

The most significant change in my life, as the years gathered momentum and began to speed away, was in my relations with those around me, especially my relatives. Outdoors, and at school, life was fairly simple, I held my own with those of my own age and size, and kept clear of the bigger boys until I could cope with them. Indoors it was entirely different. My mother I both loved and feared. I could sense her every mood by the flicker of her mobile face, the flash in her grey eyes, the nervous gestures of her workworn hands. I walked softly in her presence. Dad remained a fleeting shadow, sometimes in a good mood, sometimes bad, but always in transit. I began to notice that he came home less and less with the oil and grease of the shipyard on him. Strangely this did not seem to please my mother very much. Con, as always remained aloof, though occasionally he did condescend to speak to me.

'Li fetch this', or 'Li do that' I never argued with Con, he had a quick temper like my mother, but I learnt quickly that there were other ways of arguing. A cinder in the toe of his shoe. A spider in his favourite cup, sometimes had the most gratifying results. Bernadette, my elder sister, seemed to grow colder after I discovered her meeting a mysterious stranger each morning on her way to work. Her answers to my pointed questions became furtive. She even threatened to cut my liver out if I mentioned it to my mother. I didn't know what liver was, but the look on her face when she said it gave me the impression that it wouldn't have done me much good, so I kept my own counsel.

Only Teresa remained as always as she dressed both myself and Mick, our cat, in all sorts of outlandish clothes before I went to bed each night.

With my aunts and uncles, of whom there were legions, my stock rose and fell according to current form. Never high, it sometimes sank low enough to justify liquidation. Aunt Min, my mother's youngest sister, was my firm favourite. She never scolded, never wagged her finger at me reprovingly, mainly because within minutes of her arrival she would inevitably nod off to sleep. It was a standing joke that she could sleep on a clothes line. Nothing troubled her.

Uncle Mick and his concertina, when they were both home from sea, were next on my list of favourites. With Uncle Mick, disaster was always just round the corner, and the whole house took on the air of expectancy when he came rolling in. What drew me to him I think was the fact that he disliked his sister, Aunt Aggie, as much as I did, and of them all, she was the only one who actually took up the cudgels on a personal level.

I knew she disliked me, but I shudder to think of her innermost thoughts on the subject. My only consolation was that by the time I started school she had moved to a house several streets away, and our lessening contacts delighted us both.

For several weeks I had managed to avoid her altogether, therefore the shock was all the greater one morning when my mother called me back as I was racing down the yard on my way to school.

"Liam!" Her peremptory tone brought me to a shuddering halt. I made a quick mental appraisal of all my actions since getting up. I was innocent, but it was with a feeling of uneasiness that I returned and opened the kitchen door. She was clearing the breakfast things as I poked my head round.

"What's up, Mam?" I asked defensively. She looked at me with eyebrows raised.

"Nothin's up. I want y' t' go a message that's all".

"What now!?" I asked incredulously glancing at the clock. It was ten to nine, the school was six streets away, at five to Miss McIlroy, a red-haired, flint-eyed spinster of uncertain age, clanged shut the gate and flexed her cane in readiness for the late-comers for morning prayers. My face dropped.

"Can't it wait 'til I gerr'ome at dinner time?" I pleaded.

You cin do it on y' way 'ome," answered my mother with maddening slowness, apparently unaware of my danger. I hopped from one foot to the other, not daring to go until she said so.

"Whaddee yer want then?" She was on to the impatience in my voice like a flash.

"Watch y' tongue!" she snapped menacingly. I bowed my head. I knew that a wrong word, even a look could be fatal.

"Call in at y' Aunty Aggie's on y' way 'ome, an' ask 'er t' lend me 'er nutmeg grater."

"A what?" I asked.

"The nutmeg grater. Y'know, the thing what ..." She waved her hand impatiently. "Oh just ask 'er, she'll know." I groaned inwardly.

"Don't forget now," she called after me as I shot down the yard, with legs going like pistons as I tried to make up vital seconds.

The morning came and went in its usual pattern except that I got the cane sooner than I expected. Then after what seemed hours the home bell went, and I clawed my way through the gate with the rest of the convicts into the noisy street beyond.

I was still running as I rounded the corner to Aunt Aggie's house, and I pulled up in amazement at the sight that greeted me. The small cul-de-sac in which she lived seemed crowded. People chatted and grinned in small groups round their doorsteps, pointing, gesticulating and offering advice of all descriptions to the small round figure of Uncle Tom as he struggled to catch the shifting light with his tiny box camera.

"Sod it!" he kept repeating, as he tried to line it up at a group of my cousins outside the front door. Almost immediately I put my foot in it, as I howled with laughter at their expressions. Everyone of them was standing as though he had been transfixed in a moment between fear and laughter. Aunt Aggie, in the centre of the group, reacted at once. Without moving a muscle she swivelled her eyes in my direction and glowered. I froze and listened to Uncle Tom saying, "Sod it." It was safer.

"All right, all right", he snapped in sudden impatience, "Relax a minute. The damned thing won't go." He began to fiddle with it.

"What's up with it, Tom?" asked a mysterious voice from the edge of the group. Uncle Tom cast the voice a filthy look.

"Per'aps you've got the fil'm in the wrong way round, Tom ..." The rich Irish brogue was cut off in mid sentence as another voice broke in scathingly.

"Use y' noddle, Jimmy, will y'? It only goes in one way."

For once Uncle Tom's placid nature betrayed him as he raised his head and glowered at them. "Why the 'ell don't you fellers shurrup?" he said aggressively. " 'ose bloody camera is it anyway?"

My cousin Johnny, the same age as Con, and built like a bullock, became facetious. "Why don't y' purra penny in it, Dad?" he asked innocently.

Uncle Tom looked up, his brown eyes pools of suppressed fury, but before he could speak Aunt Aggie broke in on the tittering group. She fixed Johnny with a venomous look.

"I'll take y' photo with this in a minute if y' don't shurrup!"

She held her balled fist under his nose threateningly. Johnny gave her a sickly smile.

"I was only kiddin' Mam, honest I was," he said anxiously.

"Well don't!" she snapped.

While Uncle Tom struggled, I gazed up at the group hopefully in case Johnny put his foot in it again, but it was Bridget, the youngest, and the same age as myself, who caught my attention as she squirmed uncomfortably. I had a good idea what was the matter with her, and so had her sister Alice.

"Now don't *you* start!" She almost snapped Bridget's head off as she bent down to take her hand. "What's up with y' anyway?"

Bridget looked at her pleadingly. "I want t' go t' the lav," she answered, wriggling like an eel to avoid disaster.

"You'll 'ave t' wait" snapped Alice, shaking her irritably.

"I can't!" pleaded her sister.

"You'll 'ave to ... luk" she pointed with her free hand to a triumphant Uncle Tom. "Dad's fixed the camera."

Once again he lined them up. "Smile," he said gaily. Aunt Aggie bared her teeth and nestled her massive arms across her bosom. Suddenly he lowered the camera. "What's up with 'er?" he asked pointing at the squirming Bridget.

"Oh she's all right, Dad," answered Alice as she clutched her sister fiercely. Aunt Aggie swivelled her eyes but said nothing. Her look was enough.

"She wants t' go t' the lav," whispered Alice. Her mother's smile remained fixed.

"Then she'll 'ave t' bloodywell wait," she hissed like a ventriloquist's dummy. The whole street seemed to hold its breath as Uncle Tom's finger closed on the trigger.

"All set?" he called. "Say 'cheese'." He was a fraction too late.

Without warning the whole group disintegrated as Bridget, tried beyond endurance, snatched her hand from Alice and vanished like a wraith through the open door behind the group.

"Sod it!" exploded Uncle Tom as he lifted the camera as though he was going to smash it into the ground.

Aunt Aggie's face darkened angrily as the good-natured laughter of the neighbours filled the street. I couldn't have picked a worse moment to approach her, but with my dinner on my mind I walked towards her and tugged at her apron. I started back in fright as she spun round and glared at me like a wounded tigress.

"What the 'ell d'you want?" she roared. I was terrified. My mind went blank.

"Well?" she continued, her anger at last finding a focal point. "Don't stand there gawpin. What d'y' want?" Her voice grated harshly on my ears. Uncle Tom came up behind me as I groped desperately for an answer.

" 'ello, lad, warr'are you doin' 'ere?"

I sighed with relief as I turned away from my Aunt and faced him. "I'm on a message for me Mam." He wasn't listening. His attention was on the camera. Suddenly I felt a vice-like grip on my shoulder as Aunt Aggie twisted me round.

"I asked you a question," she said menacingly. "What is it y' want?"

"I dunno," I answered, eyes on the ground to avoid her gaze. She snorted loudly and diverted Uncle Tom's attention back to me. His eyes lit up.

"Hey, Aggie," he said, full of sudden enthusiasm, "warrabout takin' 'is photo while we're waiting for our Bridget?" I was horrified. Aunt Aggie wasn't keen either.

"What 'im!" she ejaculated scornfully. " 'is face'd crack the damn thing. Luk at 'im," she added disgustedly, " 'e's filthy."

I bridled. "I ain't filthy," I said defiantly as I held my hands out for inspection. "Anyway," I added, "I don't want my photo took."

She fixed me with her eye. "If y' Uncle Tom wants t' take y' photo, you'll 'ave it tuk. ... Stand over there," she ordered pointing to the window sill. Suddenly I remembered what I'd come for.

"Warrabout the nutmeg grater?" I blurted out, scuffing the ground with my foot petulantly.

"Warrar y' talkin' about?" she snapped. "Stand still an' stop fiddlin' with y' gansey."

I stopped pulling a loose thread on my woollen jersey and looked at her defiantly. "The nutmeg grater. That's what me Mam sent me for."

"Oh never mind that, Li," broke in Uncle Tom a little impatiently, "y' cin get that later, just stand there. It won't take a minute."

He walked back a pace or two to get me in focus. I glared at Aunt Aggie as she willed me into stillness. I seethed inwardly. I hated being in the centre of anything. It made me uncomfortable and embarrassed.

"Are y' all right?" called Uncle Tom, squinting down the sight.

Suddenly I rebelled. "I don't want me photo tuk," I yelled making a sudden dart for the entry that ran alongside the house. Johnny was too quick for me. He grabbed me by the scruff of the neck and lifted me bodily back into position.

"Smile," he said quietly, "or me Mam'll 'ave y' lights."

The neighbours grinned expectantly. I glowered and kicked a loose pebble at my feet.

"Come on, Liam," coaxed Uncle Tom good-naturedly, "It won't bite y' lad. Say 'cheese'." Once again he crouched and sighted. Overhead the narrow oblong of sky constantly darkened as a succession of clouds chased each other across the face of a watery sun. Twice he almost made it. The first time I moved. The second a big black cloud blotted out the sun completely, and each time his patience thinned a little. By this time Bridget was back. Why couldn't he take her photo I thought viciously. The sun came out. Aunt Aggie stood less than a foot away on my right. I jumped in fright as her voice hit me like a bullet.

"Stand up, lad!" she roared, "ah' for Christ's sake *smile* will y'."

Sheer stubbornness gave me courage. I put my tongue out as far as it would go and gave her a 'raspberry'. Almost simultaneously the world seemed to crash around my ears. From nowhere a ham-like fist caught me a stinging blow just under the right ear and sent me spinning into the wall.

I dimly remember Uncle Tom's startled voice in the distance as my head rang.

"Aggie! What the 'ell did y' do that for?"

I didn't wait to hear her answer. All my mind was concentrated on putting as much distance between her and myself as soon as possible, and I headed down the narrow entry like a homing pigeon, ignoring frantic calls from the whole family to come back.

Within minutes I was rounding the corner of our own entry, head down, arms going like pistons. I came to a shuddering stop as I crashed full tilt into something soft. A howl of anguish broke my whirling thoughts; moments later I was being shaken like a rat.

"Hey luk out! where the 'ell d'y' think you're goin'?"

The shaking stopped as suddenly as it began as a familiar voice sounded above me.

"Hey, cut it out, Jim. That's our kid!" It was Bernadette. I looked at the stranger as he loosened his hold on my collar. His dark sallow features looked vaguely familiar but I couldn't place him. I kicked out on principle and caught another beauty on the side of the head for my trouble.

"Nice little feller, ain't 'e?" I heard the sarcastic voice as Bernadette took hold of my shoulders and shook me. "What d'y' think you're doin'?" she snarled, "You'll kill y'self tearin' about like that. ... What's up anyway?"

"Nuthin'," I snapped rubbing my ear, "I'm goin' 'ome."

Before she could utter any protest I wriggled free and raced down the entry. There was a heavy thump, followed immediately by a startled voice as I crashed against the kitchen door.

" 'oo the divil's that!?" The door swung open to reveal my mother bending over a pile of washing and my father sitting in his usual place by the fire reading the paper. Her head cocked speculatively to one side as she looked at me.

Now that I had arrived I became filled with uncertainty. I knew instinctively how she would react to the news, and I was already regretting my precipitate action.

"What's up with you?" she asked as I stood rocking on the balls of my feet. I stayed silent not knowing quite what to do.

"Well!" snapped Dad, glancing irritably up from his

paper, "Don't stand there like an idjit. Answer y' Mother."

Still I said nothing. My mother grabbed me and pulled me right into the kitchen, then spotted the red mark under my ear. I looked from one to the other and wished I'd never come home. Her eyes bored into mine as my father waited with growing impatience for my answer.

" 'oo 'it y'?" she snapped, shaking me violently. Still I said nothing.

"We.e.ll?" Dad's voice was full of menace. Suddenly the words came tumbling from my lips.

"Aunty Aggie belted me ... she did ... honest," I blurted.

Incredulous looks passed between them. They belted me when I needed it, but for somebody else to do it ...

"She *what*" said Dad, straightening in his chair.

"She belted me," I answered defiantly, fingering my tingling ear lobe.

"What for?" asked my mother, her face darkening as she examined me. She turned to my father before I could answer. "By the luk of this she gave 'im a right fourpenny one," she said authoritatively. Dad came across to have a look.

"What did y' do?" she asked, turning to me again.

"Nuthin' " I replied sullenly. Dad snorted in disbelief. Much as he disliked Aunt Aggie he knew she wasn't as daft as that.

"Don't be so damned daft," snapped my mother. "She wouldn't 'it y' f' nothin'. Y' must 'ave done somethin'."

Every ounce of stubbornness in me welled to the surface. I was in it up to the neck. It was all or nothing now.

"No," I answered defiantly, "I didn't do nothin'. I jus' stood there an' didn't do nothin' an' she belted me."

Panic welled up. I watched her face. All my fears crystallised as the coarse apron, which she invariably wore when she was washing, was whipped from her trim waist and flung viciously across the back of a chair. Even Dad was startled as he looked at the mask of fury that was her face.

"Warr'are y' doin'?" he asked, apprehension in his voice.

"Waddee y' think? ... I'm gonna see our Aggie that's warr'I'm doin'," she snapped, brushing me to one side as she made to cross the kitchen. Her long skirt tangled in the leg of a chair momentarily baulking her. She picked it up and sent it crashing against the stairs. I cowered back against the wall, suddenly terrified at the fury I had released. Dad chased after her trying to calm her down.

"Now 'ang on, Mary," he pleaded. "Calm y'self down a bit." His voice was a mixture of anger and anxiety. "We don't want no trouble with Aggie."

Mam whirled round, hands on her hips, eyes flashing. "Nobodyd 'its my kids," she snarled. "Fetch me shawl!" she added almost in the same breath. Without thinking, Dad reacted to the order, made his way into the parlour and returned with her outdoor shawl.

I was terrified, I had never seen her as wild as this in my life.

"D'y' want me t' come?" Dad asked diffidently as she swung her shawl across her shoulder with the dexterity of a matador.

"I don't need you t' 'andle Aggie," she snapped. Relief showed on his face. She held her hand out to me. "Come on you," she ordered. With a jerk that almost pulled my arm from its socket we were off.

Up the street we went, my feet pounding the pavement as I tried to keep up with her. Past the tiny corner shop, then a crowd of unemployed hanging hopeful round the pub on the opposite side, and out to the main shopping centre with its incessant noise. Her face was masklike in its intensity. She looked neither right nor left as we clove our way through the crowds. The ordeal was nearly over. A short distance down the main street, then sharp left, and before I was fully aware of it we had arrived.

The street was like a theatre on a first night. Every doorway supported an eager audience. Rows were common in these days of grinding poverty, and the neighbours could sense one coming as a hound sniffs the wind. An audible sigh arose as mother, the leading actress, with me as supporting cast in tow, rounded the corner. Heads nodded in anticipation. Knowing elbows nudged each other quietly as the curtain trembled then rose on the first act.

Of Uncle Tom there was no sign. This was woman trouble, and like Dad he avoided this kind of trouble whenever he could. Seconds after our arrival the decks were cleared for action as the sisters faced each other across the narrow pavement, ammunition stacked and primed.

I felt limp from a mixture of fear and remorse. The scene is etched on my memory forever. What *had* I done. I struggled to escape from the billowing hate that surged like a living thing around me, but there was no escape from the vice-like grip of my mother's small but powerful hand.

"Waddee y' mean by beltin' our Liam, eh?" Mother's voice rang shrilly in my ears. "Luk at this!" These were the last words I heard clearly. Without warning, Mam's grip transferred itself from my hand to the top of my head. For one agonising second I thought my hair had come out by the roots as she twisted my head from side to side in a paroxysm of anger, inviting my aunt to inspect the damage she had done. Sounds became confused as my head rattled.

Again with startling suddenness, the intense pain on the top of my head ceased as I was flung unceremoniously to one side, presumaly no longer required as an exhibit. I swayed from side to side holding my aching head, dazed and uncertain what to do, whilst the air around me filled with vitriolic sound. I had to get away, somewhere, anywhere out of that charged atmosphere. Without hesitation I made for the dark cavern of the entry, scattering onlookers as I went, and crashed blindly into its dark comfort, emotions racing, my mind filled with the picture of the two women. Tense, hair awry. The one, a ball of fighting fury, standing one foot in the gutter, her hand outstretched in accusation. The other, framed in the doorway of the house, arms folded defiantly across her chest, her normally florid face white with anger.

I did not witness the sequel. But when time had smoothed the memory I learnt that the row, after some brief, but bitter exchanges, had ended abruptly as Aunt Aggie slammed the door in Mother's face saying that she never wanted to see her again. A sentiment with which apparently the gods concurred, for the next time they met, just four short months to the day, Aunt Aggie, her rich voice stilled for ever, lay silent in her coffin. Oh what, in innocence, had I done?

3

Farewell Aunt Aggie

1926 of which I now write, was one of those years which haunt the mind like an evil spirit. It was a year of uneasiness and change that communicated itself to even the smallest child on the district.

I didn't realise it then but this was the beginnings of the bad times. I began the painful process of growing up. For the first time I began to feel the full weight of my mother's hand. For no apparent reason tempers shortened alarmingly. I daren't set a foot wrong without getting a clip over the ear, and not only from Mam and Dad. Con, himself now unemployed like my father, now and then gave me one when they weren't looking. But the greatest tragedy to me was the fact that I lost my place in Mam and Dad's room. As soon as my sixth birthday passed I was herded into the back bedroom with Bernadette and Teresa, neither of whom thought much of the idea, and said so, with the result that they were both clipped for not watching their tongues. Justice was always both swift and impartial in our house.

I hated that backroom with its faded flowered wall paper and windows that rattled every time a train rumbled along the nearby docks, and each morning I would wake long before the knocker-up tapped his long stick against the windows for those fortunate enough to be still employed. He hadn't knocked on our window for weeks now although Dad still got up each morning and went out as usual.

One particular morning stands out vividly in my memory. It was the Tuesday exactly a week after my sixth birthday, and as usual I was wide awake, half lying, half leaning on my elbow waiting for Dad to get up. I knew his ritual off by heart, and although I never quite knew how he would react, I was so frightened and fed up in this strange dingy room that I would willingly have taken a good telling off just to speak to him. I heard the first creak of the bed as I waited tensely, and wondered what kind of a mood he was in.

"Dad!" I called in a strangled whisper, as I heard his heavy foot on the narrow landing outside. He mustn't have heard me, "Dad," I whispered a little louder this time but careful not to wake my sisters up. I could tell he was in a bad mood as soon as he spoke.

"What's samarrer?" he snapped sleepily, his hand rattling on the loose knob as he opened the door slightly.

"Nothin'," I replied defensively, half scared, yet glad to hear his voice. "Is it time t' gerrup yet?" I asked uselessly. I knew it wasn't. I heard him mutter savagely to himself before replying.

"Course it isn't," he snapped, "Now get t' sleep before y' wake the girls up." I fell silent, and lay back.

"What's up?" I heard a sleepy inquiry come from my mother's room.

"It's all right, it's all right," he answered testily. "It's only Liam askin' daft questions. Go back t' sleep."

I listened intently as he eased himself gently down the stairs, trying to avoid the second and third which always squeaked. I knew exactly what was going to happen next and listened carefully. I heard the match strike to light the gas, then the homely sound of water hissing into the kettle as he began to swing into action. Next he would let Mick in after his night's marauding along the walls.

We were all fond of our tailless cat, even though he did have a piratical look about him. I knew I wouldn't have long to wait before he burnt the toast. Of the scores of times I listened to the ritual, I never knew him not to burn the toast. Ah!, there it was, the steady scraping as he cleaned the edges before buttering it and bringing it up to Mam. My mouth watered. Right on time the sounds ceased, and almost immediately his now booted feet came clumping noisily up the stairs accompanied by the rattle of the cup as it joggled in the saucer.

"Mary!, are y' awake?"

For a few moments only the subdued buzz of voices filtered through the door. I knew it wouldn't be long before he went now. My mouth watered anew at the thought of the crispy toast on the other side of the door. Again the door creaked, and he stopped momentarily on the landing.

"Tarrawel," he said laconically. "I might get 'alf a day. If I'm not back by eight, you'll know I'm on."

I didn't know what he meant. He had been saying the same thing as long as I could remember, but I knew that within moments I would be free to try my luck for some of Mam's toast.

At long last, the sound I had been waiting for came. The back door slammed shut. He was gone. Like a flash I was out of bed, my shirt tails flying as I crossed the landing and tapped on the door.

"Are y' there, Mam?" I knew she was of course, but I had to say something, I daren't go straight in. I heard a sigh.

"Where d'y' think I am, up the chimney?" I poked my head round the door and gazed silently at her as she sat propped up against the pillow a steaming cup of tea half raised to her lips in one hand, the toast in the other. We looked solemnly at each other as I waited, half in half out of the room, an icy draught playing round my bare bottom. Suddenly her eyes twinkled, and her lips parted in a half smile as she tossed her blue black hair.

"Oh all right then ... come on," she said resignedly, " 'ere y' are." She held out the toast. Almost before the words left her lips I was on the bed, the coveted toast in my hand, and the soft comfort of her arm round my shoulders.

Of all my childhood, these few brief moments in the morning were the happiest. All the lonely hours of wakefulness in that hated back room slid from me like a tattered cloak. For these few magical moments, withdrawn from all the worries about her, she was mine, all mine. I snuggled blissfully against her.

The mournful whine of the wind outside, the heavy tramp of booted feet passing beneath the window as scores of unemployed went in search of work, seemed to emphasise my comfort. I snuggled close and chewed on the brittle tastiness of the toast and let my eye wander round the familiar room. The worn crucifix over the bed. The brilliant picture of the Sacred Heart. A battered chest of drawers with its wash bowl and jug. No palace could have given me greater pleasure at this time of the day.

Slowly an hour or more ticked away as I lay comatose, my head cradled in her arm, her head resting gently on mine. She stirred fitfully as the rolling tones of the Town Hall clock, sharpened by the wind, struck seven o'clock. With startling suddenness the peace was shattered. I found myself flung violently to one side as the front door shook to a thunderous, urgent knocking. All trace of sleep left her as she leapt from the bed, her long hair trailing down her shoulders like a black mane, and flung the window up.

Unreasoning panic gripped me as the knocking took on an hysterical note, and I dived beneath the covers. Irate protests of the neighbours blased through the open window as it squealed on its runners.

"What'samarrer?" ... "What's goin' on down there?" A high-pitched hysterical voice silenced them as Alice saw Mam's head poke out of the window.

"She's dead, Aunt Mary ... me Mam's dead. Come quick."

I peeped over the covers at the sound of the familiar voice, and saw my mother stiffen as she effectively quietened my cousin's growing hysteria.

"Shurrup, girl," she hissed. "You'll make a show of y'self. Now be quiet 'til I get down." It was like a cold douche, only the excited chatter of the neighbours sounded as she straightened, slammed the window shut, and turned to me almost in the same movement. Her face was chalk white as she pointed her finger at me.

"Now you stay where y' are, d'y' 'ear?" I nodded

silently, my head whirling in sudden fear as I watched her fling her clothes on and dash out of the room.

I heard the door of the girls' room open and Mam's sharp voice full of foreboding.

"Bernadette, Teresa, I want y'. Y' Aunty Aggie's dead." Turmoil followed the cryptic, brutal message. I held the blanket up to my nose as I listened to my sisters dashing about, then going downstairs. I lay petrified. I knew by Mam's face something terrible had happened, what it was I wasn't sure, and this made me more frightened than ever. I did the only possible thing. I howled like a stuck pig. Within seconds Mam reappeared like a genie, her hair half braided. One look at her was enough. I shut up like a clam. She balled her fist as she leaned over the edge of the bed, and shook it at me, her face was set like a mask.

"One peep," she said threateningly. "Just one!" I slid under the clothes, mouth quivering, tears rolling down my cheeks. I heard her turn and the door open. I stayed under the clothes. Mrs Taylor'll be 'ere in a minute," she said, "she'll see to y', an' any flamin' nonsense, me lad, I'll 'ave y' liver ... Understand?" I peeped over the clothes and nodded. I understood only too well.

I wasn't old enough to go to the wake, but I was taken to see Aunt Aggie laid out, to pay my last respects. I was petrified. It haunted me for months afterwards. Even now the reek of incense that pervaded the darkened room fills my nostrils at the memory, and I can feel again that gentle pull on my arm as my mother urged me towards the coffin, mounted on trestles where the dresser normally stood, and flanked by enormous candles. I edged closer when every instinct told me to run. Suddenly I found myself wafted aloft to gaze, first in fear, then in curiosity at the white-clad figure of my aunt.

Gone were the florid features I knew so well. Instead, the round white face lay smooth and unlined against the glistening white of the headrest. The eyelids, now free from the imprisoning pennies that had held them closed for the first few hours, rested against the pallid cheeks. Suddenly my mother's voice whispered in my ear.

"Touch y' auntie's for'ead, Liam, ... then y' won't dream about her."

I did though. For months that back room was filled with wavering candles and the smell of incense. It was a bad year for me.

4

Ordeal by Rats

In the two years following Aunt Aggie's death, several things happened and combined to speed the process of growing up. I learned the importance of money for instance. I also learned, and this came as something of a shock, that I could not always rely on the automatic aid of my parents when I got myself into trouble. There were some things it seemed that I had to handle myself whether I liked it or not.

Looking back from the safety of years at the grim conditions in which we lived and which surrounded us on all sides, I can see clearly that their attitudes towards any given situation were usually not only practical but essential. In our world the strong survived, the weak succumbed. It was as simple as that, and if one happened to be crafty as well, it was all to the good.

I remember I must have been about eight when I reached this particular milestone, and it was in the worst summer I ever experienced for rain. The summer holidays were almost two weeks old, and for the whole of that time, except for brief intervals, it never stopped. The gutters were awash. The cobbles glistened steamily in the humid air, and I was a virtual prisoner indoors, therefore I felt pretty annoyed when, on one of the rare occasions the sun shone and I was able to play out, I heard Mam's voice calling me from halfway up the street.

"Liam!" she yelled irritably as she called me for the

second time. I pretended I hadn't heard as I watched my paper boat floating towards the gurgling drain about five yards away.

"Hey, Liam, y' Mam wants y'." Henry Fielding, an angelic-looking, fair-haired lad of my own age, and a special friend of mine from across the road, sounded worried as he reached across and pushed me in the shoulder. I muttered rebelliously, and fixed my eyes determinedly on the boat as it gathered momentum before plunging down the grid.

"*Liam!*" Her voice hit me like a bullet. I daren't ignore it any longer; anyway the boat had gone down the grid. Henry voiced my innermost thoughts.

"You'd berra git," he said warningly, flicking his blue eyes nervously in the direction of the voice. "She'll batter y' if y' don't." He wasn't kidding either. I scrambled up and ran like a hare to where she was standing. She clipped me over the ear before I had come to a standstill.

"What's wrong with y'?" she snapped, grabbing a handful of my jersey and shaking me. "Are y' deaf or somethin'?" I rubbed my ear and remained silent. I knew when I was licked. She put tuppence halfpenny in my hand, and flicked her head sideways.

"Go an' gerra loaf." She grabbed my jersey again as I turned to leave. "An' mind Y' don't lose it," she added, nodding towards my closed fist. I tore off towards the church at the top of the street, skidded round the corner and into the corner shop. Within minutes I had got the loaf, balanced it on the top of my head and was on my way back, eager to get home and get on with my sailing while the weather held. I hadn't covered a dozen paces before a figure, slightly taller than myself and about six months older, blocked my way on the narrow pavement. I scowled as I recognised Alfie Chapman, a tow-haired, freckle-faced trouble maker, five doors up from us. Nobody liked Alfie, not even his father and mother. He bullied every kid in the street smaller than himself, including me. I hated him.

"What y' got there?" he asked looking at the loaf.

"A loaf whaddee y' think," I snapped as I made to move

past him. He counter-moved swiftly to block me. I sensed trouble.

"Mind out!" I said irritably. "Me Mam's waitin'." His eyes danced viciously as he stared at the loaf I was holding securely on my head with one hand. I felt a quiver of alarm as I noted the look in his eyes. Too late I decided to move the loaf to a safer position. A sudden venomous swipe and it was in the gutter, soaking up water like a sponge. I dived in a frantic effort to retrieve it, but his bare foot beat me to it and sent it rolling out of my reach. Savage temper swept me as I realised what would happen when I got home. I could have killed him, but instinctively I was scared of him. I fought back the tears and grabbed the soggy loaf as he grinned at me.

"Cry baby," he called after me as I began to run for home.

Mam stared in disbelief at the loaf as I edged round the door and handed it to her. Before I could utter a word she caught me a stinging open-handed slap across the face that sent me staggering against the door.

"What the hell d'y' call this?" she cried, glaring first at the loaf then at me. I muttered unintelligibly as I tried to find words.

"Don't stand there like an idjit. What 'ave y' bin doin'? ... playin' football with it?"

Her face was white with sudden anger as she raised her hand to strike again. Dad, still unemployed, broke in irritably from his seat near the grate.

" 'ang on a minute, there, what's goin' ... ?"

She whirled round on him. "It's all right you sittin' there sayin' 'ang on. Jus' luk at this!" She held the loaf up for inspection then threw it on the table and grabbed her purse. "That was the last few coppers in the 'ouse." She was almost crying with anger as she opened the purse and turned it upside down. "Luk," she said. I looked in an agony of suspense. Nothing came out. "Now where d'y' think I'm gonna get the money f' another one?" she demanded.

Dad rose quickly from his chair. There was a note of accusation in his voice as he reprimanded her. "Y' don't think 'e did it on purpose do y'?" he snapped, putting his thorny hand on my shoulder. "Somethin' must've 'appened." Mam snorted disgustedly and threw herself in a chair. Dad stared at me quietly. "What 'appened?" he asked with a gentleness that surprised me. I stammered out what had happened and his face hardened.

"The young sod!" he exclaimed, straightening up and pushing me towards the parlour door.

"Where you goin'?" asked Mam in sudden alarm.

He nodded towards the front door. "Where d'y' think I'm goin'?" he snapped, "I'm gonna see Chapman."

Mam leapt from the chair as though she had been stung and grasped his arm.

"Luk, Pat," she pleaded, "we don't want any trouble, so for God's sake watch y' temper."

I looked anxiously from one to the other. I had never seen Dad in a real temper. Normally he was easy going until something upset him, and then it was all over like a summer storm. He wasn't calm now though. His eyes shone, his jaw worked spasmodically as though he was biting something. He shook her restraining arm off irritably as he picked up the loaf, then shoved me none too gently towards the front door.

Before I quite knew what was happening he was hammering on Chapman's knocker. With instinctive intuition for impending trouble, heads popped out all along the street and gazed at him. The knocker was jerked out of his hand as Mr Chapman, tall, slim, and freckle-faced like Alfie, opened the door suddenly, an irritable frown on his face. His expression changed to one of startled amazement as Dad stuck the loaf under his nose.

"You owe me tuppence halfpenny mate!" he snapped.

Mr Chapman's jaw dropped in surprise.

"What the 'ell's up with you, Pat? ... What's that anyway?"

"What does it luk like?" answered Dad, his anger rising like a spring tide. "Luk at it." Mr Chapman looked at it nonplussed. Dad gave him the facts briefly.

"Your bloody Alfie did that," he snarled, jerking his head towards me. "Knocked it off 'is flamin' 'ead inter the gutter, and you owe me tuppence halfpenny ... so gerrit, an' quick!"

Mr Chapman drew himself up. His eyes flashed as he made to go in and close the door.

"You'll get no bloody tuppence. ..."

Dad grabbed his shirt front like greased lightning and pulled him forwards. The onlookers gasped. They obviously knew Dad better than I did.

"Gerrit!" he hissed. His tone made me jump. This was an entirely new person, and I didn't like it much. Mr Chapman went white and called for his wife.

"Annie," he roared, "fetch y' purse?"

"Waddee y' wan' it for?" A thin nervous voice floated from the back kitchen.

"Don't stand there askin' daft questions woman, fetch it."

All his belligerence faded as he waited anxiously for his wife to appear.

"An' tell 'er t' bring your Alfie out while she's at it," hissed Dad.

Alfie's for it, I thought gleefully, and serves him right.

"If our Alfie's there, fetch the sod," called Mr Chapman.

Moments later Mrs Chapman, small and worried looking, appeared behind her husband. Her eyes dancing like nervous fireflies as they flickered from one to the other. I bridled as Alfie peeped from behind his mother's skirts and stuck his tongue out at me.

"What's all this ... ?" she began.

Shurrup an' give this bloody feller tuppence halfpenny will y'."

"But I've only got threepence in the 'ouse," she answered plaintively.

"Give it 'im," he gasped as the inexorable grip tightened.

She rummaged for a second or two in her flat purse, then handed Dad a silver threepenny piece.

"I'll send Mary over with the halfpenny later," he said, relaxing a little now he had got the money to buy a new loaf. Suddenly he pointed to Alfie, and his voice grated again.

"Gerr'im out 'ere," he snapped. Chapman bridled momentarily.

"Waddee y' wan' Alfie for?" he asked petulantly.

"That bloody kid's always throwin' 'is weight about," answered Dad sharply. "Now let's see what 'e can really do, an' this time I'll be 'ere t' see fair play." He bunched his fist and pushed it close to Mr Chapman. "An' any interference from you, mate," he added menacingly, "I'll wrap this round y' ... gorrit?"

Mr Chapman nodded in alarm and gave the screaming Alfie a shove that sent him sprawling on to the cobbles. Suddenly it dawned on me what was about to happen. If my legs hadn't turned to jelly I would have run but Dad fixed me with a silent look that boded no good if I so much as whimpered. He was laying in on the line and I had to toe it whether I liked it or not.

All around neighbours clucked, some with disapproval, others, whose children had suffered at Alfie's hands, with satisfaction. I stood silent and rigid as I awaited Dad's instructions, then relief flooded through me as I heard Mam's voice right behind us.

"Pat!" she cried. "That's enough. Y' don't want the children fightin'."

He swivelled round, face set, and fixed her with his eye. Her face paled.

" 'e'll stand on 'is own two feet an' fight 'is own battles," he hissed, "Now gerr'in the 'ouse an' mind y' own business."

Neighbours gazed sympathetically at her as she hesitated.

"Go 'ome," he repeated with quiet menance. She looked daggers at him for a second then stalked slowly away. She knew him better than I did too.

My heart sank as I faced Alfie, two feet away in the centre of the street and wriggling like mad in his father's grasp. I felt sick with tension, then a surge of comfort swept through me as Dad whispered urgently in my ear.

"Don't hesitate," he whispered. "Tear into 'im. All

bullies are cowards when y' stand up t' them ... you'll see!"

With a gentle pat of encouragement on the shoulder and a quick shove forward we were at it. Everything went blank as I took his advice, closed my eyes and tore in like a windmill. Elation suddenly gripped me. He was right. Alfie howled like a banshee as he tried to break off. It was all over in a few minutes, with little damage done on either side. Mr Chapman's face was black with anger as his son suddenly ducked between his outstretched legs and bolted through the door into the house.

I stood stupified with surprise. All this time we had let him plague the life out of us. Dad grinned as he patted me on the shoulder and I felt about ten feet tall as we turned away. Alfie never bothered any of us again until it was time to fight our way through to the leadership of the street gang later on. I learnt two valuable lessons that day: the first, that Dad was right about bullies, and the second, that trouble faced is trouble halved. Nothing had frightened me so much as fear itself.

The week following the fight was misery all round. Mam and Dad hardly spoke a civil word, and of all the family only Bernadette was working. This fatal combination of unemployment, no money, and miserable weather, shortened tempers alarmingly; one could almost touch the tension in the air.

Even the odd occasion I did manage to get out of the house didn't help very much because my freedom was strictly limited by two important factors, and except for the journey to school my whole world consisted of our street, the two that ran either end, and the entries connecting them all. Further than that I dare not go without one of the family. The second reason I never dared sneak away from these confines, was a pathological fear of Chinamen, of whom we had quite a few on Merseyside. I don't know why they frightened me, but they did. All the neighbours knew of my weakness, and on the very rare occasions when inquisitiveness got the better of me, a whispered word that the Chinamen were coming was enough to send me hurtling home in fear of my life. But the morning Mrs

Taylor burst in with her startling news was so unbearable I think I would have braved even the Chinamen to get away from the tense atmosphere indoors.

Restlessness gnawed at me as I stood on a chair by the sink, nose pressed against the damp glass, gazing wistfully down the rain-swept back yard. Behind me a frigid silence was broken occasionally by a heavy thump, as Mam battered some dough against the table, preparatory to making some soda bread, or a gentle rustle as Dad turned the pages of a Western he was reading. Every few minutes I had to rub my palm on the window as it clouded with the steamy dampness hanging over the room from the lines of wet washing hanging irritatingly from the low ceiling.

"The View's flooded." I pricked my ears as Dad's unexpected remark dropped in the fetid air. I turned on the chair to look at Mam.

" 'ow 'igh is it?" she asked tiredly, without pausing in her work.

"Up to the bottom steps," he answered, finally closing the book and stretching his arms to ease his cramped shoulders.

"God 'elp them down the 'Bell's' then," said my mother sympathetically as she raised a lump of dough and crashed it down on the table amid a puff of flour. "I'll bet they're 'avin' a helluva time of it!"

I listened with interest. The 'View' as it was called ran along the bottom of our street and was one of my boundaries. I knew it and its inhabitants well. It was even more seedy than our part of the forest of bricks and chimneys that made up the district which, despite the pastoral names given to the streets by some bygone cynic, were nothing but two-up and two-down hovels of flaking plaster and stinking middens. Vineyard Street ... Pleasant View ... Woodland Street. In weather like this the whole dismal planning of the close-packed area became evident in all its pitiful inadequacy.

'Pleasant View' for some mysterious reason called the 'Bell's' was, as far as I knew, the only street in the district that had the parlour where a cellar would normally be, with access to the front down five steps into an area surrounded by railings. It was notorious during bad weather for flooding, and this apparently was what was happening now as the water from the surrounding streets cascaded down the steps like a weir.

I was still watching Mam when a sudden crash behind me made me whirl on the chair and peer through the window. I was just in time to catch a fleeting glimpse of a blurred figure dashing up the yard. Three pairs of eyes focused on the kitchen door as it opened violently to admit the muffled, dripping figure of Mrs Taylor.

"Mother'f God, isn't this the weather?" she ejaculated, spraying water all over the place as she removed the sodden shawl covering her head. Neither of my parents made any comment as she hung the garment on the back door, then blew through her pursed lips as she smoothed her hair.

"Anythin' in the pot?" she asked, turning to face Mam.

My mother nodded to the pot standing on the gas stove beside me. " 'ave a luk. Should be a drop left."

"Thanks be t' God for that," said Mrs Taylor gratefully, coming towards the stove and giving me a friendly dig in the stomach as she poured the tea.

" 'ave y' seen 'em?" she asked Dad suddenly, taking the cup to the table and pulling up a chair.

"Seen what?" he answered in a puzzled tone. "I 'aven't bin out since I came 'ome from the stand."

I looked from one to the other. He always said he'd been to the 'Stand' when he had been out looking for work. I had asked my mother what it was, and she had told me that that was what they did when they went to the shipyard. They stood outside the gates while they waited for the foreman to pick any of them needed for work.

They didn't often pick Dad. I knew that.

I looked at Mrs Taylor expectantly. I liked to watch her when she was speaking. She made all sorts of faces according to what ever she was talking about. She had a habit of waving her arms like windmills when she had got excited. They were going now.

"The *rats!*" she explode in growing agitation. Mam wiped her flour-covered arms on her sugar-bag apron and looked at Dad in consternation. "Big as Kilkenny cats, so they are," Mrs Taylor continued, waving one hand towards the back door. "Down the 'Bell's ... dozens of'm."

I felt a tremor of fear run through me as Mam and Dad gazed at each other aghast. *Rats!* ... sewer rats. I had heard the adults speak of this periodic plague which beset the district, when a combination of high tides and heavy rain effectively blocked the drains and flooded the lower, poorer quarters of the town and flushed hundreds of these vicious creatures from their myriad hiding places, causing chaos among the crowded inhabitants. I groaned inwardly as my parents warned me almost in the same breath not to stir outside without permission.

All that day I wandered from room to room peering out of the windows at the gradually rising waters, trying to spot the rats, or waving to some of my fellow sufferers, whom I could see across the street, looking just as fed up as myself. I never saw one all day. However I was still dreaming of them when something woke me up from a fitful sleep that night. I lay half awake, half asleep, propped up on my elbow listening. Outside, the continual hiss of water was broken occasionally by the harsh blaring tones of a foghorn as ships fought their way upriver through the blinding curtain. Then, with nerve-tingling suddenness, the last remnants of sleep left me as the whole house vibrated with a series of ear-splitting squeals and shrieks.

I felt the hairs rise on the back of my neck as I shot bolt upright. For perhaps two seconds I sat, frozen solid, eyes bulging, skin prickling in fright. Then I was out of bed and across the room like greased lightning, scrabbling frantically at the humped figures of my sisters.

"Bernadette!, Teresa! wake up, wake up. Somethin's up," I shrieked in a voice high pitched with growing hysteria. "Listen," I gasped as Bernadette, the nearer of the two, shot bolt upright. In a twinkling the place was in an uproar. Unreasoning fear gripped all three of us. Bernadette and Teresa shrieked in unison. Dad roared like a bull as he flew out of bed and fell over an essential article, and I yelled even louder as I stubbed my toe against the bed post.

"For Christ's sake, shurrup in there!" he yelled above the din as he struggled to light the gas with one hand, and hold his long woollen drawers up with the other. A new voice joined the tumult.

"What the divil's goin' on?" Mam's voice, shrill and angry, sliced through the hubbub. "Anyone'd think it was a bloody lunatic asylum!" All three of us shut up immediately and clung to each other for safety.

Downstairs I could hear Con threshing about in the darkness as he tried to locate the source of the trouble. All along the street sashes flew up, and tousled heads hurled imprecations into the rain-soaked air, but for a full five minutes number twelve was oblivious to the world outside as the whole family floundered and swore their way through to the sounds of maniacal battle.

At long last the gas at the head of the stairs went pop. I peeped goggle-eyed round the edge of the door and saw Dad standing in his long drawers and shirt, disbelief in his eyes and sheer horror on his face, as he gazed down the narrow stairs and saw Mick, the cat, locked in mortal combat with a rat almost as big as himself. I felt rather than saw Bernadette ease past me on to the landing, and looked up in time to see her mouth open to scream. It never came, a split second later she staggered back against the door as Dad caught her a swingeing, back-handed blow across the face.

"Get back t' bed!" he hissed savagely, "An quick!"

Bernadette vanished and so did I. I slipped round the back of Dad like a greased eel, slipped through the door of Mam's bedroom, dived over the brass end of the bed and lay palpitating in the safety of her arms. But not for long. Moments later she slung me to one side as she leapt out of bed in response to the thunderous knocking on the front door, and flung open the window.

"There's a rat in the 'ouse!" she cried, leaning right over the sill. A horrified gasp came from below, then there was dead silence as the neighbours raced back to their homes to barricade the doors and make sure the children were safe.

Outside the bedroom door was Bedlam. Squeals of shuddering hate billowed through the partly open door as Mick and the rat fought their way up, then crashed down the stairs again in a struggling mass.

Dad, now armed with one of his hobnailed boots, popped round the door now and then with a progress report on the battle alternating between the stairs and the kitchen. Shouts for information floated between him and Con downstairs.

"Con! ... Are y' all right down there?"

"I'm all right, Dad, I've gorra poker ... are *you* all right?"

"Yes."

"Is Mam all right?"

"Yeh, she's all right. She's with Liam."

"Are the girls all right?"

"Yeh."

"They're quiet, aren't they?"

"They'd berra be," I heard Dad say menacingly. "Now you watch y'self down there. There might be another one about."

"That's all right Dad; I'm standin' on the table," answered Con confidently. "I told y', I've gorra poker." There were no flies on Con.

At last it was over. An eerie silence suddenly descended on the house. Soon the landing was crowded and we all stared at the rat, stretched in bloody defeat on the second stair from the bottom, its battered body ripped almost to shreds by Mick's needle sharp claws. Mick himself was in little better shape, as Dad, now respectable in his trousers—I never did remember how he managed to get them on—gingerly edged his way past the dead rat towards him.

He lay in the well of the stairs, whimpering from a score of wounds. One ear was completely severed, and the bald patches on his skin bore mute testimony to his courage.

The kitchen and stairs were in a complete shambles. Blood and hair lay all over the place as though men and not two small animals had fought to the death. Con, who had witnessed the greater part of the fight, could not find words to express what he had seen and kept repeating over and over again, "Mother'f God Dad, what a fight!"

Tears filled all our eyes as Dad carried Mick to the table, where he was petted and bathed, stroked and admired for long anxious minutes. But it was useless. Suddenly he raised his head, whimpered plaintively, then stiffened. He could give no more.

I like to think he still lies peacefully beneath the cold unyielding bricks of the backyard where we laid him as soon as the waters subsided.

5

The World of Walls

By a strange irony, the floods which brought disaster to the whole neighbourhood, were for me a turning point. An unexpected gateway that opened up an entirely new world at the bottom of the yard.

The morning after Mick's fight dawned very uneasily. Everyone including me, was bleary-eyed from the excitement of the night. Dad had to escort Bernadette to work and missed the stand for the first time in months. Con almost trampled me underfoot as he dashed frantically around, trying to get out in time to meet his mates at the Labour Exchange, and Mam was as touchy as a smouldering volcano.

Conditions were ideal for me to put my foot in it, and with unerring accuracy I did so as I crawled in the well of the stairs, examining the bloodstains with breathless fascination.

"Gerraway from there! 'oo d'y' think you are ... Sherlock 'omes?"

I shot to my feet and gazed in alarm at my mother. She was hollow-eyed and weary. I knew all the signs. "I was only ..." I began.

"Well, don't," she snapped. "Gerrup stairs an' give Teresa a shake."

I muttered under my breath as she put the kettle on. The front door banged loudly as I made my way up.

"Cor!" I muttered savagely, "neighbours. Now I'll never gerrout." I could imagine them in the kitchen. 'Yatitty yat, yatitty yat' for hours. It was always the same when anything happened, everyone was in on it. I vented my irritation on my sleeping sister.

"*Teresa!*" I yelled as loudly as I could. She shot up, startled. "Gerrup! me Mam wants y'." I flew across the room and slammed the door before me she could grab me, and darted downstairs. I was right. There were half a dozen of them in the kitchen talking fifty to the dozen. I glowered at them, then opened the back door to have a look at Mick stretched on an old tin trunk outside the back door.

I hadn't been there two seconds before Mrs Taylor came roaring across the room and grabbed me by the scruff of the neck.

"Whaddee y' think y' doin'?" she gasped in horror. "You'll 'ave the place snooin' with 'em," she indicated the dead rat lying half submerged in the yard where Dad had thrown him until he got back. I went cold all over as she yanked me in and slammed the door shut quick. Mam's face screwed in annoyance. She flicked her free hand upwards as she poured the boiling water into the teapot.

"Gerrup there," she snapped. "An' any flamin' non-sense I'll sling y' straight out inter the entry with the rats."

"Teresa's still gerrin' dressed," I objected, knowing Mam's strict rules about modesty. Even though I still slept in the girls' room I was always in bed long before them, and they always dressed and undressed in the dark. She tossed her head in annoyance and without moving from the stove yelled upstairs to my sister.

"Teresa! warrar y' doin' there? Shift y'self before I come an' shift y'."

Scurrying sounds came from above, and like magic Teresa appeared, her long chestnut hair flying all over the place as she straightened the last crinkles out of her dress. I hovered on the bottom stair, utterly fed up.

"Can't I go out, Mam? Luk the rain's stopped." I pointed hopefully through the window.

"Y' can't go out 'til the rats 'ave gone, so don't ask." A touch of menace entered her voice. "Now shurrup, an' gerrup," she added.

"Honest, wouldn't kids get y' goat?"

I turned and glowered at the sound of the voice. Trust Mrs Threfall to stick her great beak nose in I thought savagely. I weighed the distance between Mam and myself, judging whether it would be safe to pull my tongue out at this interfering busybody. I was too close, even though she was pouring tea.

"What shall I do then?" I asked petulantly. Mam whirled almost knocking Mrs Taylor's tea out of her hand. Obviously she thought I'd gone.

"Are you still there?" she snapped. "Now git," she jerked her thumb upwards again. When she used that tone there was no argument. I got, and with as much noise as I could manage in my bare feet, clumped up the stairs rebelliously.

I hadn't been out for days. I could have smashed the walls with frustration. I slammed the door and humped by way to the window in a filthy mood and gazed at the sluggish water beneath me.

I spat into it in disgust and let me eye wander broodingly along the line of backyards and the feverish activity that was going on in every one of them. Bricks, sacks, paper. Anything and everything was being used by the men as they tried to block every possible crevice to stop the rats entering. Suddenly a yell arose from a yard about twenty yards up on the opposite side of the entry.

"Luk out. There's one in the lavatory!" Instantly heads popped up from the yards on either side. Advice poured in from all directions as the frantic householder slashed away with a broom. I didn't know the family, but every kid in the house squealed in hysterics. For a few seconds there was uproar, then a howl of laughter swept the yards as I leaned as far out as possible to see what was going on. It hadn't been a rat at all, whoever it was had panicked and battered the poor cat instead.

The brief relief that the laughter brought me soon became swallowed up in depression as my eyes flickered over the shed roofs below. I never realised before how much junk there was on the sheds. Confusion lay everywhere in a tangle of old bicycle wheels, tyres, tins, bricks and anything else that could safely be thrown up there out of the way. I was still musing among the junk when my eye caught a movement at the bottom end of the entry wall. I recognised the figure immediately. It was Henry Fielding, capering like a madman along the wall, his normally quiet features contorted with excitement. My heart bounded. I hadn't seen him for days.

"Hi y', 'enry," I yelled, waving my arms to attract his attention.

He spotted me and came hurtling along the narrow wall.

"Hi y', Li," he shouted, coming abreast, "whatcher doin'?"

"Whaddee y' think I'm doin'?" I replied tactfully. "I'm leanin' outa the winder ... Warrar you doin'?" I asked, looking at the bricks in his hands.

"Chuckin' bricks at the rats," he replied excitedly, suiting the action to the words. "Come on out, it's the gear." He held a brick up invitingly.

"Can't," I replied, hanging my head in shame.

"Why?" he asked, incredulously. Nobody ever bothered where Henry went.

"Cos I can't, that's why," I replied truculently. "Me Mam won't let me."

"Garn!" he said scornfully. His tone stung me. Blind enthusiasm swept me. But the fear of my mother was stronger. Experience prompted caution; she'd scalp me if she caught me. I crept downstairs to see how the land lay, and sighed with relief. They were still talking their heads off. I made up my mind on the spot, shot back upstairs, climbed through the window and dropped gently on to the shed roof beneath. I felt like an escaped convict, elated, yet scared.

For a moment or two I crouched where I was, peeping

over the edge of the roof to ' e it anyone had spotted me. They hadn't. Henry danced with delight as I joined him, and together we raced along to the Pleasant View end. All around us was wild activity. In several yards we passed there were guards with sticks outside the lavatory doors to protect the performers within.

"Here y'are," said Henry, suddenly stopping about four houses from the end. "Grab a coupla these." He thrust two bricks into my hand. "Luk at 'em" he said, pointing down to the flooded entry. For the first time I looked down and nearly fell off the wall in fright. There must have been twenty or thirty rats frantically milling about in the water as they sought an avenue of escape. My stomach tightened as I watched their beady, satanic eyes in morbid fascination.

About a yard away Henry cavorted dangerously on the wall despite the shouted warnings of the adults below.

"Go on, Li," he screeched excitedly. "Chuck 'em, there. Chuck it at that one over there." I followed his outstretched arm to a big black fellow scrabbling madly at the door under my feet, and together we pelted it with bricks, running like mad as it leaped up the door towards us.

Suddenly pandemonium broke loose in the last yard but one along the entry, and all hell seemed to break loose as a woman's high pitched voice sliced through the air.

"*Henry!*" it screamed. Henry and I looked at each other, startled. His normally pale face turned a shade white.

"Me *Mam!*" he cried, trying to hide behind me. He was wrong, it wasn't.

"Hi, Li ... Henry!" We looked round quickly to pin-point the familiar boyish voice that broke into the growing tumult. It was Fatty Boyle who lived three doors down from me. He hung precariously out of the window, thumping the wall beneath in excitement.

"Whatsammarrer?" we yelled in unison. He gesticulated wildly towards the sound of the woman's voice.

"There's a rat in Mr Williams' yard." Heads popped up like mushrooms as neighbours stood on anything they could find to get a better view. Moments later we were there, hanging on to the clothes post breathlessly, eyes goggling as we watched Mr Williams backed up against the lavatory door, white-faced, dinner tin raised over his head to strike at the reddish brown rat moving slowly towards him.

He must have been going for a final visit to the toilet before going to work because he was fully dressed in his Gas Man's uniform. Petrified with fear, he struck blindly in the direction of the rat with his tin. Its eyes flashed wickedly.

"Henry!" Another scream came from his wife hanging out of the bedroom window. He flicked a momentary glance in her direction.

"Shurrup!" he shouted. She recoiled visibly. Her husband being in regular work, she was normally a very 'aughty' sort of woman, who wore a coat instead of a shawl. They were a sedate family, but now, under duress, his manners seemed to have deserted him. Again he swiped at the rat. Anxiety creased her angular face.

"Henry, *please*", she cried pleadingly, "don't throw y' dinner tin at it, there's boiled 'am in them sandwiches." A howl of laughter rose from the neighbours within earshot. Henry and I looked at each other significantly. 'Boiled Ham!' They *must* be rich.

I was still thinking of the boiled ham when a small, thick-set figure came crashing over a nearby shed roof.

"For God's sake man stand still!" he roared. It was Jimmy Kiernan from the end house. His thin dark features were tense as he leaned across the wall and poked at the rat with a brush handle to divert its attention.

"*Now!*" he shouted suddenly, as the infuriated rat sank its teeth into the pole. "Run like 'ell." Mr Williams needed no second bidding. He was up the yard and through the kitchen door almost before we could blink. We were still looking at the rescuer admiringly when Dad's voice hit the back of my neck like a bow.

" 'oo the 'ell told you y' could gerrup there?" I didn't even answer him.

"See y', 'enry," I hissed as I squeezed past him and tore

along the wall. Mam's face was a blurred picture of astonishment as I burst through the kitchen door and straight up the stairs, shaking like a leaf. Dad was livid when he came in. As soon as he took his belt off I knew I was for it. That was the end of the rats for me. I got the hiding of my life, and was not allowed to poke my nose outside the door until both floods and rats had vanished, but I spent hours gazing longingly at the walls from the bedroom window.

The only bright spot that remained in the last week of that long holiday was the unexpected arrival of Uncle Mick. Things livened up miraculously for the two days he was with us, but as Mam said just before I went to bed the night he left, " 'e was a bigger flamin' menace than the rats." Life was never dull with him around, and from what I could gather, he had gone to Aunt Min's at the north end of the town, got her tiddly with some foreign stuff he had smuggled home, led her off in a wild Irish jig and nearly broke her leg as she crashed against a table. I could imagine it; she was certainly no nymph.

After that, life was at rock bottom. All too soon we were back in the damp, musty atmosphere of the school. Fatty voiced the general opinion when he wrinkled his nose as we walked into the classroom and the clammy dampness caused by the floods assailed our nostrils. "Cor!" he said, disconsolately, "it don't 'alf niff, don't it?"

I looked round the room, much as a prisoner examines his cell on his second stretch. It was long, dull, and painted a bilious green with faded green curtains on runners splitting the classroom into two. Four large windows let in any light that escaped the tall buildings around us, and in the centre, standing on a stone outcrop just below the dark beams, and immediately above a big combustion stove, was a blue robed statue of the Virgin and Child, gazing solemnly at the sufferers below.

Generations of barefoot students had passed beneath that calm unwavering gaze. I often studied those inscrutable features when lessons outpaced my mind, sometimes I gazed so long, I fancied I could see her move. I often wondered what she thought, this patient woman with her precious burden. Whatever it was it made little difference to the red-haired tyrant who sat below, and to the left on her high desk stool, Miss McIlroy, our warder and the devil's disciple.

A woman of uncertain age and temper, with piercing blue eyes that riveted you to the spot, and a fame that ran throughout the district for being faster on the draw than Wyatt Erp. All that I associated with the devil was personified in her tall angular frame. We all hated her, and the feeling was mutual.

In our class the long benches rose in a gradual slope, with the brightest boys sitting in lofty disdain at the back, but despite the possibility of sudden assault from Miss Mac, it was the front seats near the fire which were in greatest demand during the winter, because there were many among the tattered throng who not only had the flimsiest of clothes, but in many cases had had nothing more for breakfast than a slice of bread covered with condensed milk, and even this was often missing as the depression deepened.

Few, if any of us, had more than one pair of boots or clogs at any one time, and a popular expression of the times, 'Go in La, y' Mam wants y' boots' had a very significant meaning to all of us. Many a lad thus summoned, lost his boots to a pawnbroker, especially during the summer when they could be done without.

Throughout my stay at the lower school, the daily ritual remained unvaried. Some blue-eye would get the job of ringing the bell. There would be a sudden, eerie silence as everyone stood stock still. Another ring and the whole playground erupted in a frantic dash to get into class lines. Woe betide anyone with bare feet who got in the way of a flying clog! Once formed, a palpitating silence blanketed the ranks until Mr Thomas, the Headmaster, gold albert tastefully gracing his ample stomach, watch in hand, swept the ranks with bird-like intensity for faults. A fleeting feeling of bonhomie crept in as he slid his watch away and intoned his greeting.

"Good morning, children."

We made the most of our brief vocal liberty and rocked

the playground as we roared back at him. A quick nod to the waiting staff and we were on our way to the cells.

The real agony for me began with morning prayers as we lined up in front of the benches. It was always Henry's fault, straight-faced he would parody the 'Hail Mary'. Instead of 'Hail Mary full of grace', Henry's pious voice would murmur, 'Hail Mary pull a face'. Despite the consequences it never failed to tickle some perverse sense of humour in me, and I would begin to giggle. Hawkeye never failed to spot me, and as she blessed herself with one hand, she would be reaching for the cane with the other.

"Sullivan!" she'd say, eyes glinting, "you're a heathen ... I have a way with heathens." She had too; she walloped the daylights out of them.

Life in the playground was not much simpler. A fiery distrustful nature is no help to forming friendships, but after one or two hammerings from older boys, I began to learn a little tact. Not much, but a little, it helped.

Outside school, life took on an entirely new tempo, and as summer eased uncertainly into autumn Henry, Fatty—his corpulence was glandular, not over nourishment—and myself spent more and more time on the walls. We walked among the cats as though we were one of them. Gradually the leaderless gang enlarged. Young Jimmy Armfield, very small for his age, and with a peculiar twisted nose, came over from the other side of the street and joined us for no particular reason. We christened him 'Bonko' straight away. Tommy Rolf, one of the only two Protestants we had, accidentally became a member when his ball came through our front window and hit Dad on the head as he was reading the paper. Sniffer Johnson, squint-eyed and with a maniacal laugh that was to cause us endless trouble, suddenly appeared amongst us, uninvited and at first unwelcome as we squatted round Mrs Threfall's clothes-post at the end of her yard.

I remember that day well because it was the second time I got the belt off my Dad. It was a chilly Saturday morning, and with nothing much else to do, the four of us, Henry, Fatty, Tommy and myself were annoying Mrs Threfall by throwing stones at an old tin bath on her shed roof. We knew she was good for a chase if we could get her wild enough, and we could see her watching us from behind the curtains in her back bedroom, getting madder and madder as the bricks bounced off the bath. Suddenly Henry nudged me, and pointed to a squat figure just turning the corner of the entry.

" 'oo's 'e?" I asked. I didn't know Sniffer very well. His Dad was an Orangeman who lived right at the top end of the street, so they kept to their own end away from us Catholics.

"That's that cross-eyed feller from up the street," volunteered Tommy with one eye on Mrs Threfall as he crashed another brick off the bath.

"What's 'e doin' 'ere then?" I asked truculently.

" 'ow should I know?" he answered, bridling slightly, "It's a free country, in't it?"

We all turned and watched as Sniffer sauntered up a doorway and on to the wall.

"Whaddee you want?" I asked him belligerently as he came to a stop in front of us.

He rolled his good eye over the assembly, and sniffed loudly.

"Nothin'," he answered casually.

"Well you've gorrit," I said tartly. "Wrap it up an' take it 'ome."

We turned, ignored him and carried on with the game. He didn't budge.

"Bet y' can't 'it that," he said suddenly, wiping his nose on his sleeve.

" 'it what?" snapped Tommy.

"That," he answered, sniffing as though he had a bad cold, and pointing to the drainpipe running alongside Mrs Threfall's window.

"Course I can," retorted Tommy disdainfully. He jerked his thumb at Fatty. "Even Fatty could 'it it from 'ere, couldn't y', Fatty?"

Fatty grinned amiably, undisturbed by the oblique reference to his prowess.

"Talk's cheap," said Sniffer laconically.

Tommy eyed the drainpipe. I watched him anxiously.

"I wouldn't try it if I were you Tom," I said quietly. "Y' might 'it the winder." He looked at me and shrugged. The others crowded on the tiny space available.

"You're so flippin' clever, you show us!" Fatty's voice sounded petulant over my left shoulder. Sniffer's thin lips curled sardonically as he faced us. His right eye glared at me, his left at a silent Henry.

"Give us a brick," he said. Tommy passed him one about the size of a pigeon's egg, then gave him elbow room. He raised his arm and squinted along it. I saw a horrified look sweep Mrs Threfall's face seconds before it disappeared. He missed it by a foot. Then his shuddering laugh crashed on the still air as the window shattered.

"I missed it!" he said needlessly as a loud shriek came from the yard below and Mrs Threfall hurtled out. She was too late. We scattered like quail along the tiny thoroughfare.

Fatty fell into the entry with a yell. Tommy ripped his leg on an old wheel as he hurtled across the shed roofs. I nearly brained myself on Mrs Taylor's clothes-post as I flung myself over our wall, and Henry just vanished. Only Sniffer stood his ground, laughing like a maniac as he clung to the sagging clothes-line until Mrs Threfall belted him with a brush handle. We compared bruises at school next day. Everyone except Henry had had a hammering when they got home.

Gradually, as the weeks sped away, the walls became our domain until the dark nights cut off our activities. Sniffer became one of the family, unpredictable, accident prone, laughing like a hyena in whatever situation we found ourselves, and day after day we perambulated up and down, or squatted on somebody's shed until we were chased.

We got to know people more intimately in the walls than we could ever have done in the streets, because here, protected by their four crumbling walls we caught them so to speak, with their trousers down. Nature's changed completely when seen unawares through the back kitchen window. The yards were a perfect reflection of the people, and we soon became quite expert at weighing up the various families. Some were spotlessly clean. Some, at the other end of the scale, were little more than cess pits of junk. In two yards, there were minute gardens miraculously wrought from nothing, in which even the lavatories and middens took on a veneer of beauty.

Like beachcombers we would occasionally pick up a piece of flotsam from the debris of human behaviour that was pure gold, and one such occasion was when I saw the female form unclothed for the very first time.

In the time of which I write, there were no such things as bathrooms in an area such as ours, so we had what was known as 'The All Over' wash. This consisted of a series of gymnastic evolutions of which only the poorer classes, especially the miners, were the acknowledged experts. The equipment was simple. A bit of privacy, a bowl of water, a lump of carbolic soap, and a flannel. Each portion of the bather, particularly in winter time, would be washed, dried, and reclothed before proceeding to the next portion. For the intrepid, or the hardy, the whole operation could be performed 'starkers'.

Despite the difficulty of keeping clean in the overcrowded conditions time and place was always found for the operation, and, however large a family was, propriety was always maintained and the sexes strictly segregated during the performance; therefore it was all the more fascinating for me when I saw two great half moons shining at me from Mrs Mathew's kitchen across the entry.

I suppose it must have been about three in the afternoon one Saturday in the middle of Autumn 1928, when Sniffer and I, now firm friends, were sitting chatting on the wall as we waited for the rest of the lads to join us. Without warning, Sniffer nearly deafened me with his piercing laugh, and I had to grab him as he rocked dangerously on the wall.

"Luk!" he screeched, "An arse." He pointed frenziedly at the kitchen window. I sat for a few paralysed seconds, gazing at this unfamiliar sight as Rosie, an immense sixteen stone in her shift, shimmied in front of the window as she scrubbed her back. We looked at each other startled and came to the same decision simultaneously.

Leaping as though we had been stung, we tore down the wall gesticulating frantically to the rest of the lads coming up the entry.

"Come on!" yelled Sniffer, beside himself. " 'urry up or you'll miss it."

"What's up ... what'samarrer?"

We didn't wait to explain as we shot back to our grandstand seat. Neighbours popped up from all over as we howled and capered like monkeys. For a full sixty seconds the show lasted amidst shrieks and speculation. Then as suddenly as it began it was over. Our howls alerted Rosie to her precarious position. Sheer horror crossed her face as she saw us, turned and slashed the curtains across almost in one movement. But she was too late. The damage was done. We were off the wall like greased lightning spreading the news to anyone who would listen. Soon the whole street, then the neighbourhood rang with laughter as the story grew and spread.

Poor Rosie! For weeks her round, good-humoured face would colour to the roots, as she passed the gang on the way to the shops, and though she never heard a remark passed, she knew that a series of silent 'Cor's!' accompanied her on her way.

6

A Full Confession

By the end of 1928, my life was a curious blend of naivete and craft. A child, yet not a child. Loved yet unloved in the harsh practical way of the poorer working class. It was a confusing Jekyll and Hyde existence beyond my comprehension. Indoors, my place in society was strictly defined. I was to be seen, but not heard. Obey but not question.

An avid listener to adult conversation, many things they said puzzled me. A thousand questions remained unanswered, and within me the seeds of rebellion grew. Outside, in the streets and on the walls, I came into my own. Uninhibited by the superior force of my parents I flung myself into the growing activities of the gang which had now formed and solidified into eight members. Here I found equal terms I could understand. A vague pattern formed, and the fight for superiority unconsciously began.

Being a Catholic, my life both at home and at school was constantly hedged by a variety of taboos obeyed by reflex rather than reason. I found that God was everywhere, yet nowhere. An unseen companion who kept a sharp eye on me day and night. People prayed and cursed almost in the same breath. His name was on every lip. Extolled, extorted, or villified according to whim and circumstance. I went to Mass by rote, never understanding a word that was spoken. I wore my religion as I wore my skin, without thought or question. As Mr Driscoll said, I was one of *them.* It was not until this fateful year of my first confession that I realised just what being one of 'them' meant, and for the first time I gave conscious thought to sin. It was, and still is, a knotty insoluble problem.

Miss McIlroy was an authority on sin, and so she ought to have been, she had a whole class full of sinners to work on. Already a heathen in her eyes, I felt my chances of heaven at this stage were pretty slim. To add to the agony, a dose of measles on Corpus Christi earlier in the year had prevented me from making my Confession with the rest of the class, so that I was alone in my misery, harangued on every side about the pitfalls around me. Whatever I did, however innocent the intention, I found that I had committed a sin, either venial or mortal. It was a worrying time. It was very difficult at the age of eight to know just how many venials made a mortal sin, and, according to Miss Mac, once one had reached the mortal stage, there was damned little hope for one in either the here or the hereafter.

Throughout the three weeks I was given to prepare myself for the ordeal, I suffered agonies of remorse, Rosie's backside loomed large on my mental horizon. Was it a sin to look? If so, was it a venial or mortal sin? It was so difficult to pinpoint the punishment for looking at a backside.

"Examine your soul Sullivan!" exhorted Miss Mac, her eyes glinting fervently. How the devil could I when I couldn't see it? I became morose and uncertain so I decided to ask Dad about it just three days before my Confession. He was sitting by the fire nursing a splitting headache.

"Hey, Dad," I said, shaking him by the shoulder. He looked up hollow-eyed.

"Whaddee y' want?" he snapped irritably, holding his head.

"Where's me soul?" I asked.

A dull look crossed his face. "Where's y' what?"

"Me soul. ... y' know." I looked at him expectantly.

" 'ow the 'ell should I know!" he cried testily and wincing with pain. "You've got one. What the 'ell more d'y' want?"

That was that. He didn't know. Mam was too busy washing to explain, Aunt Min hadn't a clue, and it wouldn't have been any use asking Uncle Mick even if he was home because I'd heard Mam say a dozen times that he didn't have one. I was terrified. There was so much to think about and so little time left.

Did I swear? Everybody swore like troopers so I couldn't be sure. Did I answer back at home? She was kidding. I daren't. Did I miss Mass? *Nobody* missed Mass at number twelve; Dad would have had their liver. Had I ever stolen? I mused on this for hours, then I remembered that Robin Hood had robbed the rich to give to the poor, so perhaps the odd apple or cake we nicked would come into this category. God knows, the gang was poor enough.

For sleepless hours I examined every action I could remember with a sense of guilt that hung over me like a cloud. One thing kept nagging me, one act of disobedience lay across me like a great weight, and as the morning of the fateful day broke, I was still undecided whether to tell all to Father McCormack.

I felt like a condemned man as I walked up the aisle behind Miss Mac, then slipped into the tiny confessional box.

"Well, young man?"

My blood froze as the rich brogue came floating through the grill not an inch from my nose. The tip of my tongue darted out nervously to moisten lips that had turned to parchment. Outside, a hollow boom as someone kicked a kneeler in the empty church, sounded like a death knell. Should I tell him? Dare I tell him? I remembered Miss Mac's words and groaned inwardly.

"If you don't tell him everything, you'll make a bad confession, and that is worse than any sin."

"W.e.ll young man, *have* you comitted any sin?" again the priest's voice floated out to me with a slight edge of impatience. I looked desperately at the crucifix hanging just above my right ear, but the tortured face gave little comfort as it gazed back at me impassively. Suddenly a tremor ran through me, and before I quite realised what was happening, words poured from me in an avalanche.

"Father!" I almost yelled, "I ... I showed my stomach to a hen on the market, an' I saw a bum on the wall!"

For a pulsating second, only the subdued murmur of prayers in the church outside broke the heavy silence as I waited for I knew not what, then the voice, strangled with suppressed mirth said slowly, sternly, "So, you showed your stomach to a hen did you? When was this?"

Relief flooded through me. He had ignored Rosie completely.

"Before the 'olidays, Father. Fatty Boyle dared me." I suddenly remembered that I shouldn't have been at the market in the first place so I put this in for consideration. I knew Mam wouldn't find out because Miss Mac had told us that everything that was said was secret. Silence fell between us.Nervous tension began to play havoc with my plumbing.

"Anything else?" asked the unseen voice. I searched my mind frantically.

"No, Father," I said at last, squirming uncomfortably as the need to go the the toilet grew. At long last sentence was announced. Hopping from one foot to the other I listened intently.

"For your penance you will say three 'Our Father's' and three 'Hail Mary's'."

"Yis, Father." A twinge of agony entered my voice as I wriggled to avoid disaster.

"Don't forget," he added as I edged towards the door anxiously, "You mustn't go down to the market without your mother's permission. Say a prayer for me. ..."

I didn't wait for him to finish; my soul was suddenly forgotten in my overwhelming physical need. I burst out of the confessional like a cork out of a bottle, nodded briefly to a startled Miss Mac sitting rigidly on the end of the pew, then hared up the aisle to find a quiet corner at the back of the church.

Within a month of Confession my whole life turned suddenly upside down. At home, without warning or explanation, I was transferred downstairs to share the parlour with Con. Neither of us was pleased. I discovered that Con kicked like a mule in his sleep. The first night I retaliated in kind. The second and subsequent nights I suffered in silence. It was safer.

At school I was transferred to the big boys. The change was tremendous. Male masters, all experts with the cane. Giant-sized boys of eleven and fourteen, all seemingly after my blood as they crashed about the playground. Time and again during the first few weeks, a quick temper and even quicker tongue, trapped me into crossing swords with older boys, and each time I retreated, battered and defeated but a little wiser. It was a tough area. There was no room for fools or weaklings. I learned rapidly. Only once I complained at home after tangling with an older boy.

Dad's answer was short and sharp. 'Fight y' own bloody battles.' It was the first and last time I asked.

I remember this year with a sharp painful clarity. Hopeless at lessons, hammered in the playground, swept into a limbo of uncertainty at home before more pressing worries. It was a year that left an indelible stamp on my nature. I became wary, suspicious, hostile to any strange situation in which I found myself. The outer crust became hard and brittle, yet I yearned to be close to somebody, anybody. I poured my troubles out to Henry, but even he, close as we were, laughed at my dilemma one night as we sat under the street lamp talking.

" 'ow d'y' expect anyone t' like y'?" he asked solemnly after listening patiently to my flood of complaints. "You're allus argin. Y' wanna grease y'self an' slide along a bit. It's easier."

I could have thumped him as I looked into his calm blue eyes. Instead I scuffed the pavement angrily with my foot. He looked at me pityingly.

"Nobody likes y', Li, 'cause y' don't even like y'self."

I was hurt and puzzled. "You like me don't y'? " I asked half belligerently, half anxiously.

He gazed at me for a second or two, eyes half-closed, the corners of his mouth curled in a slight smile. "I'm daft!" he said laconically. I looked at him savagely as he slowly got up off his haunches. "It's no good lukin' at me like that," he added, as he walked out of the circle of light. "I ain't scared of y', an' I ain't argin." I sat silent. "Tarrar well ... see y' termorrer," he ended as his slim girlish figure merged with the blackness then vanished, leaving me staring dejectedly at the spot where he had disappeared. God I wished I was like Henry. Calm, unruffled, he never argued with anybody, yet no-one ever interfered with him. I bit my lip in exasperation. I didn't know anything of genetics then, otherwise I might have realised that a mixture of Spanish and Irish was a poor ingredient for equanimity. I was still pondering the enigma when the Town Hall clock warned me that it was time to go in.

Indoors the kitchen was packed. Aunt Sarah and Uncle Matt, Aunt Min, still awake for a change, Mam, Dad and Con all arguing at the tops of their voices about the unemployment. Dad was in the act of thumping the table to emphasise a point as I walked through the parlour door into the kitchen. His hand stopped in mid air.

"Where've you bin?" he asked brusquely.

"Sittin' under the lamp," I replied. I felt tired and edgy,

my tone must have sharpened unconsciously. He fixed me with a warning look. My senses tuned to immediate danger as I cast my eyes at the floor.

"What were y' doin'?" he asked.

I softened my voice as I shrugged and replied, "Jus' sittin' talkin' t' 'enry." We looked at each other warily. He jerked his thumb towards the parlour. "Well y' berra gerra wash, then get t' bed."

I glanced at Uncle Matt as I edged round the table to where Mam stood by the sink ready for me. He winked broadly at me. Uncle Matt always winked every time he saw me. I felt too miserable to wink back as I usually did.

Seconds later my jersey was whipped over my head, and amid a babble of conversation Mam washed my hands and face.

"Kiss y' Aunties," she ordered, giving my face a final wipe. "Then off t'y' bed." Something in her tone made me look up at her. She looked pale and drawn.

"Are y' all right Mam?" I asked solicitiously.

"No, I'm 'alf left!" she snapped as she turned to the stove to pour a cup of tea. I shrugged and gave Aunt Sarah a quick peck. She didn't like boys. It was like kissing a piece of granite.

"Ah God luv 'im, doesn't 'e look nice?" This was Aunt Min sitting alongside her. She always made a fuss of me when she was awake. I felt a sudden glow of warmth as she swept me into her arms and kissed me effusively on the cheek. Both of her children had died and she had plenty of affection to spare.

"Don't forget t' say y' prayers now," she warned me, wagging her podgy finger. "An' say one for me."

Uncle Matt laughed, "God knows, y' need all y' cin get, Minny."

I grinned for the first time that night as I walked into the parlour, blessed myself, then climbed into the makeshift bed.

It seemed as though my head had barely touched the pillow before I was violently awakened. One moment the house had the stillness of death, the next, everything erupted as a pulsating scream came from the bedroom above. I sat bolt upright, a cold clammy feeling crawling up my spine.

"What's up?" I gasped at the shadowy form of Con, already out of bed and crouched at the door listening.

"Shrrup!" he snapped.

Another cry quickly followed on the heels of the first. Low, vibrant, then racing through the scale until it reached a crescendo that seared the eardrums, then dying away to an animal like whimper. Dad's voice suddenly blasted through the house.

"Con! ... Con, y' mother's not well. Fetch Mrs Taylor; 'urry up!"

I felt the hairs on the back of my neck rise. Mam *ill*, she couldn't be. Mam was *never* ill. Thoughts and pictures crowded my racing mind. Aunt Aggie had *died* when she took ill. Cold horror gripped me as Con struggled frantically into his trousers.

I howled as I gave voice to my fears. From nowhere Con's open hand slashed against my cheek.

"Shurrup!" he snapped, grimacing fiercely. I cowered against the wall in silence. Above us, sounds of frantic activity grew more strident. The ceiling shook to the thump of urgent feet.

"I'll fetch the doctor," Bernadette's shrill voice, knife sharp with fear, suddenly rang above Mam's cries. Dad's scathing tones silenced her abruptly.

"Don't talk so bloody daft girl. We can't afford the doctor ... Mrs Taylor'll know what to do ... *Con!*" he roared, " 'ave y' gone yet?"

Con had forestalled him. He was already hammering on the wall for her.

I could sense the growing panic and uncertainty in Dad's voice; it communicated itself to me. I felt helpless and petrified. Suddenly, from deep down, a mixture of terror and love welled, and fired my shaking limbs. I had to see her. I darted out of bed and past my cursing brother, ignoring his yells to come back as I headed for the stairs with shirt tails flying.

"Liam! come outa there." Teresa, standing on the landing, yelled, grabbed at me and missed as I slipped past her and through the door. I stopped dead in the flickering light, appalled by the sight that greeted me. Mam lay half in half out of bed, her face the colour of chalk as she threshed against the restraining hands. Dad, completely unaware that he was still in his long drawers, bent holding her shoulders, eyes staring, hawk-like face, etched with shock, whilst Bernadette alternately wringing her hands, and pulling at the writhing form, seemed suddenly old.

Feet pounded on the stairs outside. I felt a hand grab the neck of my shirt, then the room whirled as Teresa yanked me bodily through the door. A split second later, Con's heavy form crashed against both of us. There was a crazy flurry of arms and legs as he cannoned off, half turned on the top stair as he scrabbled frantically to retain his balance, then toppled with a yell to the bottom where he lay, still and silent, his arm twisted grotesquely beneath him.

All hell broke loose at this new diversion.

"What the bloody 'ell's goin' on *now?*" Dad wasn't at his best in a crisis. Growing hysteria sounded in his voice as he burst through the door and glared down the stairs at us. We looked up fearfully. His eyes glittered in the uncertain light.

"Con's 'urt 'iself ..." began Teresa, trying to lift the inert form.

"Jesus wept!" he cried, dashing down and bending over the now groaning Con. "It never rains but it bloody well pours!" The words were scarcely out of his mouth when Bernadette's shrill voice, filled with alarm, froze the marrow in my bones.

"Dad! ... Dad, come quick, I think she's dyin'."

A thunderous knocking sounded at the back kitchen door as Dad galloped back to the bedroom.

"Open the flamin' door will y'?" Mrs Taylor's voice, roughed by urgency, hammered its way through the thin wood. Teresa reacted like a robot. Hair streaming wildly, eyes dull with shock, she rose and slipped the bolt all in one movement. I felt rather than saw a flurry of movement behind us, then for the second time within minutes, I was whipped off my feet and a voice hissed in my ear.

"Get back t' bed an' stay there!" snapped Mrs Taylor, as she pushed me violently towards the parlour door. She bunched her fist at me. "Poke your nose through that flamin' door, lad, an' I'll scalp y' ... Understand?"

Time has erased most of the details of that terrifying night, but nothing can erase the fever of activity that ensued, as neighbours poured in to help. I never knew who paid for the doctor, but Finnigan arrived and so did the ambulance. I can still see the pools of light all along the street as neighbours stood watching both Mam and Con taken off, one with a broken arm, the other with acute appendicitis. I stood at the window, numb with shock, tears trickling down my cheeks. My Mam was gone! Never in my life, before or since have I felt such utter loneliness.

7

I meet an Artful Dodger

My mother's sudden departure was like the removal of a corner stone in an old building. The whole house seemed to sag a little. No sudden collapse, no chaos, but a thousand little things that lacked her inimitable stamp.

Dad, now unemployed for almost two full years, became moody and unapproachable on the rare occasions he was in. Con, his arm healing well, spent most of his time round at Uncle Tom's fiddling with a crystal set that was the rage of the whole district, whilst Bernadette, never very close to me, became even more secretive than was her usual wont.

Several times I asked Teresa, who had been placed in charge of me, where my older sister was, and each time was told to mind my own business, and it was not until the fifth day after Mam had gone that I stumbled on the secret.

With approaching winter limiting our time in the streets, the gang now set up headquarters in an old shed in Fatty Boyle's backyard, and all eight of us were there on the Friday evening of this eventful week, playing pontoon for bottle tops by the light of a flickering candle. The game was good, the conversation absorbing, and time passed swiftly. Suddenly a voice roared in the night.

"Ernie! it's eight o'clock, warree y' doin' down there? Plottin' a revolution?" It was Fatty's Dad. I went cold all over. *Eight* o'clock! I could feel the sting of the belt across my bottom. Chaos suddenly filled the shed, cards and bottle tops flew in all directions as the gang, all overdue for berthing, burst through the door as though it were a speakeasy. Hurried 'tarrar's' filled the air as we dashed in our several directions.

Minutes later I was outside our backdoor, panting as I listened. Not a sound broke the stillness. An uneasy foreboding filled me. Until now I had instinctively obeyed the rules of the house as though Mam was still there. In by six-thirty, bed by seven, and now it was *eight!* I felt the hairs rise on the back of my neck.

Cautiously I opened the door, legs tensed to streak across the kitchen and straight into bed. I peeped across the room at Teresa sitting quietly by the fire knitting. For a moment we looked at each other silently.

"Is me Dad in?" I half whispered. She shook her head from side to side. I heaved a sigh of relief as I went into the warm room. "I've bin at Fatty's," I said by way of explanation, expecting a clip across the ear any second. She watched me in silence, needles clicking busily.

"Do y' wanna butty?" she asked suddenly. I looked at her in astonishment hardly believing my luck. Eight o'clock and not a word said. I eased myself towards the fire and nodded eagerly.

"Where's me Dad?" I asked stretching my hands to the flames. She shrugged. Her pretty oval face seemed strained as she rose and cut a slice of bread from the remains of the loaf on the table, then sprinkled sugar on it.

"In the pub," she answered as she handed it to me. I felt a tremor of fear run through me. Dad could be funny with drink, but I said nothing as I took the bread and started munching. For all his fire when he was aroused, Dad hated trouble at home and he would do almost anything to avoid it. His favourite refuge in a domestic crisis was the pub.

"Is 'e workin' then?" I asked. Even I knew it cost money to go to the pub.

"Course not!" she replied scornfully, seating herself beside me and watching me eat. "He's probably cadged the price of a glass off one of his mates." I sucked the last of the sugar from my fingers and glanced at the clock.

"I berra get t' bed before 'e comes in then," I announced. A flicker of alarm crossed her face. She shook her head quickly.

"Y' can't," she said, gazing worriedly into the fire. I didn't understand.

"Why not?" I asked in a surprised voice. "Me Dad'll 'ave me life if 'e catches me up."

"Don't worry, you'll be in bed before 'e comes," she replied enigmatically. I looked at her. Perversely I felt suddenly tired. All my inate stubbornness rose to the surface.

"I wanna go now!" She whipped round on her seat and fixed me with her grey-blue eyes.

"Y' can't," she snapped, "So shurrup an' siddown!" I glared back at her.

"I'm goin' *now!*" I announced, and before she could stop me I was across the kitchen and opening the parlour door. A muffled curse and a sudden flurry from the darkened room stopped me dead, then I saw two indistinct forms sitting on the settee over by the window.

"There's somebody in there!" I shrieked in fright. I felt my sister's hand grab my hair irritably.

"Shurrup. That's our Bernadette an' 'er young man," she hissed. "Now you keep y' mouth shut, d'y' 'ear?" She yanked me bodily back into the kitchen and thrust me towards the fire. Moments later the door opened and the dark sallow face of Jimmy Kiernan popped around. The secret was out. Now I knew why there had been no rollicking for coming in late. Bernadette was courting, and Mam would have her life if she knew.

"Y' didn't see me 'ere t'night," said Jimmy, wagging his finger warningly. "Y' gorrit?"

"I did see y', I did!" I yelled, "You were in there with our Bernadette." I pointed accusingly at the parlour. Teresa looked helplessly at my older sister, now standing with Jimmy inside the door.

"I couldn't stop 'm," she said pleadingly.

Bernadette gave me a filthy look. "Now I suppose you'll blab t' me Dad?" she said viciously. I sat turning the situation over in my mind as I gazed at them. Never in my whole life had an adult taken any notice of my opinion. This must be serious. I continued to stare silently. Bernadette shrugged resignedly as she spoke to Jimmy.

"You'll see, 'e'll blab as sure as 'ell, then the fat'll be in the fire."

Suddenly Jimmy dug his hand in his pocket and pulled out a penny, holding it towards me. "Now button y' lip," he said menacingly. I took the proffered coin silently. It was sheer blackmail, but this was the first penny I'd had in weeks, I nodded as he turned to Bernadette.

"Don't worry, luv," he said. " 'e'll keep 'is mouth shut." He turned and glared at me. "Won't y'?" I nodded again, fingers curled securely round the penny. "I'll give 'im a few rides on me bike, that'll shut 'im up," he continued. I liked the sound of that. I'd never been on a bike yet. He walked to the back door and lifted the latch.

"I'd berra go now anyway," he said looking at the clock. "The old feller'll be 'ere anytime, so I'll say Tarra an' see y' termorrer ... Tarrawell." With another warning look at me he was gone. Then I learned what all the fuss was about. Apparently Jimmy wasn't one of us. He was an Orangeman, and if Mam and Dad found out they were courting there would be hell to pay. I promised to keep silence. There was enough trouble without looking for more.

This tremendous secret gave me a sense of confidence I had never felt before. Safe from a hiding from either of the girls, or from Con for that matter. As long as I held it, I became bolder, enlarging my territory each day from the four streets I was normally confined to. By the second week I had progressed to the thundering world of the main shopping centre. I had seen it many times before of course, but it never looked so alluring as it did now that I was on my own.

Everything seemed to have changed. I felt myself grow in stature as I ambled, half fearfully amid the clanging throng, greedily drinking in the hectic activity around me. Huge horses, snorting with effort, dragged waggons piled high with the myriad goods that nourished the life blood of the sprawling town. Tramcars, belching motor cars, hand-carts, hauled by men in tattered rags, barrel organs, street singers, and a gigantic steamroller, all intermingled with pedestrians darting in a dozen different directions at once.

Everywhere I looked I saw a vast whirlpool of activity against a background of noise which assailed the ears like a drum roll. Human voices vied in strident competition with the noise of traffic as vendors of all descriptions extolled the virtues of their wares from the open shop fronts. But the traffic was my first love. I watched it in trance-like fascination.

"Hi ya wack!" The spell was suddenly shattered as I whirled to the sound of a high-pitched boyish voice, barking down my right ear, and I gazed, half fearfully, half belligerently at the battered, familiar figure before me. It was Dinny Devlin, a lad in the next class up from me at school, who, though I had never met him personally, I knew well by reputation.

"Hi y'," I replied non-comittally.

"What y' doin'?" he asked, answering his own question as he nodded towards the pub opposite. "Waitin' for y' ole man?"

I looked at the pub anxiously, and shook my head violently. Dad was the last person I wanted to meet just then.

"No, jus' watchin'," I answered.

Dinny grinned broadly, showing a glistening row of yellowing teeth, then, scratching his matted straw-coloured hair, he spat casually into the road. "Your name's Sullivan, ain't it?" he asked. I nodded. He pointed to himself. "Mine's Dinny. Dinny Devlin."

"Yeh, I know," I answered, scuffing the pavement with my foot.

"What gang are y' in?" he asked, picking his nose diffidently with forefinger and thumb.

"Pleasant Street," I answered laconically, then flushed with sudden anger as he burst out laughing.

"Pleasant Street!" he said derisively. "Flippin' sissies!"

I eyed him viciously, but, unsure of myself I kept silent. Almost six months older than me, he looked what he was, rough and tough, with a pair of blue eyes that fairly danced with devilment in his grimy face.

For a few seconds we teetered on the borders of open hostility then the tension broke as suddenly as it had arisen as he laughed and patted me on the shoulder.

"I was only kiddin', lad, honest." Somewhat mollified I gave him a half smile as he stood weighing me up.

"Tell y' what," he said engagingly after a few moments silent scrutiny, "I like you. You come round to our 'ouse an' we'll gerra butty apiece."

I gave him a horrified look. I had heard some lurid tales of the Devlins both from Mam and Aunt Sarah. As far as I could gather there were thirteen of them, excluding the father and mother, crammed into a two up and two down, in the next street but one to us. 'Thieves and Vagabonds' was Aunt Sarah's favourite expression when the conversation got round to them. They were taboo as far as playing with any of them was concerned. I looked furtively up and down the street to see if there was anyone who knew me about.

"Ta very much," I replied hesitantly, "but I've gorra go now. Me Dad'll 'ave me lights if 'e catches me'ere." I backed up a pace.

"What's up?" asked Dinny in a hurt voice. "I ain't got fleas y'know."

I looked at his tattered rags and wished I had his confidence. I gave him a sickly grin; it wasn't that I didn't like him. On the contrary, and despite all I'd heard, he seemed a nice lad and anxious to make friends, but ever since I could remember I had been warned about the Devlins, so I tried to disengage.

"Well tarra them," I answered lamely. "See y'

sometime." I turned to go but he seemed to have taken a fancy to me.

"Tell y' what," he said amiably, putting his hand on my shoulder. "If you won't come with me, I'll come with you. How's that?" There was little I could do about it. I nodded and shrugged resignedly.

I don't know to this day what attracted me to Dinny, but whatever it was I am eternally grateful. Without knowing it, both I, and the gang into which he was accepted without demur, had acquired not just a friend but a teacher. For his age, his knowledge of life was immense. We were babies compared with him. No situation found his agile mind wanting, and in the weeks following our meeting he amazed us all with the variety of his talents.

The gang's formal introduction into the art of surviving on nothing began the day following our first meeting, when with all our morning chores of wood chopping, cleaning shoes, and running errands done, we gathered in Fatty's shed to discuss our programme for the afternoon. The general vote was for a game of three holes in the newly tarmacked road in Pleasant View, but the new member's voice had an edge of scorn as he broke into the animated conversation.

"Three 'oles!" he exclaimed disgustedly. "Whaddee y' wanna play three 'oles for? Y' can't make nothin' outa that. Why don't we go fishin'?"

Dinny at nine, was the oldest amongst us, and none of us were allowed anywhere near the docks. We told him so in no uncertain tones.

"Not fishin' f' fish, y' idjits!" he exclaimed. "Fishin' f' pennies." Amazement must have shown on our faces.

"*Pennies!*" we said in unison.

"Yeh, pennies," he replied, shaking his head at our ignorance, "Darn grids." We just looked at him. "I'll show y'," he cried impatiently. "Anyone gorra brush 'andle?"

Fatty pointed to the corner of the shed behind him and Dinny picked up the indicated pole. "Now go an' gerra bitta soap," he ordered. Fatty nipped into the house and obliged. "Come on," said Dinny, indicating the door.

Minutes later we were heading for the shopping centre

in an excited chattering group as the master expounded his theories.

" 'ere's a grid," exclaimed Eric Daly, the youngest among us, pointing frenziedly at a grid outside a public house. Dinny snorted disgustedly.

"Luk at it," he said scornfully, pointing downwards at the diamond shaped holes. We did. It was clean as a whistle. "Pub's is no good," he said authoritatively, "They clean 'em out every day. Grocers' grids is better." He pointed to one about ten yards away, then explained to the attentive group why they were better. We nodded respectfully as we received our first lesson in psychology.

Apparently, women, especially with a pack of howling children hanging on to them, put their change into their purses on their way out of the shops, and occasionally, distractions made them drop the odd coin. The busier the shop the better the chances. Shopping days were important. Sunday was better for hunting than Monday, because Saturday was busier than Sunday.

For the next few minutes, under Dinny's instructions, and unmindful of the irritation we caused to shoppers as we lay full stretch on our stomachs, we examined four or five grids along the street. At last an excited yell announced that we had struck oil, and we looked up to see Tommy Rolf dancing like a Dervish as he pointed down a grid he had been examining, in a flash all eight of us were sprawled out peering at the rubbish below. Sure enough it was a coin. A silver threepenny piece, delicately balanced like a glistening fly on a dirty piece of paper.

At once the master took over, and we watched as he expertly spit on the piece of soap then kneaded it into a soggy mass before sticking it on the end of the pole.

"Now shurrup an' keep quiet," he warned as the pole slid through the hole. Only the steady tramp of feet against the hum of traffic broke the silence as we lay, breathlessly watching the end of the pole.

Dinny put every ounce of concentration into his task. He cued the silver coin as though he were a billiard player cueing a difficult shot. One false move and the coin would slip into any one of a thousand crevices. But he made no mistake. One or two tentative jabs to make sure he was on target, then Fsss! he stabbed at it. Sixteen feverish eyes focused as he slowly began to withdraw the pole. A thrill of triumph gripped us; it was stuck on. Dinny silenced the growing restlessness with a quick, warning look.

"It's norr-out yet!" he hissed.

We fell silent. Inch by inch he drew the pole out. There seemed to be yards of it so tense were we. At last it was out. Fatty and Tommy let out yells of delight. Eric knocked Dinny's arm in his excitement. The pole quivered, and half a dozen frantic pairs of hands grabbed as the coin came loose and bounced on the grid.

"Phew!" gasped Dinny, opening his fingers to reveal the coin, then he glared at Eric's contrite face. "Y' don't move 'til it's on the deck … gorrit?" We nodded. We got it.

Under Dinny's expert tutelage, we soon became adept at retrieving not only money, but many other unrelated items that could be turned into money, such as old hairpins, which, with the addition of a little black lacquer, sold readily at two dozen for a halfpenny. Our field of operation was wide, for most of the shops in the district had a cellar of some description, and within days every member of the gang had a pole and a supply of soap. But fascinating though we found it, this was only one of the many sources of income this tattered wizard introduced us to. There was the Pigs' bladder trade, the Manure trade, Key Hole Bombs, Winter warmers, and the Empty bottle trade, all in great demand according to the season.

Almost a month to the day she had gone, Mam came home. The house was packed with neighbours and relatives. I got a half day off school to meet her, and Dad's face, for weeks a misery, suddenly seemed lit up as he followed her through the door.

I hadn't seen her since she had gone. I was delighted, yet somehow afriad. I wanted to hurl myself at her, hug her, anything to be close to her, yet I stood rooted to the spot, blind jealousy surging through me as chattering voices engulfed her.

She looked pale and strained as she blinked in the flickering gas light. Then, for one fleeting moment her brilliant dark eyes rested on me and her mouth curled in a smile as the crowded kitchen parted into a line between us. The room stood still as she lifted her arms towards me. Suddenly I felt both happy and angry as she moved forward and swept me to her. No words passed between us in that brief, fierce hug. Red as a turkey cock I wriggled free. Didn't she know I was a big lad now? … and all those people watching!

Moments later I was swept aside as first Bernadette, then Teresa and finally a self-conscious Con, each hugged her before she was finally submerged by the rest of the company. My world was complete again. Strict though she was, she was all mine. The corner stone was back. The house unconsciously straightened itself.

For a full week after her return, with a wisdom born of experience I resisted the temptation to stay out late. They fished and played pontoon without me, but by Saturday the lure of the unknown proved too much, and when Dinny came sliding conspiratorially to me at the bottom of the street with the startling news that he had a buyer for six buckets of horsemuck, the last of my resistance crumbled. With the rest of the gang occupied collecting tin cans and cotton waste to make winter warmers, he proposed that the two of us should collect the horsemuck and share the 'Divi'.

"Are y' on?" he asked anxiously as I hesitated.

I shrugged undecidely, Mam wasn't her old self yet, but she still packed a tidy wallop, as I had found the previous day.

"Me Mam's 'ome now, Din," I explained.

Dinny looked at me sympathetically. He didn't have this trouble, nobody gave a damn where he was. "You'll be all right," he said confidently, "We'll go down the Dock Road. Them railway 'orses drop it all over the place there."

I looked at him startled. I'd never been down the Dock Road in my life.

"Warrabout Canon Street?" I suggested. The main street wouldn't be as bad as the Dock Road if I was caught.

"Na, that's no good," he replied disgustedly, "It's all

squashed flat by the carts there, anyway y' gorra keep dashin' on an' off the road for the traffic. Na, the Dock Road's best, honest, no kiddin'." He grinned delightedly as I capitulated.

Six-thirty found us pushing Dinny's ramshackle cart down the gas lit road, patiently trailing a huge railway horse that gave us all the appearance of acute constipation. All sense of time had vanished as we concentrated on the job. Dinny spat disgustedly into the four bucketsful we already had in the bottom of the cart.

"Y'd think it'd want t' drop it wouldn't y'?" he hissed viciously.

I looked at the offending horse as we plodded alongside. It didn't look to me as though it was about to perform.

"Can't we take what we've got?" I suggested, a vague uneasiness creeping over me.

Dinny shook his head emphatically. "Six buckets or it's no go!" he said shortly. "Don't worry," he added reassuringly, eyeing the tremendous buttocks. "If this one drops it we're quids in."

Suddenly a voice came through the darkness from the high seat just in front of us.

"Warr'are you kids follerin' for?"

"It's not you we're follerin' mister, it's your 'orse," yelled Dinny. "Didn't y' give it no dinner t'day? What's up with it anyway?"

A rough laugh came from the darkness.

"Y' cheeky young sod!" said the voice humorously, "Whaddee y' want me t' do, purrar penny in it?" The driver laughed at his own joke as he raised his whip and clacked the horse into motion.

Dinny's face twisted in annoyance as the horse began to trot and pulled away from us. "I 'ope y' fall off an' break y' flippin' neck!" he yelled defiantly as he turned the handcart in the direction of home. "Two more buckets," he said ruefully as he looked into the cart. "Jus' two flippin' buckets between us an' a tanner each. ..."

"Shssh!" I broke in, "Listen." He stopped the squeaking cart and stood listening intently to the steady clip clop of hooves on the cobbles. Suddenly they stopped about two hundred yards away, and out of the shadows the tinkling sound of water was born to us as the horse unburdened itself.

"Come on!" shouted Dinny exultantly. "If 'e's doin' that 'e'll do the other." Seconds later, panting from our sudden exertion, we stood watching the animal perform. I could almost feel Dinny calculating whether we would get the required two buckets.

"Giddup there!" At last the long whip flicked, the animal lurched as it took the strain, then its shadow merged into the blackness. We had made it.

An hour later, with the goods delivered, we headed swiftly for the maze of streets round our house, each holding a gleaming sixpence. I heard the Town Hall clock begin to strike as we reached the bottom of the street. We stopped and listened. One ... two ... three ... Growing dismay filled me as the rolling tones continued inexorably. I looked at Dinny in amazement across the pool of yellow light from the lamp above us. *Nine* o'clock! Realisation of what I had done clutched me with ice-cold fingers. Nothing could save me from a hammering now. Nothing. I was terrified. Dinny looked at me sympathetically. For him with his sixpence, the world was his oyster.

"What's up, Li?" he asked in surprise. "It's only nine o'clock."

"If me Dad's in, I'll get the buckle end for this," I replied with conviction.

"Tell y' what." I could sense his concern as he put his hand on my shoulder reassuringly. "I'll come with y'. After all, it's my fault."

I shook my head violently.

"No, ta," I said with growing agitation. "If me Mam knows I've bin with you, it'll make it worse."

I could have bitten my tongue off as I caught his crest-fallen expression. I knew I had hurt him and tried to apologise.

"That's all right, Li," he said resignedly. "We never go to nobody's 'ouse."

I felt sorry for him, none of the children were allowed to play with the Devlins, they were so dirty. If only they knew Dinny as we did instead of looking at the dirt that encrusted him. As suddenly as it came, the frown left him, and his cheerful smile broke through as he held his sixpence out for inspection.

"Anyway, we made a bit didn't we?" I nodded miserably. "Y' sure y' don't want me t' come now, Li?" he added. "I'll take all the blame." I shook my head negatively.

"Tarrar well," he said, "Jus' go limp when the belt lands. It don't 'urt so much that way." His advice rang in my ears as he slipped into the surrounding darkness and vanished towards the bright lights of Canon Street.

All my old fears of the darkness flooded over me as he went, yet even this fear was dwarfed by the fear of my reception when I got home. I prayed that Dad was out. How long I stood in this limbo of uncertainty I do not know, but suddenly I was aware of footsteps ahead of me. A cold clammy fear crept up my spine. Louder and louder the impatient steps sounded as they pounded towards me, then a wave of relief swept me as the footsteps gave way, first to a hazy shadow, then the familiar shape of Con.

He shook me like a rat in a mixture of relief and anger, then hauled me roughly up the street.

"You wait 'til y' gerrin'," he snarled. "Me Mam's flamin' wild I cin tell y'."

"Is me Dad in?" Even the rough treatment couldn't divert me from this vital piece of information. Then as the door opened to Con's knock, my heart took a final plunge as I saw the look on Mam's tense, pale face.

"Where've you bin?" The words grated harshly as she hissed between her tight drawn lips, and shook her fist in a gesture that couldn't be mistaken.

Evasive action was impossible. I was jammed between the two in such a way that there was no escape. I attempted diversion, and held out the coin for inspection. Anger gave way to sudden suspicion as she glared at me.

"Where did y' get that?" she snapped.

"Horsemuck," I answered laconically, holding the coin in a gesture of offering. For a long moment tension surged like an electric current as I tensed for the expected blow.

Almost two full minutes had gone by since I had come in and nothing had happened, yet I knew from long experience that Mam was swift in her justice if nothing else. Con expressed my thoughts for me.

"Arn't y' gonna belt 'im?" he asked incredulously. I waited tensely for the answer. Neither Con nor I realised the unbearable strain she had undergone in the past two hours as he and the girls had searched for me. Suddenly she seemed drained of all energy. She gazed at the sixpence still in my outstretched hand.

"Oh git t' bed before y' father comes in," she snapped. My fingers were closing over the sixpence in relief as she began to turn away. She stopped and pointed to it. "Put that in the 'oly Soul's box in church in the mornin'," she said curtly. My eyes moistened, as I slipped past Con to the sink to get a wash. The only sixpence I had ever possessed! I'd sooner she'd given me a damned good hiding.

8

World Without Reason—Amen

In the two years following my mother's operation life quickened immeasurably. It was as though my wits had been placed in an incubator and the temperature turned up. My senses sharpened, a definite pattern of life clarified.

Through receptive ears, sharp eyes, and a questioning tongue, my relations with people took on a deeper significance. I learned many diverse things. I learned the meaning of poverty and of religion. I learned that God had not one, but many faces. That going to church and being holy were two entirely different things. I saw men go to church, then to the pub, then straight home and batter their wives or children, then go to Benediction the same night. I learned from innumerable contacts that happiness and misery are relative things, with character the arbiter of both, but above all I learned from my mother to look squarely at fate and spit in its eye. In the roaring world about me I had many tutors, but none was more lucid than necessity itself.

Only at home did my place remain constant, to remind me that in years I was still only ten. Beyond its walls, in the rough hurly burly of the streets, the struggle for recognition and supremacy had already long begun. Native craft, nurtured and guided by the indefatigable Dinny, began to feel its way with ever more certainty through the labyrinth in which I found myself with religion, heredity and temperament, all playing their parts in the intricate moulding of the chrysalis character.

Cold reason played little part in our lives at this time, instead, we reacted with the clear-cut logic of children to any circumstances in which we found ourselves. If, as I did, one wanted to dominate, one didn't reason with those one wanted to gain ascendancy over, one simply fought for mastery. The yardstick was strength, both physical and mental, and on this fundamental principle, the first sign of friction arose between Dinny and me despite our natural affection for each other.

As a result of his own teachings I was no longer the pliable mite he had found staring starry eyed at the traffic just two short years before. I began to resent his knowledge, his influence in the gang, and the tentative hold he had over us all, and, with only him between me and the undisputed leadership of the gang, I began to dispute decisions which hitherto I had accepted meekly.

A crisis was inevitable, and the break came on the Saturday, two weeks before the summer holiday of 1930, a time of great significance for the leader of the gang, for without full control throughout this long break, many of our planned activities would be ruined by bickering.

It had been one of those days for me right from the start. Twice since breakfast I had run foul of Mam, once for muttering under my breath, and once for glowering, each time only my footwork saved me, but about half past nine, as I was desperately trying to get my jobs finished to get out, she lit the final spark.

I was busy chopping the last of the week's supply of firewood when she poked her head round the kitchen door and hollered down the yard. I sighed as I dropped the chopper and walked into the back kitchen.

"Whaddee y' want?" I asked, a slight edge of belligerency in my voice as I stood just inside the open door.

" 'ave y' finished the wood yet?" she snapped, flashing me a smouldering look. I could see she hadn't forgotten the earlier episode yet.

"No," I answered, more cautiously.

"Well, don't take all damned day over it will y'?" I remained silent as she reached up to the mantlepiece for her purse. "Anyway," she continued, "y' cin leave it a minute, I want y' t' gerra birra fish off the fish man." She nodded towards the parlour. " 'e's in the street; 'is bell's just gone."

I groaned inwardly as I took the proffered coin from her outstretched hand. I hated the fishman, and he hated kids. I closed my fist over the sixpence and went through the parlour door, and groaned again as I looked across the street. The cart was already surrounded with customers.

The fishmonger's face was the usual picture of misery as I sidled up to the cart and stood eyeing the slimy contents morosely.

"Slimy lukin' lot ain't they?"

I turned and glared as the familiar voice whispered confidentially in my ear. It was Alfie Chapman. I half closed my eyes as I glared at him. Alfie didn't bother me these days. I turned my back on him and fiddled with the tail of a cod as I studiously ignored him.

"Bet y' darn't pick it up?" he said with a snigger. I gave him a smouldering look and picked it up for a fraction of a second. Alfie looked disappointed.

"Bet y' darn't go near 'im an' pick one up," he said challengingly, nodding in the direction of the fishman busily weighing up at the other end. I moved round the cart deliberately and stretched my hand towards a herring.

"Take y' fingers off that there flamin' fish!" I whipped my hand back as the irate voice roared down my ear. "People's gorra eat that y'know" he added amidst approving nods from the customers. Conscious of Alfie's smirking face behind me, I looked at the fishman cheekily then poked my finger at another fish.

"I won't warn y' again!" he said menacingly as he picked up a small cod for a waiting customer. I gazed at him for a second, then on impulse stuck my tongue out at him. There was a blur of movement and almost simultaneously I felt a stinging soggy slap, as he wrapped the fish he was holding round my neck. Uproar broke out round the cart.

"Warree y' doin' with my bloody fish!?" roared the flabbergasted customer. "Don't kid y'self I'm payin' f' that mate."

"We-ell," said the fishmonger, half plaintively, " 'e keeps proddin' the damned things. Warree y' want me t' do? Pat 'is flamin' 'ead?"

I didn't wait for the rest of the argument as I skidded across the road seething with anger that I should have been humiliated in front of the grinning Alfie.

Mam's reaction as I put the money on the table with the briefest of explanations was swift. She made a frantic grab at me, but I evaded her with a quick twist, and shot through the door, straight down to the meeting place with the gang, in a raging temper. I was already well late and they were basking in the sun on our headquarter's roof when I arrived, breathless and dishevelled.

"What's up with your 'ead?" asked Tommy Rolf as I shimmied up the wall and dropped down beside him.

"The fishman 'it me with a fish!" I snapped. A howl of laughter greeted the remark as I wiped the fish scales out of my hair, but I was in no mood for laughter as I gazed savagely at the gang sprawled out around me. "Never mind the funnies," I snarled as Henry came over and joined me on the edge of the roof. "What's goin' on?"

Henry shrugged. "Nothin'," he said, "We've bin waitin' for you." I relaxed a bit.

"Anyone about?" I asked. Henry gazed at me calmly and shook his head.

"There's a funeral on this afternoon," volunteeredd Eric Daly, as he sauntered to the far side of the roof and looked down into the deserted yard below. I heaved a sigh of relief. We wouldn't be disturbed for two or three hours yet. I gazed round at our summer headquarters on top of the undertaker's roof. I was quite proud of it. It was an ideal spot for our purpose, and the warm corrugated iron gave us plenty of elbow room.

Strategically it was perfect, giving an unrestricted view of all Pleasant View, of which it formed the cul-de-sac, and with no less than three other streets, in which there were rival gangs. Without moving a muscle, we could keep an eye on virtually the whole of our district. It had been a hard won position. Twice in the past three months we had fought pitched battles with the street nearest the yard for its acquistion, and the occasional chase from the irate undertaker when we disturbed his horses was considered a small price to pay for such amenities.

Within minutes of my arrival the hot sun beat down on a squatting semi-circle as we made ourselves comfortable, with Dinny in his usual place on my right. I was in one of those truculent, angry moods that so often landed me in trouble at home, and Fatty, dangling his bare feet comfortably over the roof edge, could not have picked a worse time to put a question.

"Warrar we doin' this afternoon?"

I looked up at the sound of his voice, then felt a sudden blaze of anger as I saw him looking, not at me, but at Dinny. I was the leader, not Dinny, I thought savagely. I glanced round the gang in seething silence and realised with a shock that they were all looking at Dinny. For a moment or two only the nervous stamping of the horses below us broke the tense silence. Instinctively I knew a crisis loomed. If I made no move the leadership would automatically pass to Dinny. I glanced out of the corner of my eye at the grubby figure, trying to weigh him up.

All the time he had been with us I had never seen him fight except in a pitched battle. I tried to assess my chance with him. He was older and bigger than myself, and despite his deceptive thinness I knew he was tough. I could have kicked Fatty for placing me in this position. Everyone sensed trouble. For a full minute there was dead silence.

I like and admired Dinny, but I was in no mood to try and reason so soon after the fishman incident. Dinny made no move to refute the implication of Fatty's question by passing it back to me. He accepted the challenge, and if I yielded now I would yield for good.

At last, with the nerves of my stomach tensed, hands clasped round my knees, I twisted and stared straight at Dinny as I answered Fatty's query.

"I'll say where we're goin' this afternoon Fatty, not 'im!"

The ball was now in Dinny's court, and I waited anxiously to see if he would capitulate without a fight neither of us wanted.

A thrill of anticipation and fear ran through me as I saw his eyes narrow beneath the unruly thatch, then, with quiet deliberation he spat over the edge of the roof, narrowly missing a couple of neighbours gossiping beneath.

"If they want me t' lead 'em," he said slowly, "I'll lead 'em . . . Warree y' gonna do about it?"

I felt suddenly sick as he rose from his haunches. Dad's constant advice flashed through my mind. 'If y' gonna fight,' he always told me, 'Don't argue . . . 'it 'em an' 'it 'em quick.' I acted on it immediately. The words were barely out of his mouth when I rose and struck at the same time. Tumult broke out as the lads scattered to give us room. The horses in the stalls below, bellowed in sudden terror as our pounding feet startled them. Neighbours and grooms yelled in annoyance, but we were oblivious of everything.

"What the 'ell's goin' on up there?"

"Gerrof that bloody roof before y' fall off!"

The advice from the funeral yard was a fraction too late. All my pent-up emotion screeched for action, and a wild surging anger gripped me as I swung at Dinny and missed. For a split second I teetered widly on the edge then crashed with a startled yell on to all fours. I was still rising when I felt a stunning blow on the back of my head. It was Dinny. I twisted my head and saw a blurred fist raised to strike, ducked instinctively, then staggered as his knee caught me viciously on the forehead. My head reeled with the blow. I felt frantic hands scrabble at my jersey as women tried to separate us. Mens' voices came dimly through the whirl of action.

"Leave 'em alone ... lerr'em fight it out!" A group of unemployed yelled as they cheered us on.

No quarter was asked or given in the five hectic minutes it lasted. Hands, feet, elbows and knees all played their part in the frantic effort to conquer. I was tiring fast. I had badly misjudged my opponent, but there was no going back. His thin wiry frame seemed as fresh as ever as I swung in wild desperation. Then, as suddenly as it had started it was all over. For a split second Dinny dropped his arms as he gasped for air. Instinctively I seized the opportunity, grabbed him by the shoulders, lowered my head, and pulled him sharply towards me to give him the 'Liverpool Touch'. I was horrified at the result, blood poured from his nose where my head had caught him fair and square. I gasped for air as I staggered dazedly from the force of the blow. My legs felt like jelly as I stood facing him with wavering fists, waiting, hoping he'd had enough.

He shook his head, looked at me and grinned faintly. I had seen that trick before, and kept my fists up. Then a sigh of relief ran through me as he grinned again, pawed at the blood on his jersey, then held both arms out, palms towards me.

I made no move to shake hands. "Warrar we doin' this afternoon?" I asked, fists still clenched and raised.

"You name it!" he said laconically. I grinned and relaxed. I was safe until the next challenge.

It was the last real hurdle I remember in the streets until I left school. The gang solidified into a compact unit that was to last for the next four years. My friendship with Dinny seemed to strengthen rather than diminish. All the tensions that had been growing between us vanished after the fight, and with all the accumulated knowledge of his eleven years at my disposal, we went from strength to strength.

The normal street games during the long hot summer, now seemed to hold less and less attraction for us, and we began to systematically explore every place forbidden to us. Saturday mornings after our household chores, we spent under Dinny's astute tutelage, learning the art of dickering for jobs among the myriad stall-holders at the market. Sundays after Mass were fruitfully occupied keeping an eye open for police at a half penny an hour for the illegal Pitch and Toss schools that could be found on any piece of waste ground round the dock area. But whatever my position among my own age in the street, at home I walked both quietly and warily in an atmosphere that could reach flashpoint in a twinkling.

Mam at this time was like the irate captain of a slowly sinking ship, as she tried to keep afloat without any regular money, and weekends became purgatory when Dad put on his only suit to go to church, then inevitably to the pub.

"Watch those beer stains ... don't lean against anythin' sticky ... Mind y' don't tear it." Her instructions poured out like a Sergeant Major's and with good reason. He was putting on the housekeeping for the following week. The suit had to go to the pawnshop at eight sharp on Monday and stains were fatal.

Between the eternal worry of his suit and continual unemployment for almost three years, Dad's normally easy-going temperament changed drastically. He became moody and unpredictable and, like myself, spent as much time out of doors as he could, and Con, out of his hard-won apprenticeship a year and no job, became more and more like him every day. Only the girls seemed to have any real zest for life at this time. Teresa because of her new job as a skivvy in a house on the edge of town at seven and six a week, and Bernadette because of her illicit courtship. Mam and she lived a life of armed neutrality. Both were fiery and mule-like in their attitudes, and though Mam had long learned the secret of her courtship, Jimmy was no nearer entering the house officially than the night I caught them in the parlour, and twice during the year Mam had hammered the daylights out of her to no purpose. Orangeman or not, she wouldn't give him up. The result was that I became unofficial courier between the frustrated lovers.

As a result of his faithfully kept promise to give me rides, I came to know Jimmy better than my own brother, and from him, with the bike as my classroom, I began to learn a little of the growing unrest that filled the town in the form of gesticulating bands of unemployed festooning every street corner.

With Jimmy I entered another new world, and for the first time, went beyond the borders of the town into the cool green of the Cheshire countryside. It was pure heaven. Wide skies, open fields, long twisting roads. Questions poured from me interminably, and with them I discovered a rebel. He used me as a perfect foil for his pent-up emotions. I heard words hissed through Jimmy's clenched teeth that I had heard a thousand times in fierce arguments at home. 'Down trodden', Capitalists, Communists, Under-privileged. The more irate he got, the faster he pedalled. Most of the time I didn't understand a word he said, but liked the speed, and swiftly learned to ask the questions calculated to get his goat and set him off. For hours he would pedal me around, and as I listened, I wondered.

It was the Saturday after my fight with Dinny, and during one of our rides that Jimmy told me he was going to address a meeting at the Dock gates that afternoon, and I felt a quiver of excitement when he said his brother (another reason for Mam's dislike), newly released from Walton Jail after three months for disturbing the peace, was going to speak. This was real news. Alfie Kiernan was well known throughout the district as a troublemaker. I could hardly wait to get back to the gang to tell them of the possible excitement.

At two-thirty, together with hundreds of unemployed, the gang drifted slowly towards a piece of waste ground in front of the Dock gates where a huge restless crowd, ringed by wary police, ebbed and flowed as they waited for the meeting to get under way. Tension stalked the air like a living thing. Suddenly Eric grabbed my arm and pointed.

"Hey Li, there's y' Dad an' Uncle Matt!"

I gave a startled look in the direction of his pointing finger. Suddenly the whole gang stopped dead, and one by one they spotted fathers, brothers or uncles. Tommy put our thoughts into words.

"Let's git!" he said. "If me Dad spots me, 'e'll 'ave 'is belt off." For a second I hesitated. We had walked all the way there, it seemed a pity to waste the time.

"Luk," I said, "We've come this far. Let's 'ave a luk round the docks." Eager heads nodded, and by common consent we turned and headed towards some warehouses some three hundred yards away. It just wasn't our day. We had scarcely sauntered past the first of the huge open doors when an irate yell came from the interior.

"I'll 'ave the scuffers after you lot!" We looked at each other startled, then my eye caught a broken crate of oranges just inside the door. Conclusions were simultaneous. The watchman must have thought we had done it. Only fools plead innocence with evidence like that, and with police all over the place I gave the only order I could. "Scatter!" I yelled at the top of my voice, suiting the action to the words as I belted round the corner of the warehouse with the watchman hard on my heels.

My heart almost stopped. Slap in front of me a shunting engine painfully dragged its waggons right across my path. With a fleeting glimpse of blue overalls right behind me, I reacted as though I had been stung. There was only one way out. I hurled myself at the low footplate as it passed me, and with a mental picture of two pairs of startled eyes glaring at me, flashed like a wraith through the cab, down the other side and away like the wind.

Fifteen minuters later the gang had reassembled among the old derelict boats just inside the gates, and in the depths of our favourite one, we recounted our experiences. Dinny was especially incensed.

"Sodden cheek!" he ejaculated vehemently. "Didn't even

touch 'is bloody oranges. I say let's go back an' pinch some, then 'e'll 'have somethin' t' chase us for."

I vetoed the idea immediately. I'd had enough, and anyway I didn't want to take a chance on running into Dad. Instead I suggested we wait where we were until things cooled down, then go down to the Lirage just down the road and try and get some pigs' bladders. The idea was accepted unanimously. The weather was ideal for the trade, and at a half penny each, they would be readily snapped up for use as footballs.

I looked across at Henry. This was his special department. No one could cadge like him. With his thin, girlish figure, tattered clothes, and large appealing eyes, it was hard for anyone to resist him once he put his mind to it.

"Are y' on, 'enry?" I asked him. His full lips curled into a slow smile as he nodded.

"The usual divi," I announced. "Tuppence for 'enry if we gerr'enough, an' the rest between us, fair enough?" Everyone nodded in agreement. There was never any argument about giving Henry more than the rest because getting the bladders from the slaughterer's was the most difficult part of the job.

Within an hour we were home and dry with a dozen bladders from pigs slaughtered that morning. I took one, then split the remainder up between them for cleaning and blowing up. Then, arranging to meet them at headquarters after tea, I made my way first to the woodyard where Bernadette had recently started as a piecework wood chopper, to deliver a message from Jimmy, then home.

9

My Rich Uncle

For those fortunate enough to live in the countryside as I do now, it is difficult, almost impossible, to imagine the effects of a long hot summer in a close-packed slum community. Add to this overcrowding, an acute shortage of money, enervating unemployment, temperaments like unstable nitroglycerine, with the whole leavened by religious bigotry, it is not surprising that life never assumed a humdrum aspect.

These were the ingredients of life in the Birkenhead of 1930. A year of restless emotions among the adults which seemed to gather uneasy momentum as the months sped away. Angry meetings of the unemployed became a daily feature. Emotive words by the million poured from writhing lips on every street corner. Police and people alike walked warily, and only the intimates of the slums like Lofty retained the affections of those around them.

For us the children, running barefoot and ignored in all but the essentials of life in this iron crucible, the gang became our family. In it we found not only ourselves, but in each other the close affection we were denied by our harassed parents. We were a series of biological accidents, thrown together by circumstances over which we had no control, yet which gave us a breadth of craft impossible in gentler surroundings.

During these hectic, halcyon days, I rarely touched home except to do my essential chores and sleep. Of Dad I saw little, except when he came religiously, drunk or sober into the parlour, to say goodnight and make the sign of the cross over me. Con I saw even less. At last, frustrated beyond endurance, he had scrounged an old bike, and with a two-and sixpenny piece Uncle Matt had given him, had set off on an impossible ride to South Wales in an effort to find work. How or where he lived until the bad weather brought him home, thin and emaciated in October, no one ever found out.

Bernadette, still fighting a running battle with Mam over Jimmy, had through starting her new job at the wood yard, unconsciously bequeathed Dad's one and only suit to me; it would now be my duty to take it to the pawnshop each Monday morning.

In a strange way I welcomed the responsibility. It not only gave me status in the gang, but a feeling that at last I was contributing directly to the house. In these days of Universal Welfare, the pawnshop is an institution spoken of in hushed whispers, but in the time of which I write, these noisome caverns were among the few remaining financial pools in which the destitute could bathe. It seems incredible now that whole areas of people could exist by pawning something on Monday, redeem it at a little extra cost on Friday, then start the process all over again. But they did, not because they wanted to, but because they were forced to.

With most of the people owning only the clothes they stood in, it was an ever recurring problem to get something *to* pawn, and in this a primitive form of hire purchase by the big stores came in useful. With these 'cheques' as they were called, the stores not only ensured that any available money was spent with them, but it gave people a chance to obtain something that was pawnable.

The amount of the cheque granted depended entirely on the reliability of the customer, and ranged in amounts from one to ten pounds, although the latter was almost as rare as money itself. The average was about two pounds ten. The procedure was simple. For a deposit calculated on the amount of the cheque, the 'talleyman' arranged its issue with his firm, then, as each item was purchased, the amount was entered on the back until the whole was expended. The firm then took back the cheque, and the customer continued the weekly payments until the debt was cleared.

It was after the final purchase that the fun usually started. The talleyman still had to get his money each week. Most of them aged prematurely and died of worry! At this point the cheque system dovetailed nicely in with the pawnbroker. Having got working capital, in the form of clothing with the cheque, one was now in a strong position to seek financial aid from 'uncle' if the going got rough, and, providing that the article could be redeemed each week, everything was all right. If it could not be, then one lost not only the article as an unredeemed pledge, but still had to face the talleyman. It all required deft handling.

Like every human activity, the pawning trade had its artists, who could, in some miraculous way, raise a bundle by borrowing an article here and one there among the neighbours. It was a dangerous business. Dad lost a good pair of long woollen drawers this way. The woman who borrowed them did a moonlight flit the same night, and the pawnbroker sold them to defray expenses. I can still recall his exact words when he found out, but I will refrain from repeating them here.

The rules of the pawnshop were strict. Whatever came in *had* to be clean. Nothing, however good, would be considered otherwise, and the fact that the bulk of stuff pawned was old clothes was simply due to the fact that people had nothing else, jewellery and trinkets having gone long before I came on the scene. Looking back, I think the most alarming thing about pawning was the complete loss of dignity. This went over the counter with the bundle, but, unlike the bundle, one got nothing for it, and it was this aspect of the problem that led to the rise of a completely separate race of pawners, 'the commission women'. These ladies, hard as nails, sharp-tongued, and lightning-witted, traded on dignity as they came loaded liked Christmas trees to haggle on behalf of their more bashful sisters in misfortune. They were all artists in their own right. The greater their eloquence and ability, the greater their commission, but even these were completely overshadowed by the pawnbrokers themselves.

As students of human nature, these men were unsurpassed. I think Freud must have been a pawnbroker. Hard and cynical, they seemed devoid of emotion. Each day of their lives they watched a procession of degradation which could not fail to harden them. They *could* be kidded, but it took a virtuoso to do it.

Our particular 'uncle', Mr Caldwell, one of four in the district, had spent his life in the trade. There were few chinks in his armour. Tall, thin, and with deceptively gentle brown eyes, he had a cold flickering smile that swept across his thin features with the brevity of summer lightning. There was a permanent air of faint amusement about him which suggested that he knew the personal history of almost every bundle in the district. Few could equal him in verbal battle, but there was one, or rather two, who could more than hold their own. Commission bundler 'Dirty' Gerty Armstrong. Fat, sassy and fifty. (Reputed never to have washed since she accidentally fell into a puddle after the relief of Mafeking), and Ernie her cat. They were inseparable. If anything, Ernie was the more villainous of the two. A shaggy tom of indiscriminate colour and morals, he looked like a feline Marquis de Sade, and was just as debauched.

He was, said Gerty proudly, a 'fightin' cat' and his tufted coat bore mute evidence of her accuracy. Like everyone except Gerty Mr Caldwell hated him, and on the several occasions I had been in the shop with Bernadette when the pair came in, I had noticed a sudden silence, as all eyes, not least the pawnbroker's, turned to Ernie, strutting, tail up, besides the varicosed legs. A hard cynical look would come into the cat's eyes as it surveyed the place with a proprietory air before leaping lightly on to the sacred counter. Mr Caldwell always reacted violently.

"Gerty! ... get that mangy bloody cat outa 'ere. Why the 'ell don't y' gerrit destroyed!"

Gerty leapt to its defence as she stroked her furry friend lovingly. "Ah where's that didum's lad then?" she cooed, "Did that skinflint shout at 'im?"

Sheer exasperation took hold of the pawnbroker at this display.

"Gerty ... I won't tell y' agin, gerrit out ... the flamin' thing's not 'ygenic." A sudden swipe, a howl of protest from Gerty, a spit from Ernie as he leapt off the counter and he was gone until the next time.

As a boy I loved these visits. All the world and its mother assembled there, Catholics, Protestants, Hebrew and Hottentot, all rubbing thin clad shoulders and finding laughter where only tears had an hereditary right.

Despite its ignominy, the ramifications of the pawnshop on the close-packed society was immense. Born of necessity, it survived on the poverty which surrounded it, and it served a vital purpose in the era in which it survived. Without it, many would surely have starved. But overall resided 'The *Bundle*'. Enigmatic, yet eloquent, shy, yet flamboyant as it screamed its owner's poverty for all the world to see.

I looked forward eagerly to my first official visit in charge of the suit. It had an air of excitement out of all proportion to the job, and throughout the weekend I felt a superiority towards the remainder of the gang who, as yet, were not allowed to perform this vital function.

Monday dawned with a clear blue sky, and the parlour was bathed in soft sunlight as Mam's stentorian voice rang through the thin door in time with the striking of the Town Hall clock. Seconds later she popped her head round the door. As always she was fully dressed, hair braided into a neat bun, clean apron over her long black dress.

"Come on!" she snapped, "It's seven o'clock. You'll be at the back'f the queue if y' not careful."

I was quick to react to the sharpness of her tone, and in a twinkling was out of bed and dragging my trousers on as I headed for the sink to get washed. The all important bundle, already wrapped in brown paper, lay waiting on a chair near the open door, and as I moved from the sink to the piece of bread and condensed milk laid out for me on the table, I listened to her detailed instructions.

"Don't forget," she said earnestly, "when 'e asks y' 'ow much, just say,'Me Mam said the same as last week, seventeen an' a tanner'. Can y' remember that?" I nodded, chewing steadily on the tasty bread. She laid her hand gently on my shoulder. "Now don't forget t' say 'Please', will y'?"

Her voice suddenly grew impatient as I continued to chew without replying. I snapped sharply into focus as her finger tips flicked painfully across my neck.

"I 'eard y', Mam, honest I did!" I cried, swivelling round quickly on the chair and gazing at her. "I say the same as last week!"

" 'ow much?" she snapped.

"Seventeen an' a tanner!" I whipped the answer out like a shot. The next time she flicked her hand, her fingers might not be open.

Within minutes of my mother having satisfied herself

that everything was all right, I had bolted the last of the bread, and, with the bundle balanced on my head and butterflies in my stomach, I set off for the entry leading to the main street. I was on my way at last, and for the first time began to feel alarm as the awful responsibility of Dad's suit began to weigh on me. Half past seven sharp I rounded the corner and stopped dead. There; right in front of me was the tall forbidding figure of Taffy Jenkins on point duty.

I lowered the bundle in front of my face in an effort to conceal myself. It was barely three days since he had caught Dinny, Henry and me hanging on to the back of a tramcar, and threatened to take us to our parents. Had he forgotten? Would my presence remind him? I peeped cautiously over the bundle, scuffing one bare foot against the other uncertainly. There was no way out. To get to the pawnshop opposite I *had* to pass him. I was still in a fever of indecision when he called to me.

"Come on young feller. You're gonna be late f' school if y' stand there all day." He nodded to the lengthening queue outside the shop. As he spoke I became aware of something huge materialising beside me, and I looked up to see the biggest woman I had ever seen in my life. To my startled eyes she looked like a mountain, more so because of the vast array of bundles that hung about her. I gazed in astonishment at the florid, sweat-streaked face surmounting her massive bosom.

"Jesus it's 'ot!" she exclaimed, splaying her bunioned feet as she gave a frantic hitch to her slipping load. Slowly, and with awe, I examined her, from the iron-grey wire sticking out in wild disarray from her bullet-like head, to the threadbare galoshes that struggled to enclose her enormous feet. Her eyes, brilliant blue, and deep sunk beneath beetling brows, glared belligerently at Taffy as he waved his arms at the traffic.

"Hey, Taff!" she yelled suddenly, in a high-pitched squeaky voice that contrasted sharply with her generous build. "Whaddee y' think y' doin' there ... conductin' a bloody orchestra? ... We're waitin' t' cross."

She threw me a quick nod. Taffy grinned broadly.

"Sorry, Annie," he roared back above the noise of the traffic. "I thought y' were waitin' for the Ferry! Anyway why don't y' gerrup in the mornin's. ... They've bin there 'alf an hour." He flicked his head to the queue. Annie's toothless mouth writhed in a hideous grimace as she tried to find a suitable answer, but before she could speak he held his hand up, and like a liner with a tug in tow, she waddled across amid a stream of ribald comment. Even I came in for a bit of friendly advice from Taffy as we passed him, with a warning to keep off the trams.

Across at last, Annie, burst in among the queue like a bomb as she jammed her slipping bundles against the wall to get a better grip. Without a word she seemed to have adopted me, and I hovered close to her voluminous skirts as she shooed me this way and that until we were settled in the noisy line. I felt myself pressed and squashed on all sides. It was difficult to breathe. Suddenly there was a disturbance behind, and without warning I was squeezed like a pip as Annie jammed my head between one of her bundles and the woman in front, as she turned to see what was going on.

I felt her quiver as she roared at the interloper.

"Gerty!" I heard her shout, "You've gorra bloody cheek. You get t' the back where y' belong!" Seconds later, a feline screech, followed immediately by an indignant cry from Gerty, confirmed that the terrible twins had tried to jump the queue and Ernie had been booted, but before an argument could develop, a new diversion broke out in front of us. Caught as I was I couldn't see a thing, but a sudden surge forward, coupled by the irate cries of those in front as they hammered on the door, told me that they were getting impatient.

"Warree y' doin' in there, y' old skinflint?" shouted someone. "Countin' y' shekels?"

"Fiddlin' the bloody books more like," answered an authoritative voice from the back.

The restive queue frightened me. I felt stifled. I never did like people too close to me, and I felt a growing panic as I struggled for air between the pulsating bodies. But even greater than the fear for myself was the fear that

Dad's suit might get damaged. Then, as always when I was badly frightened, I reacted violently, and a howl of anguish rose from the small rotund woman in front of me as I lashed out with my feet.

"Y' little sod!" she cried, whipping round like a wounded tigress.

Like lightning she stamped on my bare foot to prevent my escape as she raised her hand to strike. I sensed a huge bulk tower over me as I prepared for the blow. It was Annie, her mouth set hard as her blue eyes bored into the woman's face.

"You lay a finger on 'im, Maggie Kenyon, an' I'll flatten y'!" she hissed menacingly. " 'e's with me." My would-be assailant scowled as she lowered her hand.

"An' gerrof 'is bloody foot while you're at it," added Annie as she glanced down at my trapped foot. I gazed at her with almost doglike affection as she forced an opening in which I could stand in comfort. "If anyone wants t' know," she announced loudly, "You're with me. ... What's y' name anyway?"

"Liam Sullivan," I answered respectfully.

"Not Mary Sullivan's lad from Pleasant Street?" she cried in astonishment.

I nodded.

"Mother'f God," she exclaimed looking me up and down, "You've grown like a bloody weed. ... What does she feed y' on ... horsemuck?"

I gazed dumbly at her.

"Where's your Bernadette anyway?" she asked as I remained silent.

"Workin'," I answered laconically.

"Is she now!" she said, surprise in her voice. "Wonders'll never cease. Where's she at?"

"Mickey Joyce's woodyard," I answered, clutching my bundle tightly.

A look of concern crossed her florid face. The woodyards were tough places for a girl.

"An' she's welcome to it!" she said, "That feller's. ..."

I never knew what Annie thought of my sister's new employer because without warning the doors opened and I was swept irresistibly forward into the dim interior of the shop.

Around me pandemonium broke loose as the customers struggled against the counter in an effort to get served first, and the hot, humid atmosphere became filled with high-pitched badinage that would have not been out of place in a barrack room. I felt completely bewildered, but fortunately my suspense was short lived. With remarkable efficiency the first few customers were dealt with and I was still dithering when the bundle was suddenly whipped out of my hands and banged on the counter, level with my eyes.

" 'ow much did y' Mam want, luv?" asked Annie in a strangled whisper that could be heard all over the shop.

"Same as last week," I answered promptly.

" 'ow much was that?" she asked.

Panic gripped me as my mind went a complete blank. I suddenly felt in urgent need of the toilet, it was too late. I went crimson with humiliation. Not only could I not remember the vital amount, now I had wet trousers as well. I felt like a tiny speck of dust as Mr Caldwell leaned over the counter and glared at me.

"Well 'ow much?" he asked impatiently.

" 'e said 'is Mam said the same as last week," volunteered Annie.

" 'ow much was that?" he asked.

Annie raised her ample eyebrows. " 'ow the 'ell should I know!" she exclaimed, then her mouth curled in a half smile as she fingered the suit and made an opening gambit on my behalf.

"Birra good stuff this, worth a coupla quid at least," she said without batting an eye.

Mr Caldwell looked at her cynically. "Pull the other leg, Annie luv," he said quietly. "It's got bells on."

Annie shrugged, she'd tried.

The pawnbroker sighed disconsolately as he thumbed through his ledger.

"Hmn!" he said at last, "Seventeen an' a tanner," I watched anxiously as he rubbed his chin thoughtfully, a sure sign that the pledge was losing its value. I felt helpless. My wet trousers stuck to my legs, I was way out of my depth, and with a mixture of anger and shame I knew it.

"Seventeen an' a tanner's a lot, Annie," he said, examining closely for marks. He nodded knowingly. "It's bin in a few times too."

I gazed from one to the other, as the fate of the suit hung in the balance. It had never even entered my head that I wouldn't get the specified amount, and I didn't know what to do if he offered less.

Suddenly all the glories of my new office vanished. All I wanted to do was get out. I looked appealingly at Annie, and like the good soul she was, she brought all her powerful armour to bear on the wavering target. Harshly, yet with humour skilfully infused into her voice, she leaned confidentially over the counter.

"Go on, y' old skinflint," she said quietly, "That's a bloody good suit an' you know it. If y' gave 'im eighteen bob, y' wouldn't be strainin' y'self."

Mr Caldwell looked at her as though she had suggested something indecent. "Whaddee y' think this is, Annie, a mission or somethin'? ... anyway," he added, a note of triumph in his voice, "luk at the beer stains." His long bony finger pointed to the lapels where Dad has spilled a drop.

Annie looked at him as though he had crawled from beneath a stone. "Y'know," she said confidentially, "the older you get, the worse y' get, I'll tell y' one thing for nothin'."

"What's that?" he asked, thin lips curling in a slow smile.

"You'll never die of 'eart disease, not you y' won't."

"Why not?" he asked innocently.

" 'cause you ain't bloody well got one! ... I'll lay two t' one y' die of cramp givin' money t' charity ... go on," she urged, "give 'im eighteen shillin' so 'e'll die thinkin' well of y'."

Mr Caldwell wavered slightly, and my heart leapt.

"Come on," urged Annie persuasively. "Y'know they've 'ad a rough time round there. Y' cin take the extra tanner off one of my bundles if y' like." Her voice purred gently on, oblivious of the rest of the customers as she pointed at me teetering uncertainly from one foot to the other.

"Ah God luv 'im," she said soothingly. "Luk at 'im; 'e's that worried 'e's wet 'iself." I flushed anew and wished I were dead, then I leapt as a harsh rasping voice blasted from the other end of the shop.

"Warree y' doin' up there, Annie, courtin'?"

"I wouldn't be seen dead with 'im," laughed Annie, digging him playfully in the shoulder. At last with the other customers getting impatient, he capitulated.

"All right, Annie," he sighed, reaching for a pawnticket, "You're a flamin' nuisance, but just this once I'll give 'im eighteen shillin'."

Annie smiled delightedly. "I'll knock the tanner off yours mind y'!" he added warningly.

I could have wept with relief. My hand trembled as I reached up for the money and the ticket, then, with stammered thanks for the impossible, I headed for the door and raced home.

Words tumbled from me as I burst into the house and triumphantly spread the money on the table, and even now as I write, I can see every line on my mother's careworn face as she fingered it disbelievingly. For the first time since she had come out of hospital she swept me into her arms and hugged me. For one brief, fleeting moment I was a child, and we were one again.

10

Sailor Beware

My introduction to the pawnshop, vivid though it was, was not the only reason why the late summer of 1930 stands out sharply in my memory. An unexpected telegram, an even more unexpected lodger, a near riot in the house and my first taste of the sea, all combined to leave an indelible impression.

It all started quite innocently, on the second Saturday after the pawnshop trip with a thunderous knock on the front door just after breakfast. Actually I was on my way to chop firewood when it happened. Dad was shaving and nearly slit his throat with shock, and I stopped in midstride as Mam leapt to her feet spilling her cup of tea.

"Jesus Mary and Joseph!" she exclaimed. "The Bailiffs!"

Dad dropped the razor like a hot brick and, still lathered, hurled himself through the parlour door. By the time Mam and I joined him seconds later, half the street were standing on their doorsteps watching interestedly as the telegram boy stood waiting for an answer, with hordes of chattering youngsters pawing at his uniform.

"What is it?" gasped my mother, as Dad ignored the expectant look on the boy's face, thanked him, and closed the door.

"It's a telegram," he said, turning the buff envelope end over end as he examined it. Mam snorted impatiently.

"I cin see *that!*" she snapped tactfully, " 'oo's it from?" Dad shook his head as he tried to puzzle it out.

"Well, for God's sake open the damn thing, then per'aps we'll find out," she cried reaching forward.

At last he slipped his fingernail under the thin flap and flicked it back. A smile spread over his face. "It's from your Mick," he said with relief.

Mam gasped in surprise. "Our Mick! ... Why the hell didn't 'e send a letter instead of frightening the wits out of us? ... What does it say?" she added straining forward trying to see. He read it out to her as I danced about excitedly.

"I'm comin' ... it says," she looked at him expectantly.

"Well?" she asked, "What else?" Dad shrugged and puckered his mouth.

"That's all ... 'I'm comin' '."

"Nothin' else?" she queried. He shook his head and handed it to her. She gave it a quick glance, then went off like a bomb. "Well, of all the daft sods!" she snapped,

"That's just typical of our Mick. We know damned well 'e's comin'. What the. . . . ?"

"Isn't that the way t' talk to y' lovin' brother now!"

We all whirled in astonishment as the rich slurring brogue came softly from the door behind us. It was Uncle Mick, still in his pea—jacket and sea boots, grinning like a Cheshire cat as he leaned against the door jamb.

Muscular arms encircled me as I flung myself at him and was swept high in the air, while Mam and Dad stared as though he were a ghost. Suddenly they realised that their legs had been pulled. Grins spread over their faces. Mam's arms were raised to greet him when a sudden movement in the kitchen caught my attention.

"There's someone in the kitchen!" I yelled. Instantly Uncle Mick put his finger to his lips.

"Whisht now. You'll wake 'im," he said, tip-toeing through the door.

We followed in mystified silence, then Mam's eyes opened wide as she saw the thin, emaciated form, eyes closed, wispy gingery hair straying over the heavy lids, sprawled in the chair she had recently vacated. "Mother'f God!" she gasped, " 'oo's that?"

Her brother gave her a slow wink. "That's Archie, me ship mate." He looked affectionately at the crumpled figure, "God 'elp 'im," he added.

"What the divil's 'e doin' 'ere?" asked Dad, wiping the remains of the soap from his half-shaven face.

Uncle Mick's eyes half closed, a whisper of a smile hovered round his lips. "Ah well ... T' tell y' the truth of it, it's like this."

Mam put her hands on her hips as she glared at her brother. "Cut the blarney, Mick. I know you too well." She unconsciously lowered her voice as the slumbering figure moved uneasily. "Now 'oo is it?" A hardness crept into her voice. "If it's another one of your waifs and strays the answer is *No!* "

Uncle Mick was like a magnet for down and outs. A contrite look crossed his face as he lowered me to the ground, then as he straightened his expression changed to one of mock astonishment. His voice quivered with synthetic emotion as he put his arm affectionately round her shoulder.

"Is this me sister talkin'?" he asked, looking at Dad. "Is this Mary Sullivan, me very own favourite, the one I'd. . . ." Dad grinned as he poured cups of tea for everyone. Uncle Mick hugged Mam to him as Dad sugared the tea. "It 'urts me 'ere," he patted his heart dramatically, "t' think, that the poor man," he pointed to gently snoring Archie, " 'as nowhere t' go, 'omeless, friendless, me own shipm. . . ."

" 'e's not stayin'!" snapped Mam, wriggling from his arm, "so y' cin cut out the soft soapin'." There was a note of finality in her voice as she moved towards the sleeping form.

"Right!" said Uncle Mick, suddenly all business. "I'll tell 'im. It'll break me 'eart but I'll tell 'im 'e'll 'ave t' go t' the Mission, an' me with 'im."

Alarm showed in Mam's voice as she laid her hand on his arm. "It's not that I wouldn't 'ave 'im Mick, y'know that . . . but where the 'ell would we purr'im?"

"Anywhere's as good as nowhere," he answered, eyes dancing as my mother wavered.

"Is 'e a shipmate, Mick, no kiddin'?" asked Dad, thoughtfully sipping his tea.

"Me blood brother," answered Uncle Mick solemnly. " 'e bailed me outa jail in Valiparaso." Dad nodded understandingly, then looked at Mam. "They could 'ave Bernadette's room," he said slowly, eyeing the slumbering Archie.

"An' where's she gonna kip?" asked Mam, "In the coal 'ole?"

I watched anxiously. I didn't want Uncle Mick sleeping anywhere but in our house. I didn't see enough of him as it was.

"She cin go up t' Minnie's, can't she? . . . she's got room, an' it's only f' six days."

"I'll go t' the woodyard an' tell 'er, Mam," I volunteered.

She hesitated. Uncle Mick's soft voice poured over her

like syrup as Archie grunted, moaned slightly, then drowsily raised his head.

"I didn't do it!" he mumbled, glaring belligerently at Dad.

I suppressed a titter as the toothless face writhed its way to consciousness. Uncle Mick grinned at Mam's puzzled expression.

"Pay no heed," he advised. " 'e 'ad a heavy night last night. 'e'll be all right when 'e comes to."

She looked uncertainly at Dad. "Whaddee y' think?" she asked.

Dad looked first at my uncle then the half-conscious Archie. "Is 'e clean?" he asked.

Uncle Mick's eyes twinkled. "Bath's once a year whether 'e wants it or not," he said promptly.

Dad looked at him solemnly. "I asked y' if 'e was clean," he said quietly.

Uncle Mick nodded.

"Don't worry, Pat, Archie's O.K." Dad shook his head in satisfaction, looked at Mam for confirmation then nodded to me. Minutes later I was on my way to the woodyard to tell Bernadette that she had been dispossessed for a week.

She was delighted. She and Aunt Min got on famously, and she knew Jimmy would be welcome there, Orangeman or not. So everyone was happy and we had a lodger for a week. And what a week! Archie turned out to be a rare treasure.

A toothless Yorkshireman of uncertain age, he was a natural born waif, whose rubbery, weatherbeaten skin hung in loose folds on an elongated face like a spaniel's. Despite his solemn air, he was a comic who exuded a strange old-world detachment and dignity that was awesome in its innocence. Each morning he greeted my mother with a peculiar courtly bow as though she were a queen.

Except for his gnarled leathery hands and the absence of a bosom, he had the physique of a woman more than a man, with pale watery eyes that shone lack lustre from beneath overhanging brows. I fell in love with him the moment he was sober, and during the brief span of his first visit he taught me how to splice a rope, spit downwind, sew buttons, press trousers, make a pancake and a dozen other things. He took me down to the docks, and for the first time, though I had been born among ships, I really saw them. Like Uncle Mick, they were his life and his mistress. He knew no other home and loved every nut and bolt in them. In his slow deliberate way, he turned every ship we passed into a magic carpet to anywhere in the world, and I became the envy of the whole gang.

With the gift of the true wanderer he settled down amongst us as though he had known us all his life. Both he and Uncle Mick, with pockets full after a long voyage, seemed determined to sail as flat broke as possible on the following Saturday. Every night became party night, and I slept when and where I could as the house rocked to the wail of the concentina and sea shanty. Within forty-eight hours Uncle Mick's bounding spirit brought us the first of two visits from Lofty Rourke, the tall rangy policeman from Wexford.

I heard Uncle Mick's voice just as darkness fell on the Monday night. The house was full of singing dancing figures.

" 'ave y' no soul, Lofty?" I heard him shout above the din. "An' you a Wexford man," he added accusingly.

Archie's thin wailing voice sounded strangely horrifying as he continued to sing in the sudden silence as I made by way through from the kitchen. Lofty seemed to fill the whole doorway as he glared into the room.

"Yiz'd wake the dead," he said, enviously eyeing the bottle of stout less than a foot from his hand on the table.

"Ah sure it's all his fault!" said Uncle Mick taking one hand from the concertina and grinning tipsily as he pointed to Archie, standing unabashed in the centre of the room. " 'e won't shurrup."

"I don't give a damn 'ose fault it is," snapped Lofty. "Jus' cut it down a bit." He jerked his thumb towards the street, "They can't gerrany sleep out there."

"Anybody for 'Silent Night'?" shouted Archie.

Uncle Mick was right on cue and every man in the

house crashed out the opening bars, as a white-faced Aunt Sarah dashed in from the kitchen.

"Matt!" she cried to her husband, standing on Lofty's right, " 'ave y' no more se. . . ."

Uncle Matt just looked at her.

"Ah would y' whisht woman!?" Mam laid her hand on Aunt Sarah's shoulder giving her a warning look as her husband shushed her to silence. Aunt Min turned her towards the kitchen.

"Leave 'em be Sarah. The mood they're in it'll be no sooner the word than the blow," she whispered.

Lofty continued to eye the company threateningly.

" 'oo complained?" asked Dad, pouring himself a drink from the crate Uncle Mick had brought in.

"The O'Malley next door," answered Lofty.

A howl of laughter rang out.

"Well, bad cess t' the O'Malley!" roared Uncle Mick. "An' him that cin sup it outa dead man's boot. Send 'im in, I'll tear 'im apart."

"You do that," snarled Lofty, "an' I'll run y' straight in."

There was alarm in Mam's voice as she sensed the delicate balance between jocularity and trouble. They were all half-seas over.

"Ah go on, Lofty," she said persuasively as she eased herself between Uncle Mick and the policeman. "They're off t' sea agin Saturday."

"I don't care wha. . . ." Lofty stopped in mid sentence as Archie, hair awry, face flushed, took Mam by the shoulders and eased her to one side. He gave her an elaborate bow then stood square in front of Lofty gazing up at the jutting jaw unblinkingly.

"Sir," he said, with tremendous dignity, "you trespass!"

There was an awed silence as the whole company gazed at him. I put my hand to my mouth to stop a titter. Lofty's eyes bored through him. "Y' what?" he asked.

Archie swayed gently from side to side. "You trespass, sir," he repeated.

Uncle Mick roared with laughter. "You tell 'im Arch!", he cried encouragingly.

Archie turned solemnly to acknowledge the support then, turning back to an astonished Lofty, and drawing himself up to his full five foot two, he slowly poked his index finger in the policeman's chest.

"I repeat, sir, you trespass on the property of this good lady." He nodded to a worried looking Mam, "So *git!*" He removed his finger and jerked his thumb at the open door.

"For Christ's sake, Archie, shurrup will y'?" cried Dad, as the astounded Lofty bent down and stuck his nose in Archie's face.

"You poked me!" he said accusingly.

Archie gazed at him unmoved, then raised his finger again. For perhaps two seconds they glared at each other silently, every eye in the room on the wavering finger, then a gasp of horror rippled through the company as Archie, well oiled and supremely confident, waggled his thin shoulders and said slowly, "Yis, mate, I poked y', an' if y' don't gerrout ... I'll throw y' out."

There was a stunned silence. Mam's eyes popped out of her head as Lofty straightened, eyes gleaming, and placed his huge hands on Archie's shoulders.

"Right," he said menacingly, "that's it. I know just the place for comedians like you!"

Uproar broke out. Uncle Mick dropped his concertina like a hot brick. Aunt Min screamed as he crossed the room in two short strides. Aunt Sarah, never one for trouble, tried desperately to hide herself on a hardbacked chair, and Mam flung herself between Lofty and Archie as Dad and the rest crowded round to his defence.

"Tell 'im y' was only kiddin' Archie!" she pleaded, "Go on, tell 'im."

Uncle Mick's mercurial temper was no good in a situation like this, and I crouched against the door anxiously as he raised his fist at Lofty.

"Take 'im," he roared, "an' y' take the bloody lot!" He swept his arm round the room. "Go on try it," he challenged.

"Mick!" hissed Dad. "Shurrup will y'. Y' makin' it a bloody sight worse."

But Uncle Mick wouldn't. "Go on, Lofty," he challenged again. "Try it."

Lofty suddenly looked worried. It was developing a bit too fast for his comfort. Mam tried to pour oil on the troubled waters.

" 'e didn't mean it, Lofty. Go on Arch, tell 'im y' didn't mean it."

Archie turned his pale watery eyes on her; his whole attitude breathed solemn defiance.

"Go on tell 'im," pleaded Mam.

Somewhere deep down in his hazy mind, Archie must have sensed impending disaster. Lofty made it easier for him.

"Apologise an' I'll forget it," he said magnanimously.

Uncle Mick was outraged. "Apologise … to a *copper.* … Never!" he roared.

Uncle Matt clamped his hand over Uncle Mick's mouth to shut him up and grinned at Lofty. "It's the drink talkin'," he explained.

Lofty nodded understandingly then turned to Archie swaying gently in front of him. "Well?" he said.

Archie looked from him to Mam, hiccupped, then back again.

"In deference to this good lady," he said with supreme dignity, "I apologise for pokin' y'." Mam sighed with relief. Lofty relaxed. "But," he added deliberately, "I still think you've got a bloody cheek tresspassin' … ."

Dad's hand clamped itself over Archie's mouth. "That's enough, Archie!" he cried as Lofty bridled anew. "For Jesus sake don't say any more … 'ave a drink" he added to Lofty, nodding to the bottle on the table.

Uncle Matt took up the invitation as Lofty looked at it uncertainly. "Go on," he urged. "It'll wet y' whistle."

"I'm on duty," said Lofty wistfully.

"Ah go on with y'," snorted Dad, "When did duty come between a Wexford man an' a good bottle'f stout?" he asked, "Go on. We won't split on y'."

Lofty grinned as he closed the door.

"All right then, just one … but for God's sake keep the noise down."

It had been a close thing. Archie couldn't apologise enough the next day when he realised how near he had come to causing a riot, and in the afternoon, to clear his head before they went up to Aunt Min's that night, he took the whole gang for a treat on the Ferry boat, and for the first time in my life I set foot in Liverpool.

We were thrilled to bits when we saw the great liners from mid river. Archie knew the busy highway like the back of his hand, and held us all enthralled as he told us a little about it. He showed us the old colonades at the Liverpool landing stage where the slaves used to be chained before transportation to America. We listened breathlessly as he explained the history of the great 'Liver Bird' which stands atop the Liver building overlooking the water, and how King John first granted a charter to the monks to ferry people from Birkenhead to Liverpool. He trailed us along the Birkenhead side to show us the great gun that fired at one o'clock every day, a sound which I had known and feared from birth. Without knowing it, he enlisted eight recruits for the Merchant Navy.

Suddenly, without warning, this glorious week came to an end. I could have wept as my two fairy godfathers packed their sea bags and took the ferry across to Liverpool to join their ship. Even Mam's face glistened with a tear as she clung momentarily to the restless, unpredictable spirit that was her brother.

It was as though the house had died.

11

Victims of Circumstance

The weeks following Uncle Mick's departure had a flat, brooding quality about them which was enhanced by the cold swirling mists creeping up from the river each day and engulfing the shivering population. They were weeks of tiny crises, all insignificant in themselves, yet each contributing its quota of relief.

Dad got two separate half-day's work. Bernadette almost severed her hand off in the freezing winds of the woodyard. Aunt Min slipped coming out of church and sprained her arm, losing all the grace her recent Communion had given her, as she swore like a trooper, and finally Mrs Chapman across the road, threw some paraffin on the fire and nearly burned the house down. Small palpitating lights that pierced the overall gloom as Christmas, the eighth in succession that Dad had been unemployed, came and went with the minimum of food and presents.

Everywhere the slow remorseless turn of the economic screw was evident. Pawnshop queues lengthened. Women grew old before their time as their children thronged the local Mission for free soup and bread, and their fathers waited four deep in the dole queues muttering rebellion. No house in the district was free from the possibility of internal explosion as the men, rotting from idleness, short-tempered and dangerous with frustration, were forced off the streets and into homes that were charged to flashpoint.

Money, already a museum piece, became even scarcer. Food, light, heating and clothing became hard-won luxuries. Then, like the plaything of mischievous gods, influenza swept the town. Four times in as many weeks the plumes of the funeral horses tossed in the icy winds as old neighbours, emaciated and defeated, succumbed to the unequal struggle.

Priests and nuns worked like Trojans to comfort, but the word of God alone could not fill empty stomachs, cover frozen feet, nor yet ease the plaintive cries of a sick child, in a district where illness was not just a problem for the afflicted, but a catastrophe for the whole family.

Looking back on these times, my heart bleeds for my mother, for all the mothers of this terrible era.

For us in the gang, inured to the rough and tumble of the life around us, these were weeks of frenetic activity. No part of our day was unoccupied. From waking to sleeping our minds were filled with a myriad schemes, all hatched and discussed round a smouldering five-gallon drum of cotton waste in Fatty's shed. With the manure trade dead until the spring, we turned our energies to winter warmers, candle lanterns, wood chopping, snow clearing, key bombs and occasional grid fishing, with Saturdays reserved solely for jobs on the market.

Throughout the week, Tommy Rolf and Sniffer, experts at making winter warmers, scrounged cotton waste from the shipyards, while Bonko punched holes in the bottoms of cans already collected. Fatty and Henry, I put on special missions, alternately working the bottle trade round the various shops, and keeping us supplied with a succession of broken biscuits, cadged from the dozens of confectioners around the town. Henry, demure and angelic, was the front man in both activities, with Fatty in close support, pinching the bottles round the back of the shops, and Henry innocently handing them in at the front door for the penny deposit that was usually charged.

For the Catholics in the gang it was a permanent struggle between conscience and necessity, with the latter winning hands down. Saturday after Saturday, we went to Confession, then straight back to the shed to think up as many new fiddles as we could.

My own speciality, apart from twisting wire to make handles for the winter warmers, was the making of key bombs, which were either sold for a farthing each, or swapped for anything we could get. It was a simple, dangerous contraption. A key, a nail, a piece of string to connect the two and to swing it by, and I was in business. The instructions for use were equally simple and dangerous. Stuff the hollow shaft of the key with as many match heads as possible, insert the nail, then swing the whole affair against the nearest wall. Several things could happen once it hit the wall and exploded, but that wasn't any of my business. It was while testing one of these bombs that I ran first into Mrs Webster, a drunk, then into Josh Evans who was punch drunk.

It was about the third Friday after Christmas that the lads and I were testing out some newly made bombs and winter warmers under the lamp at the bottom of the street. Sniffer and Bonko were cavorting about, swinging their winter warmers over the heads and shrieking like madmen. Dinny and the rest of the gang were crowded round me as I stuffed the bomb with match heads. It was a beauty, one of the biggest keys I had ever had, and I was just inserting the nail when I felt a tap on the shoulder, and looked up to see Dinny nodding his head at a house across the road.

"There's old Light'ouse watchin'," he said. I glanced across at the tall angular figure of the widow Webster, silhouetted against the parlour light and watching us with silent intensity.

"Ah take no notice," I said, carefully adjusting the nail. "She can't see straight anyway. She's always 'alf cut."

Dinny giggled as he watched the brooding hawk-like features, surmounted by a lump that stuck out of her sandy hair like a light-house in a desert. I swung the key experimentally. Her shrill voice blasted across the road.

"Warrar you lot doin' over there?" she demanded coming to the edge of the pavement.

"What's it gorra do with you, Light'ouse?" challenged Sniffer, warming his hands on the glowing tin. She stiffened with sudden anger as the gang roared with laughter.

"I'll give y' Light'ouse!" she shrieked, shaking her bony fist at us as she took a step forward. "You're a lotta young sods that's what. ..."

"Ah why don't y' go an' polish y' flippin' lump!" snapped Dinny straightening up and glaring at her. For a second there was dead silence. Then everything seemed to happen at once as Sniffer's piercing hyena laugh rang round the narrow street. At the same moment I crashed the key against the wall.

There was a cry as she grabbed for Sniffer, missed and slipped on the icy road. The explosion of the key vibrated for a split second, then another even sharper cry broke from her as she clutched at her leg.

"Y' shot me!" she screamed, "bloodywell shot me!" I gazed in horror at the gash in her leg where the key had struck her when the bomb disintegrated, then she rose to her feet like a rocket. I smelt the sickly odour of meths as she grabbed me round the neck and shook me until my teeth rattled. Then, with the protesting cries of the lads ringing in my ears, she dragged me unceremoniously along the road.

Before I quite realised what was happening I was outside our door. Vicious words swept over me as she told Mam what had happened. Grips were transferred. My feet left the ground as Mam yanked me inside, then a sudden blur as her hand caught me a cracking blow on the ear. Again she raised her hand to strike, but with a quick twist I was free and outside running like mad. There was still an hour to go before bedtime, perhaps she would cool off. But my luck was right out. Within five paces I crashed into a darkened form. Another hand grabbed me.

"Where the 'ell d'y' think you're goin'?"

It was Dad. My heart sank then raised slightly as I saw there was someone with him. "Gerrin' the 'ouse!" he snapped. I got. Mam's eyes gleamed as I came through the door, and I was still dodging round the table when Dad followed me in.

"What's goin' on?" he asked in astonishment.

" 'e shot Mrs Webster, that's what's goin' on," she shouted, making another grab at me.

"Shot Mrs Webster? ... Whaddee y' mean? I've just passed 'er goin' down the street swearin' like a trooper."

"That's why she's swear. ..." Her whole manner changed suddenly as Dad's companion came through the door, and my mouth opened in astonishment as I looked at the battered, grinning figure, blinking uncertainly in the light.

"This is Josh. ... Josh Evans," said Dad, turning to the shaking figure behind him. "An' this," he added to Josh as he jerked his thumb in Mam's direction, "is the Missus, Josh."

I watched fascinated as the full drooling lips writhed a greeting. I sensed trouble ahead in her bleak smile. Already there had been one or two arguments over the past two weeks when Dad, forgetful that there was barely enough money to feed us, had brought several of his cronies home to talk politics and boxing.

With her face set hard, she completely ignored both Josh and me as she nodded towards the kitchen.

"Come in 'ere," she snapped to Dad, "I wanna word with y'."

Dad's face darkened in annoyance. I felt the hairs rise on the back of my neck as Josh, obviously insensible to the sudden tension, stood leaning amiably against the sideboard gazing short-sightedly at me. At any other time this grotesque figure, with its two cauliflower ears, would have fascinated me, but my ears and senses were tuned to the rising voices in the kitchen, and, scared as I was, I felt I must see what was going on, edging nearer the door in time to catch Mam's impatient voice.

"Whaddee y' think this is?" she asked Dad as I peeped round the edge of the door. "A flamin' cafe? ... Where d'y' think I'll get the stuff from? Off a Christmas tree?"

I saw his face harden as she turned, back ramrod straight, and begin to fiddle irritably with the tap. His voice held infinite menace as he answered, slowly and deliberately, "If I wanna bring anyone inter this 'ouse, I'll flamin' well bring 'em."

She whipped round on him, eyes flashing dangerously. "An' where the 'ell d'y' think I'm gonna get the food t' feed 'im? It takes me all the bloody time t' manage as it is ... this is not a Mission y'know!"

"A cuppa tea won't 'arm y' will it?" he snapped, " 'onest you get a damn sight worse you do," he added exasperatedly. In a blur of movement she snatched the tea-caddy off the shelf over the sink and flung it on the table. Nothing came out as the lid flew open.

"All right," she said sarcastically, "you're so bloody clever, you make a cuppa tea outa that!"

If looks could have killed she would have dropped dead on the spot as he glanced from her to the caddy and back, then he became truculent.

"I wanna cuppa tea!" he hissed, "So gerrit!"

She retaliated instantly, blue grey eyes flashing like ice cold diamonds.

"Why the 'ell don't y' gerra job, then per'aps we could afford t' feed y'. ..."

Her hand flashed to her mouth to stop herself, but it was too late. He staggered as though she had slapped him across the face. Fear clutched at my throat as every ounce of colour drained from his face and his fists clenched. He took a step towards her, visibly fighting to control himself. I saw Mam tense for the expected blow. "Mother'f Jesus!" he exploded, shaking with anger. "What a thing t' say!"

"I'm sorry Pa ..."

He swept her stammered apology aside in a torrent of emotion.

"Day in, day out, I tramp round the yards lookin' for work. What more d'y' want woman? ... Is it *my* fault? ... Well, *is it?*"

I felt myself go cold inside as he leaned forward, knuckles white, vibrating with temper. "D'y' think I *like* bein' out ... Do y'?" he roared waving his fist under her ashen face.

"I'm sorry Pat," she began again.

"*Sorry!*" he shouted, "By the living Christ y' will be!" He shook his fist at her again as she sagged wearily against the sink. "Believe me, you *will* be!"

Suddenly, violently, he swung around, squashing me unnoticed against the door jamb and muttering wildly to himself as he passed. She rushed across the kitchen and tried to grab his arm but he was already half way through the front door pushing a bewildered Josh before him.

She looked a hundred years old as she walked slowly back into the kitchen, flopped in a chair, folded her arms on the table, lowered her head and sobbed uncontrollably. Tears rolled down my cheeks. I felt terrified and helpless. If only I had had sixpence I would have given it to her. For long minutes I stood watching silently.

"Mam," I said at last, "are y' all right?" She raised a tear-stained face.

"Oh for Christ's sake get t' bed will y'?" she said wearily.

Unwashed and frightened, I went.

He said she would be sorry and she was. We all were.

For two days and three nights, despite the most diligent search by the whole family, we saw neither hide nor hair of him. Even Lofty, with his finger on the pulse of the whole district, couldn't help us. Then he turned up, and dumped him on the doorstep, blind paralytic drunk. Where or how he got the money we never found out. In my few short years I had seen many drunks, and I had seen Dad tipsy more than once, but never had I seen him in this condition. Looking back I think my predominant feeling was revulsion. I found it difficult to associate the clean, lively figure of my Dad with the helpless bundle that Mam, Con and Bernadette dragged in and dumped on the bare boards of the parlour.

Mam's uneasy fear of the past few days changed suddenly to violent unreasoning anger as Con tried to get Dad's coat off. She slapped him hard across the sagging features. I stood unnoticed in the doorway as Con pleaded with her to calm down.

"Just let's gerr'im upstairs, Mam, and sleep it off," he pleaded. He recoiled sharply as she whirled on him.

"Leave the stupid sod where 'e is," she shouted, "Helluva lot 'e cares," she added, poking him viciously in the thigh with the toe of her shoe.

"Ah Mam, please!" joined in Bernadette, "We can't leave 'im 'ere; it's freezin'. 'e'll catch 'is death'a cold."

"Serves 'im bloodywell right!" Mam snapped, her face white with temper. Suddenly she spotted me in the doorway.

"Warrar you gawpin' at?" she cried, "Get t' bed."

Con answered for me. " 'ow cin we get t' bed with 'im lyin' there?" he asked.

She had evidently forgotten for the moment that Con and I slept in the parlour. She shrugged irritably. "Oh go an' ask the O'Malley t' give y' a hand t' gerr'im up then."

Con sighed with relief as my sister went to get some help. Ten strenuous minutes later they had him upstairs and settled for the night. Then with Mam bunking in with Bernadette, the house settled down uneasily.

I never closed an eye all night, and with Con tossing and turning restlessly, I was glad when the first streaky fingers of dawn paled the window. Brooding tension stalked the air, and all my fears of the night were renewed as Con woke, put his finger to his lips and whispered urgently to me.

"Now for God's sake, Li, don't say, or do anythin' to upset things this mornin' ... understand?" I nodded fearfully. "One wrong move," he added. "One word, an' the 'ole bloody caboodle will go up." I crept back under the blankets silently. In the kitchen I could hear Bernadette, a full hour earlier than she need be, quietly getting ready to get out of the way. Con eased himself out of bed and into his trousers. The back door opened and closed on my sister as Con walked silently into the kitchen. Mam's footsteps on the creaky top stair followed almost immediately. I counted each step she took as I waited for her to speak and gauge her mood. Then my neck prickled as she curtly refused Con's offer of the tea she had borrowed from Mrs Taylor the night before.

I crept out of bed and peeped quietly round the door. Her face was set like granite. Con flashed me a warning look.

"Are y' all right, Mam?" I asked. She ignored me and began to bang the fire irons about as she always did when she was in a temper.

"Shsss!" whispered Con involuntarily.

She almost bit his head off. "Don't you bloodywell shush me!" she snapped. "If I wanna bang, I'll flamin' well bang!" She crashed the poker down to emphasise the point and Con winced as a muffled groan came from upstairs. He half rose from his seat, face drawn with worry.

"Don't wake 'im, Mam, *please!*" he begged, "Lerr'im sleep it off. Y'know what 'e's like when 'e's 'alf drunk."

It was like setting a match to dry kindling. She picked up every fire-iron in turn and hammered it down, then stalked to the bottom of the stairs. I went rigid with fright as Con leapt from his chair, ashen-faced. "Please!" he begged, "Don't wake 'im."

"You gerrout to the stand," she snapped, "Y' should've bin there 'alf an hour ago."

Con faced her, trying desperately to calm her down.

"There's nothin' in the yard, Mam, I'd sooner stay 'ere 'til Dad sobers up ... We don't want no trouble now, do we?"

She jerked her thumb upstairs. "*Trouble!*" she shouted, "What the 'ell does *he* know about trouble? ... blind rotten drunk an' not a penny in the bloody 'ouse. Don't you talk t' me about trouble."

Con put his hand on her shoulder. She shrugged it off impatiently.

"Now be fair, Mam," he begged, "It's not 'is fault 'e can't get work. God knows 'e's tried 'ard enough, you know that."

Mam's face hardened even more. She knew she had been unjust in the first place, but it had gone beyond that now. Months and years of poverty and frustration had taken over from reason.

"Don't y' think *I've* tried?" she shouted.

"Course we do," said Con desperately, "Nobody coulda done berra, but causin' a row isn't gonna help is it? An' y'know what 'e's like after the booze. Jus' leave 'im be for a few hours."

Suddenly there was a scrabbling upstairs, followed by a bump. Alarm spread over Con's face.

"Now you've wakened 'im," he said accusingly, " 'e's tryin' t' get outa bed."

Mam pushed him roughly to one side, her eyes flashing angrily as she roared up the stairs. "An' I 'ope 'e falls an' breaks 'is bloody neck!"

That did it! There was a sudden deathly silence as I hovered, still in my shirt tails, between the kitchen and the parlour. Then there was a series of grunts and groans as Dad tried to guide his wandering legs into his trousers. Some sixth sense warned me of impending disaster. I grabbed my own trousers as his voice, slurred and truculent, hammered down the stairs.

"What's all that flamin' noise down there?" he roared.

With incredible suddenness, dialogue changed into frenzied action as Mam shrieked something intelligible. Seconds later she stumbled against the back kitchen door as

Dad floundered down the stairs, and without warning, struck her a vicious open-handed blow.

I had a blurred vision of Con ducking out of the way as every movable object in the tiny room became airborne. Cups, saucers, teapot, fire-irons, anything they could lay hands on flew between the two. Con, caught squarely between them, stood dazed against the wall uncertain what to do. Then, without warning, near tragedy took a hand. An involuntary scream of terror left my parched throat as Dad, in a blind paroxysm of anger, picked up the bread knife from the littered table. Mam's mouth dropped in horror. Reasoned thought stood still as Con hurled himself instinctively between them. Moments later as he lay stretched unconscious on the floor, blood streaming from his forehead, where a heavy enamelled jug, thrown by Mam in desperation, had caught him.

My heart hammered, my throat constricted as Dad raised the knife. Then somewhere deep down in his fume-crazed mind, instinct sounded a warning. With stunning force he flung the knife from him and began to rampage round what was left of the room, smashing chairs, pictures and anything he could lay hands on. Dimly above the appalling noise I heard Mam's screams.

"Fetch Father! Fetch Father!" I stood paralysed for a fraction of a second. "Fetch 'im" she screamed. "For Christ's sake 'urry up." I had a last momentary glimpse of her. Hair awry, face chalk-white, backed up against the sink, I shot through the crowded neighbours gathered round the front door. Minutes later I was hammering on the front door of the priest's house.

"Father McCormack!" I gasped as Mrs Hannagan, the housekeeper open the door. She took one look at me and yanked me inside.

"Mother'f God Liam, what's up?" she cried. I had no time for formalities.

"Father Mac," I shouted, "Gerr'im quick. Me Dad's batterin' me Mam!"

"Jesus, Mary an' Joseph!" she gasped. "Sit y' down lad. I'll gerr'im."

I couldn't have sat down for a hundred pounds, and the

few seconds it took the short stocky figure to join me seemed like hours.

"Liam. ... Whatever's up lad?" I repeated my information. His cheerful face hardened to stone.

"Is 'e now?" he snapped, "Well, we'll soon fix him!"

I sighed with relief as I watched the broad shoulders shrug impatiently into his outdoor coat, his long cassock dangling beneath like a skirt. Everything would be all right now. Father was tough as they came. He knew his flock and he knew how to treat them, especially drunks, and Dad wouldn't be the first he had challenged to get his coat off. Even the Orangemen respected this forty-year-old whirlwind, and I knew men personally who wouldn't hesitate to spit in the eye of the police, yet who would draw the line at the 'Cork Divil', as he was sometimes called.

By the time we turned the corner of our street, word had already gone ahead of his impending arrival, and the crowd outside the door grew rapidly as he approached. Nobody was going to miss anything if they could avoid it.

"Ah come on now!" he cried as he neared the crowded doorway. "Away with yiz an' let these poor divils be."

The crowd retreated a few paces, forming a lane between him and the open door. Inside, the house was a shambles. The hard-earned bric-a-brac of a home lay in tangled heaps as though a tornado had struck. In a fever of beserk anger, Dad had ripped the work of a lifetime to shreds. Of Mam there was no sign. Sudden surging fear gripped me.

"Where's me Mam?" I yelled distractedly.

A hand gripped my shoulder. Mrs Taylor's worried voice poured over me like a balm. "Come on, luv," she said soothingly. "Y' Mam an' Con's in our 'ouse. Come an' 'ave some breakfast." I gave one last startled glance through the door then broke from her grip and hurled myself through number ten.

What happened once Father Mac entered the house, no one ever quite knew, but whatever it was, he came out with neither coat nor collar, and the light in his eyes was that of battle rather than religious zeal. Certainly I never knew a priest to cut his knuckles blessing anyone.

Within ten minutes of his arrival it was all over. A deathly silence emanated from our house as he popped into Mrs Taylor's, making final adjustments to his collar, a broad grin on his face.

"He'll be all right now, I've had a word with 'im," he said quietly as he scrutinised Mam and patted me on the head. "Are y' all right now, Mary?" he added. She nodded briefly. He ran his finger round the edge of his collar to seat it comfortably. "I've told 'im t' be at the church at eleven," he announced.

"What for?" asked Mam. His eyes twinkled briefly.

" 'e's takin' the pledge," he answered laconically, "an' if 'e's not there," he added, "I'll come an' fetch 'im."

Dad took the pledge. ...

12

The Panel Man

The smashing of the home in 1931 had a tremendously sobering effect on me. Violent argument I understood. A flash of temper accompanied by a sudden blow, were all part of life. Fighting rows in the district were expected, but never in my whole life had I seen such savage violence in my own home. In those few minutes I experienced a terror which I have not felt since. In one searing flame of animal hatred my whole perspective of life changed, and from that moment until I grew to manhood I watched Dad closely, especially in drink.

This whole year stands out in startling clarity as a year of violent changes and finely drawn emotions, a year in which my generation were taken by the scruff of the neck and flung into early adolescence. It was also the year in which I, in company with the other Catholic members of the gang, were uprooted from the cosy routine of 'Our Lady and the English Martyrs' and transferred to the

Central Catholic school which drew all its pupils from the four Catholic Primary schools. I didn't care much for it, or the two mile walk to get to it.

It was an old converted house, which smelt as it looked, musty. The pupils, many from a district at the north end of the town nicknamed 'The Blood Tub' were tough, but the masters, disciplinarians to a man were tougher than any of their ragged pupils, and within a month I was up to my neck in it.

Several things combined to make me truculent from the moment I set foot in the place, but it was Dinny, six months my senior, and already an old hand at the school, who led me into my first clash with Mr Denson, the Headmaster. It must have been about three weeks after the row at home when we were walking through the park on our way to school when Dinny suddenly grabbed me by the shoulder and whispered excitedly in my ear.

"Luk!" he said, pointing frantically to an old chap walking along the footpath about thirty yards ahead, "The Captain!"

" 'oo?" I asked.

"The Captain," he repeated. "Y'know, the feller what smokes cigars. ... Remember I told y' about 'im."

I nodded understandingly as I eyed the old sailor, now leaning over the railings feeding the ducks.

"Luk ... see," Dinny said, nudging me violently, " 'e's got one on now."

Sure enough the old boy, bowler-hatted, and with grey spats poking from beneath his trousers, was smoking a cigar butt about an inch long.

"So what?" I asked.

" 'e's a toff," said Dinny in a hushed whisper. "You'll see, 'e'll throw it away in a minute."

"So what?" I asked again.

Dinny looked at me disgustedly. "Warree y' talkin' about?" he asked, "You gone dim or sommat? ... As soon as 'e drops it we'll grab it an' 'ave a puff, that's what."

I looked at him horrified. I'd never smoked in my life.

"Don't be so damned daft," I snapped. "I don't wanna smoke. Anyway, 'oo says 'e's gonna throw it away?"

Dinny winked knowingly. "You'll see," he answered. "Jus' wait 'til 'e gets t' the bridge." He pointed to an ornamental bridge spanning the narrow part of the lake.

"When 'e gets there, 'e'll 'ave another gander round at the ducks, then 'e'll chuck it away an' push off."

I watched fascinated as the old man, now out of bread, moved on towards the bridge. Dinny became impatient as he watched him slowly mount the steps then lean over the side. "Go on, y' silly sod!" he muttered. "Throw it."

The Town Hall clock boomed the quarter hour as the old man raised his hand and took the butt out of his mouth. I felt Dinny tense as the hand hung over the water.

"Cor 'ell!" he ejaculated irritably, " 'e's gonna chuck it in the water."

He didn't, instead he turned, looked at us benignly, threw the butt down the steps, then sauntered off. Moments later he was out of sight behind a clump of bushes. Dinny pounced on the butt triumphantly, stuck it in his mouth, and eyes rolling ecstatically sent clouds of smoke into the crisp morning air. I watched him incredulously. None of the gang had ever mentioned smoking, let alone tried it.

" 'ere," he said after a few seconds, " 'ave a puff. It's the gear."

I shook my head as he held out the butt invitingly.

"You cin stick that where Paddy stuck 'is ninepence," I said tartly.

"What's up?" he asked grinning at me. "Are y' windy?"

I felt a surge of anger. "Y'know bloody well I'm not windy," I snapped.

"Talk's cheap," he countered, "Prove it ... go on, take a drag an' swaller it."

Eyes narrowed irritably I snatched the butt out of his hand, inhaled deeply and almost died on the spot. A writhing serpent seemed to grip my throat as the stinging acrid smoke burnt its way down into my tortured lungs. Ground, sky, and water merged into one as my head reeled in a violent fit of coughing. For what seemed an age I alternately struggled for air then coughed it out, and all the time, dimly yet persistently came Dinny's piercing laugh. I could have murdered him as he slammed me on the back.

"Cough it up, Li," he encouraged. "It might be a gold watch."

At long last the pain eased, and still fighting for normality, I glared at him through tear-dimmed eyes as he puffed contentedly on the remains of the butt.

"You stupid sod ..." I began, then stopped as the clock struck again.

We gazed at each other in horror as the chimes went on unendingly. Nine o' clock, and we still had half a mile to go. I could visualise Mr Denson slamming the main door as he always did on the stroke of nine, leaving the late-comers until morning prayers were over.

"We're for it!" I said.

"You're not kiddin'," answered Dinny as we hurtled up the path.

At five past, we skidded through the basement to avoid the main door, up the stairs and into the classroom.

"We've bin to the lavat. ..."

Mr Cartwright, our classmaster, looked us over cynically. "Pull the other leg" he said. "It's got bells on." He jerked his thumb upwards. "Git!" he added. We walked slowly up to Mr Denson's room. A quick trial, no evidence for the defence was admitted, two on each hand, and we were on our way down the corridor rubbing them together to ease the pain. It was several months before I tried smoking again.

The worst thing I found about the school, apart from having to attend, was the fact that as a direct result of changing schools I lost the first regular job I ever had. 'Tally boy' in a bakehouse. It had been a peach of a job, landed after a great deal of backstairs negotiations and in the face of tremendous competition from a score of lads, all under pressure from home to get work and ease the frightening poverty.

The hours were long and the wages low, but in the first flush of enthusiasm for regular work, it had seemed a mere bagatelle to work from six in the morning until eight, followed by an hour at lunch time, then a further stint in the evening until seven, in return for one and threepence per week and two balm cakes every day.

In these days of multiple bakeries, the job of Tally Boy has now vanished, but in those days, people mainly mixed their own dough and brought it to the bakehouse in tins provided by the baker. Each evening I sat on the bakehouse steps with a pile of tin tallies. One I gave to the customer, the other I stuck into the dough, then according to whether they wanted their bread early or late, I put the tins on the appropriate table ready for first or second baking. Next day the reverse happened, when I redeemed the tallies and handed out the bread.

It was recognised by all the lads as a snip, especially in winter and with it I had been the envy of the whole gang, but with my new school it had come to an abrupt end. I asked for a change of hours, instead, but, with competition fierce, I got the sack. For Mam the loss of one and a penny wages was disastrous, for me, the loss of the tuppence she gave me was catastrophic.

Except for Eric Daly, now lying dangerously ill with diphtheria, I was the only member of the gang unemployed. It stung my pride, and for two weeks after I lost it I was completely at a loose end, then, on the day I nearly choked on the cigar butt, and just a week before St Patrick's Day, came another offer.

It must have been about seven o'clock when I was squatting under the lamp at the bottom of the street waiting for some of the lads to knock off before we could gather in Fatty's shed. I felt cold and fed up. Even the new winter warmer in my hands failed to cheer me as I alternately swung it and glanced warily at Lighthouse standing broodingly on her step watching me. She never liked me after I shot her with the nail. I had just got the warmer going nicely when a familiar voice sounded behind me. It was Father Mac, loaded with parcels. I leapt to my feet.

" 'ello Father ... did y' want me Dad?" I knew he kept a sharp eye on Dad especially with St Patrick's Day coming round. He grinned and shook his head.

"Anyway," he asked, "what are y' doin' hangin' about here? I thought you were working for the baker?"

I scuffed my foot against the pavement as I explained what had happened.

"Well, the divil take the man!" he hissed, "Your mother'll feel the loss."

"She does that, Father!" I replied feelingly. "An' so do I!"

He cast a speculative eye over me.

"You're a strong lad, Liam," he said after a moment or two of silence.

I puffed myself up.

"D'y' think y' could handle it if I had a word in Harry Bailey's ear for you?"

My eyes gleamed. Harry's butcher shop was one of the liveliest places in the district, especially on Saturdays. I would give anything to work there.

"Oh would y', Father!" I exclaimed, "Honest?"

His eyebrows raised in mock anger. "There's a thing to ask a priest!" he exclaimed, "Is he honest?"

I looked at him abashed. He gave his parcels another hitch and winked at me.

"We'll leave it like that then. No promises mind, but I'll try ... by the way," he added, "what are you doing now?"

"Jus' waitin' for the gang t' finish work, Father."

"Right then," he said in business-like tones. "Just so the divil won't have idle hands t' tempt, y' cin give me a hand with this lot, but first, take this to your mother."

He handed me a parcel and I shot up the street and waited a few seconds while she opened it. Her eyes lit up. It was a pound of sugar, a quarter of tea, and an egg wrapped in newspaper.

"Thanks be t' god for that!" she exclaimed. "Sure 'e's a man an' a 'alf that one."

Within minutes I had joined him as he made his way along the darkened doorways. We stopped outside Tommy Rolf's. I looked at him in amazement.

"They're *Protestants* 'ere Father!" I exclaimed. He looked at me and grinned as he handed me a parcel.

"*All* stomachs ache when they're empty, lad," he said laconically, nodding at the door.

"What shall I say?" I asked as he moved on down the street. He looked back over his shoulder.

"Nothin," he called, "Just hand it in. It'll speak for itself."

Ten minutes later I dropped him at our door and went to Fatty's to see if the lads were home.

It was two full days before I heard from him again, and by that time, the cold that had been creeping on me for the past few days, worsened to tonsillitis and laid me flat on my back.

I could have wept when Father Mac told me that Harry was willing to give me a start at two shillings a week. I was terrified in case he took someone else on, but Father reassured me that he would see him and explain.

For three more days I tossed and turned, alternately sweating and shivering as Dad applied sock after sockful of hot salt round my throat, and rubbed evil-smelling camphorated oil on my chest.

Suddenly I found myself the centre of attraction. Mam and Dad rarely left me for more than a few minutes. Bruised fruit, nicked from the market, began to make a mysterious appearance as the lads came to inquire after me. Then, on the day Dinny came to tell me that Eric had been taken to hospital seriously ill, I got, for the first and last time as a child, a whole egg to myself.

It was a strange, fearful experience looking down at the inert body of Eric. Even as we crowded round the tiny coffin we could not believe he was dead. Not young Eric, it seemed so unreal, so unfair, so final. Even Sniffer, for once tense and subdued, edged uneasily as we jammed into the crammed parlour to pay our last respects.

Death came more and more frequently to others in the district but why us? Why the gang? Oh how I wished at that moment that I was God, to breathe life into that pallid shell, to wipe away the tears of Mrs Daly sitting stunned and silent at the head of the coffin, staring, just staring at the girl-like face with its long lashes resting against the waxen cheeks.

For three days now the house had been restless with a constant stream of neighbours and friends, each to stare a moment, touch the forehead, and say a prayer over this tiny piece of jetsam overwhelmed by the turbulent stream around him then cast on the shores of oblivion. Tonight he would be taken to church. I shuddered at the thought of him lying there all night, alone by the altar. He was always so frightened of the dark. Tomorrow the black-robed priest would intone the De Profundis, sprinkle the polished wood with holy water, commend him to the care of God, then bury and forget him. It seemed such a stupid waste. Unwanted and in tears he had arrived, rested like a gadfly for one brief moment on a tossing rock-strewn stream, and now, with nothing achieved, he would be borne away on a fresh flood of tears. Why? How many times since that day have I touched the foreheads of a corpse and asked this unanswerable question.

But Eric was not the only one. In the four weeks since I had taken ill, three other children and one adult had died on the district, many were still ill and death stalked haughtily among the destitute as work and food got scarcer. It was the oft repeated tale, too little help and always too late, and always the very old and very young took the brunt.

It seemed like hours since we had first come in to see him, and I could feel the growing restlessness of the gang when the first tentative sounds of uproar attracted my attention. I felt suddenly irritable, but it was Eric's Auntie who gave voice to my unspoken thoughts.

"Y'd think people'd 'ave a bitta respect at a time like this wouldn't y'?" she whispered irritably to her husband. He nodded then went to the window and raised the blind to see what was happening.

Sniffer nudged me and flicked his head towards the door.

"Come on, Li," he whispered urgently. "Let's go. It gives me the flippin' creeps 'ere!"

He cast a furtive glance at Eric. Dinny nodded agreement. I turned to Mrs Daly sitting silent as a sculpture.

"We've gorra go now, Mrs Daly, so I'll say Tarra. ... I'm sorry 'e's dead." I added lamely. I felt a hot breath in my ear.

"Tell 'er we'll chop 'er wood for 'er." whispered Dinny.

She must have heard him. A ghost of a smile flickered across her drawn features as she raised grief-glazed eyes.

"Ta very much," she said, then, with an imperceptible nod, she dismissed us.

I signalled the lads to pay their last respects and one by one, dry eyed and uncomfortable, we edged to the head of the coffin, laid our hands on his ice cold forehead, knelt with a quick prayer then left. Tommy and Sniffer came last, and without the comfort of Catholic ritual, just stood uncertainly for a moment then followed the rest of them out.

Soon I had to cast off the over-riding gloom that had settled on me with Eric's death. He was gone, there was nothing I could do about it, and without further thought I threw myself into my new job at Harry's.

I loved it. Harry lived up to all my expectations as a boss. Invariably cheerful, his ruddy face, surmounted by a mop of snow white hair, and set on powerful shoulders, gave him the appearance of an elderly elf. He showed me all the tricks of the trade. Skinning sheep's heads, separating ribs from carcase, dressing hogs' heads, dry scrubbing the cutting block, and making interminable sausages from yards of intestine. I was never still and time passed swiftly in the lively atmosphere of the shop, and with the gang fully occupied before and after school, I worked as many voluntary hours as I could get. For this I was paid in meat, not money. A few sausages, a bundle of ribs, and occasionally if we had been extra busy, a piece of meat which Mam could spread over two or three days. But the most valuable thing I got from the shop was a deep insight into human nature, and, through the ribald conversations to which I listened avidly, a stark picture of the appalling economic conditions in the town.

Throughout 1931 rumour ran riot. Talks of cuts in the already low social benefits, despite the existing poverty, were rife. But it was not until three weeks after I started work that I ran into officialdom in all its harshness.

It had been one of those days for me from the moment I opened my eyes. Late for school, fighting in the playground, just one slice of bread for tea, then a hard night, dry scrubbing the chopping block in the shop. I was glad when the clock struck seven so that I could dash home, have a quick wash, then round to Fatty's shed where we had some black puddings stashed away. It wasn't to be. I was just on my way out when Mam came in from Mrs Taylor's.

"Where's Bernadette?" she asked. I shook my head and shrugged. "What's up with you?" she snapped. "Lost y' tongue or somethin'?"

I bristled but answered quietly, "I dunno where she is."

"Well, y' berra go an' find 'er," she cried in sudden agitation, "She's on the Panel."

"What difference does that make?" I asked, surprised.

She glanced at the clock, worry written all over her face.

"If she's not in by nine, they'll stop 'er benefit, that's the difference it makes, so go an' find 'er, an' quick."

I shrugged helplessly. "Well, I don't know where she is ... do I?" I complained.

Her tone hardened. "Go an' find 'er."

"But I was jus' gonna see the la ..."

She jerked her thumb towards the door. Her tone was ice-cold. "Git!" she said, "an' quick."

I bit my lip in frustration. I hadn't seen the lads for two days. We had a million things to talk about. None of us finished in time to play as we used to, besides I was hungry and we have seven black puddings to eat. I would have liked to glare at her, but daren't, instead I nearly took the door off its hinges on the way out.

Eight o'clock came and went. I couldn't find her anywhere. I looked in every place I could think of but not a sign. Defeated at last I returned home just as the Town Hall clock struck nine. Mam was fuming.

"Well!?" she snapped as I poked my head round the door, "Did y' find 'er?"

"Never saw hide nor 'air of 'er," I replied, seating myself wearily by the empty grate.

She went off like a rocket, crossing and recrossing between the parlour and the kitchen. "Where the 'ell *is* she?" she kept repeating. At five past nine the knocker on the front door crashed loudly. She stopped dead in her tracks, her face drained of colour. "I knew it!" she gasped. "I bloodywell knew it. I'll lay a quid that's the Panel Man." She flicked her head at me. "Go an' open it," she said abruptly.

I went and it was.

"Name of Sullivan?" inquired the natty, bowler-hatted visitor. I nodded.

"I'm from the ..." he began.

"I know," I said, "You're from the Panel aren't y'?" He inclined his head in agreement. My mind whirled. I could hear Mam dashing in and out of the back door trying to *will* Bernadette to come home. I had to stall him if I could.

"Well?" he said.

"Well what?" I asked innocently.

"Is she in?"

"Is 'oo in?"

He gave me an old-fashioned look. "You know perfectly well who lad ... your sister." A note of irritability crept into his voice. "I 'aven't got all night y'know," he added.

I shrugged. "Well I've got two sisters," I answered. "Which one d'y' want?"

He consulted his notes. "Bernadette," he said at last, "She's the one that's sick isn't she?"

" 'ow about our Teresa?"

"What about her?"

"That's what I'm askin' you."

"Luk," he said slowly, "I don't care if you've got sisters in every cupboard in the house, lad, all I'm interested in is Bernadette. Now is she in or isn't she?"

I was getting desperate. There was still no sign from Mam that she had arrived. I couldn't hold him much longer.

"Tell y' what," I said brightly, "I'll go in an' 'ave a luk. I shan't be a tick." He sighed disconsolately.

"May I come in?" he asked.

I shook my head vehemently. "You'd berra not," I suggested. "Me Dad might come in an' 'e's funny." I left him standing open-mouthed on the step and dashed in.

"Is 'e still there?" asked Mam quietly.

"Yeh," I replied, "an' 'e wants t' come in." She looked from me to the clock. It was ten past nine.

"All right," she said resignedly. "Y' berra lett'im in, we can't keep 'im standin' on the flamin' step all night, can we?"

A minute later he was facing her across the kitchen table. Her attitude was a strange cross between defiance and pleading as she answered his questions.

"She's not in then?" he said with a faint note of triumph.

Mam leaned across the table. "She's only across the road on a message," she pleaded, " 'ave a 'eart the poor kid's bin stuck in for days."

"You know the rules as well as I do, Mrs Sullivan," he answered silkily. "If she's sick she's sick, and sick people drawing panel money should be in by nine o'clock. ... There's nothing I can do about it," he ended triumphantly. He looked so smug and self-satisfied I could have kicked him.

"Warree y' gonna do then?" asked Mam, knowing full well what he was going to do.

He shrugged his well clad shoulders eloquently. "I have a job to do Mrs Sullivan, you know that."

His round face was dead pan. Suddenly all her bottled-up temper flooded over, she had nothing to lose now, and alarm spread over his face as she leaned over the table, shaking with temper.

"Yeh," she snarled, "you've gorra job t'do, an' you're gonna bloodywell do it arn't y'? It doesn't marrer t'you does it? ... Your belly's full, isn't it? Whaddee y' think we're gonna do without 'er Panel Money, eh?" She jerked her thumb at the door. "Gerrout while y' safe," she grated.

He muttered something unintelligible as she followed him through the parlour and slammed the door behind him.

That was that, there was no appeal. The money would be stopped automatically, and, since work was impossible for her at the moment in the freezing woodyard, it was either an appeal to the Guardians or go without. Mam was just coming through the door, face dark with anger, when a new diversion occurred. I groaned as the back door opened and the thin, pinched face of Mrs Dempsey, popularly known as 'Nunny Ann', popped round, eyes gleaming excitedly. I, in company with the whole neighbourhood, hated her. An inveterate churchgoer and gossip, she had all the propensities of a pious rattlesnake, and was one of those unfortunate people who take a delight in causing trouble. Whatever her news was, she picked a most unfortunate time to impart it.

"Mary! ... are y' there luv?" I looked up narrow-eyed at the sound of her cringing, ingratiating voice. Mam was there all right, and in a flaming temper.

" 'ave y' eard ...?" Nunny got no further. She was still half in half out of the room when the stream of invective hit her square between her saucer-like eyes.

"Jesus, Mary an' Joseph!" exclaimed Mam. "The bloody Panel Man at the front, an' a cross-eyed hypocrite at the back!" Nunny's head withdrew like a jack rabbit, leaving Mam staring blankly at the paint-blistered door. Seconds later there was a rush of footsteps in the yard. The door burst open, and in dashed Bernadette, straight into Mam's pent-up emotions.

I took one practised look at the tense faces, slid quietly round Mam, through the parlour door, and left them to it.

13

Faith of Our Fathers

Whether it was the result of the Panel Man's visit, or a gradual accumulation of irritations I shall never know, but relations betweem Mam and Bernadette, already strained to breaking point over Jimmy, deteriorated rapidly as April gave way to May, and Teresa, now very 'aughty as a result of working among the 'toffs', didn't help much by her condescending attitude during her last visit before she left England altogether for a job near Phoenix Park in Dublin. I came somewhere in the middle of it all, light of tread, eyes wide open, ears cocked for trouble.

Altogether this was a rough period, and what between going to the pawnshop, working at Harry's, trying to make time to scrounge extra work on the Market, holding the scattered gang together as a cohesive unit, and running into trouble at school, life assumed a hectic round. The only bright spot was that Uncle Mick and Archie were due home at any time. Even my name began to sound monotonous round this time. 'Sullivan ... late again, two strokes. Larking about ... two strokes, slovenly work ...' I was beginning to look like a zebra.

It was mostly Fatty's fault, giggling, slyly knocking my elbow as I wrote, pulling faces to get my goat. I hammered him unmercifully, but it made no difference. Ever since Sniffer had joined the gang he had been the same. He was in one of these skylarking moods on the last Thursday of a very hectic May. Class had barely started as Dinny, Bonko Armfield, Henry and myself returned from the Headmaster's room, rubbing our stinging hands after being late, and Dempsey, the master, was in an ugly mood when a monitor came to the door just as he was settling down, and asked him to step up to Mr Denson's room. He glared at us as he got up.

"Just watch it!" he said in dark brown tones as his eyes swivelled the room then focused on me. "I've just about 'ad enough of you lot. One peep while I'm out an' you'll all get it ... got it?"

We sat frozen-faced as he walked to the door, and with a final menacing glare, left. His footsteps had barely receded before bedlam broke out. Fatty leaped for the empty desk.

"Watch it you lot," he mimicked. "Jus' watch it ... gorrit?" The class howled. I felt a surge of irritability.

"Hey Fatty! ... gerroff there will y'? He'll hammer the flamin' lot'f us if 'e comes in."

He ignored me and began to sing in a screeching falsetto as paper darts and ink-stained blotting paper flew round the room. I jumped from my desk to shut him up. The door opened and the tousled head of the look-out popped round.

"Hech, hech, lads, 'e's comin' down the stairs."

The time lapse between the warning and Dempsey's arrival was seconds. With a frenetic burst of activity the class settled as though they had all been stuffed, all except me. I stubbed my bare foot on the front desk and fell flat. I felt the cold fishlike stare as I picked myself up and flung myself into the desk, then looked up into the hard blue eyes.

"*Sullivan!*" he yelled. I rose obediently.

"Whats-a-marrer, sir?" I asked innocently. A ghost of a titter ran round the class.

"If y' wanta sing," he said sarcastically, "go an' see the Canon, an' ask if y' can join the choir."

I looked at him incredulously. If ever I get hung for singing, I shall die innocent. I couldn't and still can't sing for nuts. Venom flashed in my voice as I answered.

"I can't sing, an' you know it!" His face darkened at my tone and he pointed silently to a spot immediately in front of him. I didn't move.

"I'll give you just three seconds t'get out 'ere," he said slowly, reaching for the cane behind his desk. All my stubbornness rose to the surface.

"It wasn't me," I said defiantly. "An' I'm not takin' the stick for somethin' I didn't do."

A subdued mutter ran round the room as he glowered at me. Fatty leapt to his feet, face wrinkled with concern.

"It was me, sir. Not 'im. ... Honest it was."

"Shurrup an' siddown!" snapped Dempsey.

"But ..." gasped Fatty.

"Shurrup!" Dempsey snarled, walking down the gangway, "or you'll get it." He jerked his thumb to the front of the class. "Out!" he said to me menacingly. I glowered at him as defiance consumed me like a flame.

"No!" I answered flatly. The class gasped. He didn't ask

again. I felt myself grabbed by the jersey, shaken like a rat, then hauled down the gangway.

"Get y' hand out," he ordered, flexing the cane in an atmosphere that had become electric. I knew instinctively that I was being punished for cheek, not just singing, but the devil had a firm hold on me. I stuck my hands behind my back and stared at the flushed, angry face.

"No!" I said again. His anger burst like a torrent as he slashed me across the thighs. I reacted as I would in the streets. Body tensed, head down in blind anger, I swung a hard right and caught him square in the stomach.

There was a moment's shocked silence. I went cold at the enormity of my offence. For one split second the whole room froze in silent tableau, then, I was on my way, struggling and cursing to the Headmaster's room, where after one of the briefest interviews of my academic career, I was given six absolute beauties, and told to report to him again before I went home. It was the longest day of my life. I was given a letter for my Dad and told to bring an answer the next day or he would call and see Dad himself. I was right out on my own. None of the gang could help me, and I daren't destroy the letter. For the first time I missed going to work, and it was not until almost half-past-seven that I plucked up the courage to go home. I couldn't have picked a worse time.

The house was full, and right in the middle of the parlour like a great fat duck was Ma Bloomfield, pointing her podgy finger accusingly at Aunt Sarah. No one even noticed me as I stood quietly in the kitchen doorway, crumpled letter behind my back, listening and taking stock of the agitated faces around the room. Then I gasped in surprise. There, right in the corner by the front door, tense and silent, sat Jimmy Kiernan with Mam looking daggers at him across the room.

The arguments must have been going on for sometime, but before Ma Bloomfield even spoke I knew what it was all about. She confirmed it with her first words as she turned to Mam.

"I'm Orange," she said aggressively, "We're friends aren't we?" Mam nodded. They were good friends. "All right then, so what the 'ell. 'e's a good lad, what more d'y' want?" She jerked her thumb at Jimmy. He flushed but said nothing as Bernadette squeezed his hand in encouragement.

"That's all very well," snapped Mam. "Me mother'd turn in 'er grave if she knew one'f mine'd married an Orangeman."

" 'e's not askin' t' marry y' mother is 'e?" Ma's three chins wobbled violently as she shot back her answer.

"There's no need for that Maggie." Dad admonished her as he cast a quick anxious glance at my mother.

"I don't trust Orangemen," muttered Aunt Sarah darkly.

Aunt Min was obviously on Jimmy's side despite the opposition. "What's up with 'em?" she asked, "They're all built the same aren't they?"

Aunt Sarah misunderstood her. "*Minnie!*" she gasped.

Aunt Min shook her bullet like head irritably. "Oh, shut up, Sarah, an' don't be daft. Y'know damned well what I mean. Anyway," she added in a tone of exasperation, "I think it's a lotta tommyrot."

"What is?" asked Dad.

"Well, all this 'ullabaloo. If they want t' get married, lerr'em. It's their lives isn't it?"

"You're a damn fine Catholic you are!" snapped Mam accusingly.

Aunt Min flushed. "Well, I'd sooner 'ave a good Protestant before a poor Catholic any day I cin tell y' that," she answered spiritedly.

" 'e's not even a good Protestant. . . ." began Dad.

Jimmy shook off Bernadette's restraining hand and jumped to his feet angrily. "Jus' because I don't go t' church an' thump me craw every day doesn't mean t' say. . . ."

"All right, Jimmy," drawled Uncle Matt, sitting alongside him. "Ease off an' batten y' hatches." He winked slowly. Normally Jimmy and he got on very well together. "Keep y' shirt on, son; everythin' 'll be all right."

"You're worse'n 'e is," cried my mother.

"They're trouble makers," broke in Dad. "That's what I've gorr'against them."

Again Jimmy jumped to his feet angrily.

" 'oo is?" he demanded.

"You are!" snapped Dad. "You an' y' 'ole flamin' family. Always 'ave bin. Where's your Alfie now eh? Tell me that!"

Jimmy flushed hotly as several heads nodded in agreement. Dad had a good point there. Alfie was in Walton Jail for disturbing the peace, his second spell in two years.

"Well, somebody's gorra speak up," snapped Jimmy, defending his absent brother. "We're not gonna gerr'anythin' done about the unemployment sittin' on our arses, are we?"

Aunt Sarah sat bolt upright. "Jimmy," she said primly, "there's no need t' bloodywell swear!"

Uncle Matt roared with laughter. His wife flushed a deep red as Dad pursued his point.

"You're a lotta Communists, that's what you are, an' I don't want 'er—" he flicked his head at Bernadette—"mixed up with it."

Bernadette leaned forward defiantly. "I don't give a damn what 'e is," she said heatedly.

Dad pointed his finger at her. "You watch y' language," he snapped, "an' speak when y' spoken to."

She flushed hotly, eyes glinting in silent fury, but her voice was calm as she spoke. "I'm norra child y'know, Dad, I'm twenny-three."

"Y' not too old t' feel the weight of this!" cried Mam, clenching her fist and shaking it at her. My sister glared but said nothing.

Suddenly the conversation swerved violently as Mam pointed her finger accusingly at Ma Bloomfield. "It's all your fault, Maggie!" she cried irritably, "you've encouraged 'em."

"All right then," agreed Ma, "I've encouraged 'em, so what? Where did y' want 'em t' do their courtin'? Down the entry? ... Y'know your trouble don't y', Mary Sullivan?"

"You seem t' know the lot," answered Mam sarcastically, "go on tell me."

"Y' bigoted, that's your trouble. ... If 'e was a Catholic, y' wouldn't care if 'e pinched the Town 'all clock would y'?"

I thought Mam's eyes were going to pop out of her head.

"*Me! ... bigoted!*" she gasped. "Y' must be off y' flamin' rocker, woman."

"All right then," challenged Ma, "prove it, prove you're a good Christian as well as a good Catholic, lerr'em get married."

"Over my dead body," snapped Mam, folding her arms over her breast and drawing in her lips.

It was deadlock. Aunt Min tried to pour oil on troubled waters. She waved her hand at Ma, now squashed uncomfortably between Aunt Min and Bernadette.

"Ah take no notice of 'er, Maggie, she didn't mean that. She's upset, she'll come rou. ..."

"I'm not bloodywell upset," cried Mam.

Aunt Min persisted. "Yes y' are. Luk, I'll tell y' what, I'll make a cuppa tea. 'ow's that?"

She eased herself painfully out of the hard-backed chair, but Bernadette intervened.

"Warr-about me?" she asked irritably. "Anybody'd think I wasn't 'ere t' listen to y'." She looked more like Mam than ever at that moment. Eyes flashing, long black hair cascading down her back, oval face grim and determined. Ma Bloomfield glanced from her to Mam and back, laid her hand on Bernadette's shoulder.

"Easy girl," she said quietly. "That's y' mother y' talkin' to y'know."

My sister shrugged her off impatiently and glared defiantly at Mam. "Warr-about my feelin's?" she demanded. "Nobody's asked me. You'd think I was about this 'igh." She held her hand, palm down, about three feet from the ground. "Anyway" she continued, "I don't care what anybody says. I luv 'im an' I'm gonna marry 'im."

Jimmy flushed a deep red as Mam snorted disgustedly.

"*Luv!*" she said scornfully. "Whaddee you know about luv? Warris it anyroad? A ticklin' at the 'eart that y' can't scratch," she answered herself. "Wait'll y' get 'alf a dozen kids round y' then come an' talk t' me about luv ... don't make me bloody sick."

"When poverty comes in through the door," intoned Aunt Sarah melancholicly, "luv flies outa the winder."

"Trust Sarah t' be cheerful," said Aunt Min. She turned to her sister-in-law, "Why the 'ell don't you purra sock in it Sarah?" she asked confidentially. Aunt Sarah sucked in her lips and fell silent.

"They're trouble makers," muttered Dad out of the blue.

Jimmy leaned forward, his lean dark face tense as he jabbed his finger at Mam. "Trouble makers!" he snapped, "Warrabout your Mick?"

She flushed. "You leave our Mick outa this," she cried. "Mick's all right."

"Oh aye," answered Jimmy sarcastically, "Mick's all right. 'e's a Catholic isn't 'e? It doesn't matter that 'e's bin in 'alf the jails round the world does it?"

"Nark it, Jimmy!" Uncle Matt's slow voice rumbled ominously beside him.

He flashed Uncle Matt a quick grin. "No offence, Matt, but it gets y' flamin' goat doesn't it? Mick's bin inside more times than I've 'ad 'ot dinners, an' 'ere's me bein' condemned just because I was born Orange."

Again the conversation took a swerve as Mam introduced an unexpected point.

"Warrabout 'er wages," she snapped suddenly, immediately clapping her hand over her mouth and flushing crimson as Ma whipped up an accusing finger at her.

"Now we're comin'to it!" she cried triumphantly.

Mam looked uncomfortable. This I knew was one of the real problems. Apart from my two shillings, and Dad's bit of Parish money, Bernadette was the only one really contributing.

"It's all right for you, Maggie," cried Mam in retaliation, you've got y'' lodgers, an' a hell of a lot more if I know you, but if she goes, we're on our uppers."

"I'll see y' don't go short," promised Jimmy seizing this unexpected opening.

Dad was on his feet in an instant, bristling. "I'll luk after me own, Kiernan," he roared. "An' I don't want any flamin' Orangeman doin' it for me." The temperature shot up. Aunt Min stepped straight in.

" 'e didn't mean it that way, Pat, an' you damned well know it, so don't go lukin' for trouble where there is none."

Suddenly Bernadette jumped to her feet. I could see by her expression that she had come to a decision.

"I'm gonna marry 'im," she said flatly. "I'm twenty-three an' I'm sick an' tired of 'avin' t' creep round corners t' see 'im." She leaned forward and glared at Mam sitting rigidly by the kitchen door. "An' if y' don't like it," she added grim-faced, "y' cin flippin' well lump it!"

The room erupted. Mam jumped to her feet, white with anger. Dad grabbed at her, missed, and her open hand slammed hard across my sister's face. Jimmy leapt to his feet to go to her assistance, but stopped dead as Uncle Matt's ham-like hand descended on his shoulder.

Leave it, son," he advised, as Mam's high-pitched voice cascaded over the sudden tumult.

"All right!" she cried, struggling with Dad as he tried to hold her. "If y' want t' marry a bloody 'eathen ... *marry* 'im, but don't come cryin' t' this 'ouse if y' in trouble. Once you've made y' bed me girl you'll flamin' well lie on it. Make no mistake about that."

"Sssh, Mary, calm y'self," urged Dad.

I watched anxiously as the opposing factions gyrated round each other with Aunt Min and Ma trying to restore what little good will there was. But it was useless. Bernadette's blunt statement was like a match to a powder keg. Mam wouldn't be calmed.

"Out!" she roared. "Get 'er out before I screw 'er flamin' neck."

Uncle Matt nodded to Jimmy to get going.

Bernadette tried to regain lost ground and make friends. "Mam," she said pleadingly.

"Out," roared Mam again, "an' don't bloodywell come back!"

Jimmy took my sister's arm and nodded to the open door.

"Leave it luv," he suggested. "Y' can't talk to 'er now. It'll only make things worse."

"Mary ..." began Aunt Sarah, but Uncle Matt had other ideas.

"Come on, Sarah," he ordered. "Let's go before y' tie a knot with y' tongue that y' can't undo with y' teeth."

She gave him a reproachful look, fixed her pot like hat with a huge hat-pin, sniffed heavily, then hurried out. Only Aunt Min remained, looking pityingly at Dad as he prowled disconsolately up and down the room, then she looked at Mam quietly.

"One of these days, Mary Sullivan, your tongue'll 'ang you. Why the 'ell don't y' calm down a bit an' make it up."

"I don't want any bloody Protestants in this family," cried Mam, rising from her seat in renewed agitation. "She'll rue the day, you mark my word ..." Suddenly she spotted me, half in, half out of the door. Her anger focused.

"Where the 'ell 'ave you bin?" she yelled. "An' what's that y' hidin' behind y' back?"

I shuffled uneasily as Dad's eyes swivelled in my direction.

"Y' mother's talkin' t' y'," he snapped. "Answer 'er."

"Now don't take it out on 'im!" pleaded Aunt Min coming over and putting her arm round my shoulder. "It's nothin' t' do with 'im is it?"

"You mind y' own business, Minny," cried Mam. "When I want your advice, I'll ask for it."

Her sister's face crinkled in annoyance as she picked up her shawl and threw it over her shoulders irritably. "Honest our Mary," she said, "I don't understand you at all. They glared at each other silently for a second or two, then Aunt Min flicked her shoulders. "Oh I'm goin'!" she snapped exasperatedly.

"Go!" cried Mam, "An' t'hell with y'."

"I'll go," rejoined Aunt Min in one of her rare flashes of temper, "but it won't be me that'll go t' hell. It'll be you ... y' bad-tempered bitch." She waddled to the front door, paused a second then turned back. "Goodnight t' y'," she cried. "An' t' hell with you too!" she added as she slammed the door behind her.

My heart sank. With her there I stood a chance. Without her, retribution would be swift. I shifted about uneasily, crumpling the letter in my hand.

"Well," roared Dad, "what is it?" He looked at me suspiciously. "Are you in trouble?" he asked menacingly. "We've just about 'ad enough t'night with the other faggot without you."

Heart pounding I handed over the letter in silence, then stood petrified as he read it. Icy fingers prickled my spine as his expression changed.

"You did *that!*?" he asked incredulously as Mam strained to see the letter.

"I ... I ..."

"Shurrup!" he snapped. " 'ere read this," he added, handing the letter to my mother. "Just read it." My mouth was like parchment as her face paled.

"Holy mother'f God!" she hissed, poising to strike. Dad held her arm.

"Gerrin there," he said quietly and nodding towards the kitchen as he unbuckled his belt. "I'll deal with this."

Desperately I tried to find words to explain what had happened. "It wasn't my fault Dad, honest it wasn't, I ..."

To this day I cannot recall what followed nor do I recall the lightning grip that flung me across the nearest chair. But oh how I remember the hammering. All his pent up emotions surged in the right arm as the broad leather seared my shoulders, arms, and buttocks. For days the dull throb reminded me of the respect due to my elders, but it was years before I forgot the basic injustice. I had picked the one moment in time, when all the forces of diabolical fate had conspired to bring my sister's turbulent courtship to a head in which to commit this cardinal sin. But if my sin was great, Bernadette's, in that day and age, was by far the greater.

Only one ray of sunshine brightened my life during the four days that followed, and that was the impending arrival of Uncle Mick. I was at work when he and Archie arrived on the Monday, and the first intimation that my idol had come home was the sound of argument as I passed the window on my way back from work with Dinny.

I stopped dead at the sound of raised voices, and, spine prickling in case of trouble, put my ear to the window pane cautiously.

" 'ose that?" asked Dinny.

"Ssh!" I quietened him irritably.

"*Never!* ... she can't." There was no mistaking that rolling brogue.

"Tarra, Din," I cried excitedly, "it's me Uncle Mick."

"I thought we were goin' round t' Fatty's?" he complained.

"Not t'night," I replied. "Not with me Uncle Mick 'ome. Tell the lads I'll see 'em termorrer o.k. ... See y'."

Without waiting for a reply I hammered on the front door. Moments later I was inside, embraced in a bear hug, first from Uncle Mick, then Archie. I gave a quick glance round for their sea bags to see what they had brought me.

"It's no good lukin'," cried Mam irritably. "Y' Uncle Mick'll see y' later. We're talkin'." I knew better than to argue.

"Our Bernadette's gerrin' married." I announced by way of conversation.

Mam looked daggers at me.

"You shurrup an' mind y' own business," she said sharply. "Go in an' gerra wash." I sighed disconsolately as she jerked her thumb towards the kitchen.

"Ah lerr'im be, Mary," cried my uncle, stretching his arms towards me, " 'e's doin' no 'arm. You come an' sit by me, Li," he suggested. I looked at him gratefully and snuggled myself between him and Dad.

"Where's she livin'? " asked Uncle Mick as I settled myself. Mam buttoned her lips.

"Up at Ma Bloomfield's," I volunteered.

"I told you t' shut up!" she said menacingly.

"What's 'e like this 'ere feller?" asked Archie in his slow drawl.

"I don't wanna talk about them," replied Mam sharply. Archie shrugged.

"You know 'im, Arch," broke in Dad, "short, thick-set feller. ... You remember we 'ad a drink with 'im last time you were 'ome."

"Not the one we watched speakin' at the Park Entrance, the one. ..."

"That's 'im," answered Dad, scratching the back of his head. "A real trouble maker. Always spoutin'. The 'ole family's the same. Their Alfie's in Walton now."

"What for?" asked Uncle Mick.

"The usual," answered Dad laconically. "Politics. I tell y' they're a lotta bloody Commies."

"I thought 'e was pretty good," said Archie thoughtfully.

"Oh 'e's good all right," conceded Dad. "Talk a flamin' bird off a tree Jimmy could, but I don't want 'im in this family, there's enough trouble as it is." Mam nodded agreement.

"Orangeman as well eh?" muttered Uncle Mick.

"Red 'ot," said Dad. "No kiddin', y' could fry an egg on 'im."

"Bloody cheek of 'im!" answered Uncle Mick vehemently. "I've 'alf a mind t' go up there an' land one on 'is sodden ear'ole, upsettin' the 'ouse like this."

Alarm registered on Mam's face. "You keep outa this, Mick; y'know what you're like. We've enough on our plate without fightin'. Jus' leave 'er. Don't worry, she won't 'ave an ounce of luck gettin' married in a Registry Office."

"*Registry Office!*" gasped Uncle Mick, "She'd never do *that* would she?"

"I 'ope not," answered Dad, "but she's stubborn. I wouldn't put it past 'er."

Throughout the conversation Archie wore an air of puzzlement. Several times his lips pursed to ask a question but each time he seemed to change his mind at the last moment. At last, hand rubbing his forehead thoughtfully, he leaned forwards towards Mam.

"How long've they been courtin', Mrs Sullivan?" he asked quietly.

She looked across at Dad and shrugged. But he didn't know either.

"I know," I volunteered.

"You mind y' own business," snapped Mam.

"Dad ignored her as he turned to me. "Well," he said, "go on."

"I saw them together in the entry the day me Aunty Aggie belted me." I blurted out.

"Don't be daft," said Mam tartly.

I was adamant. "It's true, honest. I crashed into 'em in the entry on me way 'ome."

Mam looked at Dad startled. "But that's nearly five years ago. Did you know anythin' about it?" He shook his head. " 'oo!" she hissed. "She's as deep as a drawn well that one."

Archie laughed lightly. "Well, whatever the ins and outs of it," he said, "y' must admit, they must be fond of each other."

"What's that got t' do with it?" said Mam sharply.

"Oh, no offence, Mrs Sullivan," said Archie hastily, "but if they love each other. ..."

Uncle Mick roared with laughter. "*Love!*" he said scornfully. "Come off it, Arch. 'e's an Orangeman."

Archie looked more puzzled than ever. "What's that got t' do with it?" he asked.

"You're kiddin', Arch?" broke in Dad equally puzzled.

"No, I'm not," replied Archie. "Y' say 'e's Orange, and that's that as though 'e 'ad 'orns growin' outa 'is 'ead. It's just like sayin' y' don't like fellers with wooden legs. ... What difference does it make?"

There was dead silence for a second or two. Everyone, including me, looked at Archie as though he had gone mad.

"What difference does it make!" repeated Uncle Mick incredulously.

" 'e's a Protestant!, that's what difference it makes," cried Mam in agitation.

Dad shook his head warningly at Archie, but he missed it completely and pressed manfully on to dangerously thin ice.

"I don't understand all this," he said, shaking his head in disbelief. "After all, y' don't seem to know what 'e's like even, as a man I mean. I'm a Protestant myself, yet y' make me welcome enough."

"Ah yes," broke in Dad, "but you're different, you're not Orange are y'?"

Archie looked at him, scratched his head, then shrugged.

"This is not Yorkshire y'know Arch," said Uncle Mick. "This is Merseyside mate. Y' don't know 'em 'ere."

"But I know a lot'f Orangemen," began Archie.

"Aye, so do we!" broke in Dad, sardonically. "We've gorra live with 'em."

"Well," said Archie quietly, "it cuts both ways. They've gorra live with you too, 'aven't they?"

"Whaddee y' mean?" asked Dad.

"What I say," answered Archie. "With all due respect, Pat, it sounds like six of one and 'alf a dozen of the other t' me. It's a free country, isn't it? Surely a man's religion is 'is own affair."

"You go round to the Orange Lodge an' tell 'em that," suggested Uncle Mick with a grin, but Archie remained serious.

"I don't see why I couldn't," he said thoughtfully. "I wouldn't mind. I'll bet they're a lot more reasonable than y' give 'em credit for."

A sudden gleam came into Uncle Mick's eyes. Mam noticed it immediately. "Warrar y' thinkin' about, Mick?" she asked suspiciously.

"Nothin'," he said innocently. "I was just wonderin' if Archie would like t' put 'is theories to the test that's all."

"*Mick!*" she cried in alarm.

" 'ow d'y' mean?" asked Dad.

"I thought per'aps he'd like t' come round t' the Lodge termorrer. . . ."

Mam shot to her feet. "*No*, Mick, now cut it out, we don't want no more trouble. It'll be bad enough when the twelfth comes round."

He spread his hands and shrugged, blue eyes dancing with devilment. "Now y'know me. . . ." he began.

"Too bloody right I know y'!" she shot back. "So jus' forget it."

"Mary's right," cut in Dad. "Jus' forget it, Mick. Archie doesn't know 'em around 'ere."

"No, Mick's right," said Archie, scratching his cheek

thoughtfully, "I think you're exaggerating. I'll lay y' ten t' one you'll be surprised once y' start talkin' reasonably." Dad looked at him sceptically.

"Luk," said Uncle Mick, "better still, we won't do any talkin' at all."

"What's the use of goin' then?" asked Mam, a tentative note of relief in her voice.

"We'll sing instead," suggested her brother.

"*Sing!*" they chorused.

"Yeh," he answered, eyes gleaming in growing excitement. "We'll give 'em a few bars of 'Faith of Our Father's' an' see what 'appens!"

Dad roared with laughter. "Y'know bloodywell what'll 'appen Mick."

"No, no kiddin'," replied Uncle Mick, suddenly serious, "I think Archie's got somethin' there y'know. Reason, that's what's wanted."

Mam and Dad looked at him suspiciously, then he stared straight at Dad. "Still," he added, shrugging resignedly, "if you're scared. ..."

Dad's eyes glinted viciously as he jumped to his feet. "Scared!" he roared. "*Me*, scared of a bunch of bloody Orangemen? You're kiddin'. What time are y' goin'?"

Mam's face went dead white. "Pat don't!" she pleaded. "For God's sake don't ... *Please!*"

Uncle Mick had sent the shaft unerringly to a vulnerable spot. All hell wouldn't stop Dad going now, and Mick knew it. Mam looked daggers at him as he rubbed his hands jubilantly.

"Good on y', Pat. What time do they meet as a rule?"

"Seven o'clock," answered Dad.

"Right, seven it is," he replied. "We'll wet our whistles with a few scoops first, then we'll show 'em. An' now let's 'ave a drink on it."

Mam was beside herself as they put their coats on in high good humour. She tried everything to dissuade them without success, and within a hour of them leaving Mrs Taylor came in breathless.

"I've just 'eard," she gasped, as she came through the kitchen door. "They're never gonna do it, are they?"

"I see it's got round then!" said Mam laconically.

"But there'll be murder!" cried Mrs Taylor agitatedly. I gazed solemnly at her from my seat by the grate as Mam nodded agreement, then shrugged.

"It's no use talkin' to our Mick," she said in a dejected tone. "Y' might as well talk to the wall. 'e just loves trouble. It's in 'im."

"What about Archie? Can't 'e do anythin' t' stop them?" suggested Mrs Taylor. " 'e seems a sensible sort'f feller."

"It's all 'is flamin' fault!" snorted Mam, cupping her chin in her hand as she leaned disconsolately on the table.

"*Archie!*" cried Mrs Taylor, "but 'e's such a nice quiet feller."

"That's just the trouble," answered Mam. " 'e is . . . 'e thinks 'e's still in Yorkshire; 'e doesn't believe anyone's daft enough t' fight over religion.

Mrs Taylor rolled her eyes in disbelief. "Jesus," she said, "it's nice t' be some people! Anyway let's 'ope somebody talks some sense into 'em round at the pub. There's enough trouble in the town with the work, an' this'd be just the sort of excuse the 'ot'eads would like."

No one talked any sense into them, and at six fifty-five precisely the following night, well primed by Uncle Mick's generosity, the trio weaved their way down the street, along the main road a short distance, then left into the long narrow street where both Church and Orange Lodge were situated within three hundred yards of each other. The gang and about twenty adults were close on their heels.

"What did y' say they were gonna do?" asked Henry, walking alongside of me.

"They're gonna sing 'Faith of Our Fathers' on the Orange Lodge steps," I replied.

"What for?" asked Fatty.

"Search me," I said as Henry rolled his eyes and blew through his lips.

"I reckon this should be funny," said Dinny laconically.

"You might think it funny!" snapped Tommy Rolf, one of the two Orange lads in the gang, "but me Dad say's there'll be ructions if they try it."

"They're all gonna be there y'know," joined in Sniffer, Tommy's co-religionist. "An' they'll get battered if they try anythin'."

I looked from one to the other. They were both good pals, but I didn't fancy standing by and seeing my Dad get battered without doing anything.

"Your lot berra not start anythin' with me Dad an' Uncle Mick," I said threateningly. Tommy stopped dead and glared belligerently at me as the crowd thickened in the last few yards to the Lodge.

" 'ow would your lot like it if we started singin' 'King Billy's March' outside your church?" he demanded.

We never did find the answer because a sudden cheer broke out immediately ahead of us, and in the split second it took me to focus the street erupted. I had a momentary glimpse of the trio poised on the steps. I saw Uncle Mick's mouth open, then a human avalanche descended and they vanished beneath a struggling, kicking mass. The tiny flame, lit as a half joke, was suddenly fed by long years of blind bigotry. All the years and years of frustration and unemployment found an unexpected outlet, and by seven-five, the street shuddered to a tumult of hate as co-religionists plunged to the help of their fellows.

Harsh Irish voices grated in breathless curses. Women screamed as they tried to drag their cheering children away. Then suddenly, strident with urgency, the church bells crashed above the noise. Every Catholic in the heaving crowd gasped with shock. The heathens were within the church precincts! Like turbulent water, the seething melee stampeded towards the alarm bells to protect sacred ground. Everywhere, threshing arms and kicking legs blurred the vision as the Orangemen made a determined effort to get to the altar and tear the tabernacle down.

"This way ... this way!" Dinny's voice screeched excitedly somewhere to my left. I looked round frantically, then howled in anguish as a heavy boot trod on my bare foot.

"Li, Li, come quick ... this way!" Fatty's voice seemed to blast down my ear as I threshed about just inside the church gate. I turned my head. His face gleamed ecstatically less than six inches away. "Cor!" he yelled. "Luvverly, in't it?"

"Where's the gang?" I yelled.

"There's 'enry," he cried pointing. I turned, crashed to the ground as someone hurtled into me, picked myself up and looked for Henry. He was sitting on the church wall, laughing like a maniac and belting everyone that passed beneath him with a roll of newspaper. I turned away disgustedly. Trust Henry to get himself the best of both worlds.

"Where's the others?" I yelled.

"Dinny an' Bonko's in church," he screeched above the noise. "An' Tommy an' Sniffer's joined the other lot."

"Fair enough!" I shouted back. "Foller me."

Together we slipped round the side of the church where the fighting was not so heavy, through the vestry and into the church near the altar.

It was like a scene from Dante. Above us, the bells crashed ceaselessly. All four priests stood on the altar, guarding the Tabernacle behind a score or more of ragged unemployed. The body of the church was a writhing mass of cursing figures, threshing amid the most appalling noise as pews overturned, and prayer books, kneelers, candles and everything movable flew.

Father Denison, young, inexperienced and terrified, arms spread-eagled protectively in front of the Tabernacle, constantly opened and shut his mouth in prayer. Below and to his left, eyes blazing with fury, fists clenched, Father McCormack roared at his unfortunate colleages as a determined Orangeman slipped through the cordon of unemployed, evaded his grasp and made for the Tabernacle and the Host within.

"Don't *pray*, Father!" he roared. "*Belt* him!" All three priests made a dive for the intruder as police whistles screeched outside.

For one of the longest half hours I can remember, the church rocked to the cacophony of hate. But at last, with every available Catholic in the district manning the church in a solid phalanx, it was finally cleared, leaving behind a scar which has not healed even now.

Dad was black and blue. Uncle Mick had the time of his life. The rift between Bernadette and Mam was a chasm that seemed impossible to bridge and the whole district smouldered dangerously as it waited for the twelfth just one week away. Archie put it in a nutshell as Mam bandaged a deep cut on his forehead.

"You were right y'know Mrs Sullivan," he said magnanimously. "They really *don't* like each other do they?"

14

The Black Eighth

The eighth of October 1931. A day that left an indelible scar on two generations and sowed the seeds of discontent in one unborn.

I remember it as though it were today. The stunned huddled groups on every street corner. The shocked, chattering women. The raw icy winds sweeping mercilessly from the foam-flecked river. My mother tight lipped and bitter. My father, cursing as I had never heard him curse before.

It had come. 'The National Economy Order 1931', the Means Test!

For those fortunate enough to be on the dole, it meant a cut to fifteen and threepence a week for each husband, eight shillings for his wife and two shillings for each child. For the great bulk of the people, long since ineligible for dole, and existing solely on Public Assistance, it mean much more. It meant inquisition on an unbelievable scale. Degradation unthinkable in a civilised society. It meant the splitting up of whole families to foil the probing inspectors. It meant lies, evictions, hunger marches, suicides, and finally, an abiding hatred which became the springbroad of unprecedented greed and irresponsibility on the part of those self-same masses when, in the fullness of time, they became the masters.

To me, the half-understood ravings of the adults seemed to be the culmination of an emotive year. First Bernadette, now married and already on Public Assistance. Religious strife, Uncle Mick and his fiery eloquence, and now political meetings. The house seemed never still, and, to add insult to injury, Dad lost his only suit as an unredeemed pledge. Actually its value had been dropping sharply as a result of a tear during the near riot in July, but the final tragedy had not occurred until the last day in September. It all happened quite simply. The Assistance money just collected had dropped through a hole in his overall pocket and vanished. That was that. No money, no suit. Mam had to sell the pawnticket to get food, and for the first time I could remember he went to Mass in his overalls.

For the gang, the few remaining weeks of good weather after the abortive riot passed swiftly, and with religious feelings safely tucked away until next St Patrick's Day we were able to enjoy the few precious hours of leisure together. For once, I was glad Uncle Mick had gone back and from the end of July, when his ship had sailed on a six months voyage, the house had been comparatively peaceful, but now, with the weather closing down, the raging emotions created by the new order, the peace was soon shattered and life resumed its normal uncertainty, and within days of the Eighth, the first of many hundreds of visits by Government inspectors took place in our street.

It caught Bonko's Mam both unawares and innocent. She was too truthful. Like a fool she disclosed that the two daughters were contributing a little, a married son helped where he could, her husband scrounged, chopped and sold firewood at a farthing a bundle, and that she herself, worked like a black, taking in washing to make ends meet. It was fatal. Their Assistance was stopped immediately. The people learned fast. Consultations took place on every doorstep. Arrangements were made to lie in support of each other. The stage was set for a battle that was to last for four bitter years.

Our turn came two days before Bonfire night. The first intimation that anything was amiss was when Mrs Taylor came bounding through the back door, breathless. I was just getting ready to go to work. Mam was scrubbing the table, and Con having a strip down wash at the sink.

" 'e's comin!" she gasped, smoothing her ruffled hair with her hand.

Mam looked up inquiringly. " 'oo?" she asked.

"The Means Test feller," replied Mrs Taylor in agitation. "If you've ..."

"*Con!*" roared Mam, "get t' 'ell outa 'ere!"

Con looked up startled. For official purposes he was supposed to be living with Aunt Min. If the inspector came in and caught him it would be fatal. Water dripped from his chest and arms as he stared uncertainly at her.

"Come on," Mam roared again. "Shift it. If 'e catches y' 'ere 'e'll stop the lot." She turned to Mrs Taylor. "Y' sure 'e's comin' 'ere?"

"Don't worry, 'e's comin' all right," she replied. " 'e inquired at Maggie Bloomfield's, an' I've jus' run straight down from there."

" 'ell!" said Mam, "I wish Pat was 'ere."

"Y' might be better off without 'im," answered Mrs Taylor with conviction. "Y'know what 'e's like when 'e loses 'is temper."

Mam nodded as Con flew round the kitchen grabbing his things. I looked at the clock. Twenty minutes to five. I still had a little time to go to get to work, with any luck I would see him. I had heard so much about these inspectors lately I wouldn't have been surprised if he walked in with horns on. I hovered near the door. Mam spotted me.

"Hey you," she cried, as Con struggled madly to get into his shirt. "You get t' work."

My face dropped with disappointment. "Ah, Mam," I pleaded, "can't I wait an' see 'im?"

She didn't have time to answer. The knocker thundered.

"Hell!" cried Con as he ripped his shirt trying to force

his damp arm through it. Mrs Taylor held the door open for him.

"Never mind that," yelled Mam impatiently, "y' can't go out like that, gerrup stairs an' keep y' trap shut." Again the knocker crashed.

"Warrabout the washin'?" cried Mrs Taylor in sudden agitation, and pointing frantically to a pile of freshly laundered clothes that Mam had been preparing to iron for customers. "These fellers 'ave gorreyes like 'awks."

"Go an' answer the door before 'e takes the bloody knocker off!" shouted Mam to me as she dashed across the room and hastily covered the clothes with newspaper. They were still tearing around as I went through the parlour and opened the door.

I was disappointed. Instead of a big man with horns, our visitor was quite small, with a pale oval face that sprouted above his winged collar like an elderly choirboy's. I noted his snug, well fitting coat with envy, and admire intensely the natty fawn spats, partly hidden by well creased, pin-striped trousers. He smiled bleakly under my frank scrutiny, opened a folder he was carrying and studied it for a moment or two. Behind me I could hear sounds of frantic activity as they hid anything he might consider of value.

"Name of Sullivan?" I nodded my head in the affirmative.

"Your father in?"

I turned my head slowly from side to side, hoping to God Con had settled himself upstairs.

"Your mother in?"

"Yeh, she's in."

"Can I see her?" he asked softly.

I shrugged and bought a little time. " 'oo are you?" I asked. He pursed his lips impatiently.

"I'll explain that to your mother," he snapped, "just go an' fetch 'er."

All along the street, whispering groups of women watched closely as I shrugged resignedly, half closed the door and went in. There was no sign of Mrs Taylor or Con.

"Is it 'im?" asked Mam in a strangled whisper as I came

into the kitchen. I nodded. "Little feller with a bowler 'at an' spats," I answered. "Should I lerr'im in?"

"I don't suppose we cin flamin' well stop 'im, can we?" she replied irritably. I returned to the front door.

"Me Mam says come in," I flicked my head and he followed with an air of disapproval, eyes flickering round the parlour as he passed through.

"Ah there you are, Mrs Sullivan," he greeted her with simulated bonhomie. "You *are* Mrs Sullivan I take it?"

"I 'ope so," she said non-committally.

"Just a few particulars," he added, opening his folder and laying it on the still damp table. His eye caught the crystal set Con was fixing for Uncle Tom.

"That's a nice crystal set, Mrs Sullivan," he said looking at it thoughtfully. "A bit expensive aren't they?"

Mam was on to it like a flash. "Oh don't worry," she retorted sharply. "It's me brother-in-law's. We can't afford stuff like that on the Assistance."

He gave her an old-fashioned look. "Quite so," he answered flatly. "Your son's at home?" he asked out of the blue.

I gasped and looked at the ceiling. She didn't bat an eye.

" 'e left weeks ago," she lied.

"Oh?" he replied suspiciously. "Is he married then?"

"Not that I know of," answered Mam, seating herself by the table, without inviting the visitor to do the same.

But why doesn't he live at home, Mrs Sullivan. Surely it would be of more help to you if ..."

" 'oo are you kiddin'?" she snapped, suddenly losing her first nervousness. "If 'e lived at 'ome you'd knock 'is money off Pat's."

"Pat?" he said inquiringly.

"Me 'usband!" she snapped.

"Could you give me your son's address please, just for the record y'know."

Mam smiled. She was on safe ground. They couldn't touch Aunt Min. She lived on a small pension in lieu of compensation for her husband's death some years before. She gave the address to him. He still wasn't convinced.

"You know," he said quietly, "according to my information your son is still living at home, Mrs Sullivan."

Her eyes hardened. She was in full control of herself now. She leaned across the table, eyes boring into him.

"Well, y' information's wrong isn't it?" she retorted.

I looked from one to the other, anxiously praying that Con wouldn't cough or do anything to give the game away. Suddenly the roving eye caught the pile of washing, jutting out from beneath the papers. A smile crossed his face.

"You seem to have a lot of washing, Mrs Sullivan," he said silkily. "All yours?"

Her eyes narrowed, and a slight flush came to her cheek. She knew what he was thinking and so did I. She brazened it out.

"If y' thinkin' what I think y' thinkin'," she said irritably, "y' wrong."

He gazed at her calmly. "Oh? and what was I thinking, Mrs Sullivan?" he asked, a slight smile hovering round his full lips.

"You think I take in washin' don't y'?" she answered. His head moved a fraction in the affirmative. "Well, I don't see an' if I did it's none of your bloody business." Her voice trembled with rising anger, but he remained unmoved.

"But it *is* my business, Mrs Sullivan, very much so. You can hardly expect the State to give you money, when you're earning, now can you?"

He looked so smug I felt like kicking him.

"They're not strainin' themselves are they?" countered Mam sarcastically.

"These are difficult times, Mrs Sullivan, difficu ..."

"Your bread's buttered though isn't it?" she snapped.

He ignored the remark and made a note in his book.

"You *did* say this was all your washing?" He lifted the paper and looked meaningfully at it. I jumped as she reacted explosively.

"No I didn't!" she roared, getting up, snatching the paper out of his hand and re-covering the washing. She glared at him as she resumed her seat. "Where the 'ell d'y' think we'd get money for stuff like that?" she asked, calming a little.

"Oh, it's somebody else's then?"

Her eyes flashed with temper again.

"Y' don't give up easy do y'?" she snapped, "Course it's somebody else's."

"Whose?" he asked shortly. She trotted out the prearranged excuse glibly.

It belongs t' Maggie Bloomfield up the street ... 'er with the lodgin' 'ouse." She outstared him ferociously, visibly trying to hold herself in, "an' if y' don't believe me," she added, "go and flamin' well ask 'er."

He looked at her cynically. Suddenly his eyes hardened and darted to the ceiling as Con moved and the bed creaked.

"What's that noise?" he asked, indicating the ceiling.

Rats!" she snapped. His eyes gleamed as he checked his notebook.

"This *is* your son's address?" he asked pointedly. I prayed he wouldn't go upstairs.

"You callin' me a liar?" challenged Mam.

He shrugged silently, eyed me speculatively as I leaned against the door, then went off on a new tack. I shrank back as he raised his arm and made to pat me on the head.

"You've a fine lad there, Mrs Sullivan," he said softly. She sniffed, and smoothed her hair silently. He gazed at me thoughtfully. "Still at school?" he asked. He knew damn well I was. I nodded in silence. Suddenly the restless eyes caught the bloodstains on my trousers where I had been carrying meat during the lunch hour. "Cut y'self lad?" he asked quietly.

I looked at the dried streaks and almost fell for it, but Mam was quicker.

" 'e cut 'iself shavin'," she said sarcastically. I giggled. He opened his mouth to reply but she forestalled him.

"If y' probin'," she said, " 'e doesn't work either."

"There's no need to be sarcas ..." He stopped in mid sentence as the back door flew open and Dad walked in. The neighbours had obviously told him who our visitor was, and one look at Mam's strained face was enough to give him the picture. His eyes glittered in his hawk-like face.

"Well?" he said menacingly, "warree y' want?"

Mam registered immediate alarm. Up to now she had been doing nicely. With Dad in this mood anything could happen. I backed into the well of the stairs as he advanced on the visitor.

"I asked you what y' wanted," he repeated sharply.

The inspector drew himself up defensively. "I'm ...," he began.

"I know damn well 'oo y' are," retorted Dad. "Now what is it y' want?"

Mam tried to calm him. "It's all right, Pat," she said rising and laying her hand on his arm, " 'e's just askin' a few questions."

"I'll bet 'e is!" replied Dad, turning to the inspector again.

" 'ave y' got what y' want?" he questioned.

"Not quite," answered the visitor calmly. "There are just one or two things I'm not quite satisfied about." His eyes wandered suspiciously to the ceiling then back to the notebook. "Your son no longer lives here I believe?"

Dad was off guard; he didn't even know Con was in. Mam jumped up and stepped between them.

"You've gorr'is address 'aven't y'?" she snapped. "Isn't that enough?"

He returned her look steadily. "Not quite," he answered quietly.

"What's up?" roared Dad in sudden temper. "D'y' think 'e's 'idin' upstairs or somethin'?"

I felt a prickle up my spine as I glanced across at Mam's chalk white face.

"Possibly," replied the inspector non-committally.

Two pairs of eyes bored into Dad trying to will him to shut up. He didn't.

"Of all the bloody cheek!" he roared in exasperation. "If that's what y' think, mate, go an' 'ave a luk!"

Mam gasped. "*Pat!*" she cried. She was too late, the inspector had already taken up the invitation and was on his way up the stairs with both of them in his wake. I waited tensely for the discovery. Nothing happened. I scratched my head in puzzlement, then the miracle was explained as I caught a blur of movement through the kitchen window as Con dropped swiftly from the shed roof into Mrs Taylor's backyard.

The inspector came down, a triumphant gleam in his eyes. Con had left his boots behind!

Seventy-two hours later we knew the result of the visit. The sharp eyes had missed nothing. We had lost. Dad got no money, just a seven and sixpenny food ticket.

"What's that?" asked my mother as he threw the bright yellow card on the table.

"That's it," he said dejectedly. "That's all we get."

"No money?" she asked incredulously.

He shook his head. "Seven an' a tanner's worth of grub and nowt else," he replied.

She looked at him disbelievingly. "They can't do that!" she gasped.

He gazed at her solemnly. "They've bloodywell done it, 'aven't they?" he said disgustedly.

"But warrar we gonna do?" she asked helplessly. "Warrabout the rent, coal, clothes ...?" He shrugged.

"Don't ask me," he said resignedly. "I'm no magician. What we 'aven't got we'll 'ave t' do without won't we?"

Her face was white as she sank dejectedly into a chair near the empty grate and put her head in her hands. I felt helpless. I wanted to go to her, comfort her, put my arms round her, but I daren't. Dad suddenly flicked the local newspaper across the table to her.

"Read that," he said quietly.

She picked the paper up and studied it for a moment, then read it aloud.

'Eighteen thousand pounds to be spent on a new cemetery in Landigan.'

"Jesus wept!" she ejaculated. "That's just what we need now isn't it?" She paused a moment speculatively, then flicked her head towards the card on the table.

"I'll tell y' what though, if that's all we're gonna get, they won't be long fillin' it, not with this weather."

For a few moments there was a brooding silence as she

picked the card up and turned it over and over in her fingers. At last she flicked it back on the table as Con came through the door.

"What's that?" he asked.

"Read it an' see," answered Dad laconically.

Con picked it up then blew through his lips. "God!" he said despairingly, "we can't get much lower can we?"

Dad shook his head dejectedly. "We'll eat," he said, "but that's about all!" He turned to Mam sitting on the other side of the table. "When will y' pick the stuff up?" he asked casually.

She flushed. "I'm not goin' for them!" she cried in alarm.

Dad looked at her irritably. "Well, y' don't think I'm goin' do y'?" he snapped. "Y' won't be the only one y'know," he added. She looked at Con pleadingly. He put his hands up in horror.

"Don't ask me t' go, Mam. Honest I'd die of embarrassment."

I suddenly felt uneasy and began to ease myself towards the parlour door as they glared at each other uncertainly. I didn't want to go either. Dad caught the movement out of the corner of his eye. His face brightened.

"Send 'im," he suggested. "They can't 'urt 'is feelin's. Kids don't understand these things." I seemed to curl up inside as they gazed at me.

How wrong he was! Oh, how wrong. I can still feel my spine crawl as it did when I entered the shop next day and put the distinctive ticket on the counter. It seemed to scream aloud.

For the first time in my life I was conscious of the rags that draped me, my battered thin-soled boots, my grubby knees. From the dark recesses of my nature, unsuspected and outraged pride, welled and consumed me, as the assistant, sleek-haired and glossy-faced, picked up the ticket with exaggerated care between finger and thumb, and dangled it in front of me.

"Would *Sir* like them delivered?" he asked with a silky half smile.

It was agonising. I felt myself flush with shame as the

nearby customers sniggered. Suddenly I felt a new sensation. I began to grow smaller. Down-down-down, until I felt no bigger than an insect, and from the depths of my misery, I marked every feature of the smirking face. Years later I met him again, thin, emaciated, and but a stone's throw from death. His smile no longer crucified me, but I felt no pity.

Yet we were among the lucky ones. Mam still had a few shillings from Con, and an occasional five shillings from Teresa in Ireland, my two shillings, and what she could make from the washing, and we were healthy. For others with large families and ailing children it must have been a nightmare.

Within two weeks of the Order, old enmities were forgotten in the common need. The street and district welded together in mutual help. Nothing, however small was wasted. Men and boys searched the town and docks for anything burnable to keep the fires going, and the gang, wide-eyed and alert, crafty and resourceful, came into its own. Fagin never had more apt pupils than us. From our individual jobs and a thousand other sources we scrounged, stole or borrowed tit-bits, which, under normal circumstances would have been thrown to the dogs. It was the first of four hard, bitter winters, and whilst the winds shrieked, the town bubbled like an uneasy volcano. Tragedy stalked the air, and within eight days of Christmas, it struck. Suddenly, violently and with appalling results.

It was a freezing night. The Town Hall clock was just striking half-past-eight as Dinny, Henry and I walked down Pleasant View towards the pool of light from the gas lamp at the bottom of our street. We were all dog tired. The street was deserted as we paused for a final word beneath the lamp. Suddenly our blood froze as a piercing, pulsating scream, more animal than human, blasted from Mr Simpson's, two doors from the corner.

We looked at each other with bulging eyes. Moments later, the door flew open, a shaft of light stabbed the darkness, and two of the younger children, screaming dementedly, hurtled out and careered blindly up and down.

All along the street, serried rows of light ripped aside the stygian blackness as doors and windows were flung open. The whole world seemed to go mad as Mrs Simpson, eyes rolling wildly, mouth opening and shutting in horror, stumbled out clutching the youngest child in her arms.

"Gerra Doctor! ... For Jesus' sake gerra Doctor!" she cried as neighbours rushed from all directions, gathering her terror stricken family as they went.

"What's up? ... What's that bloody 'ollerin' about?" A dozen different voices chattered irritably in the night, then the marrow froze in our bones as she swept past us.

"Jimmie's cut 'is throat!" she cried dementedly, " 'e's done 'iself in!"

A grasp of horror seared the gesticulating crowd like a flame as Mr Simpson himself suddenly appeared, silhouetted in the doorway, struggling blindly to keep upright.

My tongue clove to the roof of my mouth as he sagged, straightened momentarily, then moved crabwise into the street, blood pouring from a terrible gash. We stood paralysed with shock, terrified, yet fascinated as we watched the thin form slowly sink down the wall and on to the pavement. Pandemonium broke loose as he hit the ground. Mrs Simpson unconscious of the screaming child in her arms, dashed deliriously round the stunned crowd, pleading, cajoling, imploring.

" 'elp 'im!" she cried. "For Christ's sake somebody 'elp 'im. *Please!*"

"Get Lofty!" somebody yelled.

"Never mind Lofty," cried another voice. "Get the flamin' Doctor or 'e'll be a goner."

"It's too late!" A shrill, high pitched woman's voice scythed through the night as a neighbour bent over the inert form. "Fetch Father."

" 'e'll never gerr'ere in time," shouted a stunned voice.

He was right. Father was too late. Everyone was too late to help this destitute wraith, especially the Government.

15
Eviction

"Why the hell don't y' keep still? 'ow d'y' think I'm gonna get this down y' if y' keep 'oppin' about like a hen on a hot griddle?"

I tensed as Dad's eyes flashed in sudden temper, and looked nervously at the small brown paper cone he held between finger and thumb.

It was Spring. We were going through the sulphur ritual, and I dreaded it.

"What's up with y'?" demanded Mam as she hovered between me and the open door to prevent escape. "Gerrit down y'. It'll do y' good."

I looked at her disbelievingly as Dad re-charged the cone with sulphur. I had had it every Spring since I could remember, but it hadn't done me any good yet. I backed away.

"Come on!" he snapped. "Any more bloody nonsense an' I'll ram it down." I stiffened at the thought. His voice gentled a little. "Come on, don't worry, it'll clear y' blood."

I moved forward to where he sat by the grate. Terrified but obedient.

"Open y' mouth," he ordered.

I closed my eyes, opened my mouth and went rigid. He put the cone in and blew. Blind panic seized me as the dry powder hit the back of my throat, and stuck, choking me.

"Are y' all right?" His words came faintly through the pounding in my ears as I staggered about the room clutching desperately at my throat.

"Ah take no notice of 'im!" cried Mam irritably. "Makes a fuss about nothin' e does." I glared at her through tear-dimmed eyes. It was murderous treatment. I'd sooner suffer with clogged blood.

Even without the sulphur, there was no mistaking that Spring had arrived after a hard, bitter winter. Life seemed to renew itself under the warming sun. The whole district buzzed with activity. Backyards were sluiced, front steps scrubbed and sandstoned until they shone. Blank spaces appeared all over the street as curtains were taken down, washed, dried, and put back again. Children swarmed like so many prisoners just released. Women gossiped, whilst husbands, with nothing else to do, stood in huddled groups on the street corners arguing and planning. Even school did not seem quite so bad at this time of year.

But it was all a facade. Nothing had changed. Beneath the surface resentment smouldered. There was still no work, no money, and nothing to pawn. Threadbare clothes could not be replaced, rent could not be paid, and food was becoming more and more difficult to obtain as the activities of the inspectors intensified. But for me it was Sunday. The sun shone. I had been to Mass and the rest of the day was my own. I couldn't wait to get down to the shed to see the lads. I was still gasping for breath as I made for the door.

"Where are you goin'?" demanded Mam.

"Down t' see the lads," I answered, hoping she wasn't going to find a job for me at the last moment.

She nodded dismissal. "All right," she said, "but don't go gerrin' y'self inter trouble."

I shook my head and hurtled through the door gratefully. They were all there, gazing rapturously at Dinny when I arrived.

"Where you bin?" he asked in a lordly fashion.

"Gerrin' me sulphur," I snapped, spitting the residue out of my mouth.

They howled with laughter.

"D'y' wanna drag?" asked Dinny as I glared at them. "It'll do y' good."

They howled again as I stared at the minute dog-end he was holding out invitingly.

"Y' know what y' cin do with that don't y'?" I replied shortly.

"Yeh," he said, puffing casually at the mangled remains, "smoke it."

I bridled. He seemed a bit cocky. I was in no mood for cheek. "Watch y' lip!" I snarled.

He spat the butt on to the ground deliberately, then

stared fixedly at me. I felt suddenly uneasy. It was the first time we had really got together since we had all started work. Something was up, but I couldn't quite put my finger on it.

"Right," I said, "let's go t' the docks an' gerra raft out."

Fatty was the first to react. He rose from his seat on the ground.

"All right, Li," he said peevishly. "We're not kids now y'know. We're all workin' now, so there's no need t' order us about."

So *that* was the trouble. I decided to stamp on the rebellion swiftly. "We're goin' to the docks!" I snarled, "an' if y' wanna argue, take a sniff at that first." I stuck my fist under his nose. He looked startled, then shrugged.

"O.K.," he said, "I'm with y'."

"You might be," broke in Dinny scathingly, "but I'm not."

I gazed at him belligerently, but he ignored me. "I'm broke," he continued, "so I'm goin' grid fishin'."

Before I could answer Tommy Rolf chimed in. "We'll talk about it, then we'll decide what we're doin'," he said flatly.

I was in a dilemma. Authority was slipping from me rapidly. Silently I weighed Tommy up. He was bigger than me now. It might be disastrous to start anything, beside there was Dinny. I couldn't manage two fights in a row. I tried another tack.

"What's up, Tom?" I said scathingly. "Y' scared of the water or sommat?"

He flushed angrily. "You're kiddin'," he hissed savagely.

Fatty, Sniffer and Bonko shifted uncomfortably as we faced each other. None of them liked trouble much. Then, with tempers at flashpoint, Dinny butted in again.

"Luk," he said amiably, "I don't mind the docks burr'I'm broke; we're all broke. There's nowt at the docks, but there might be in the grids." I nodded. That was reasonable. "Then," he continued, "if there's nowt there we cin 'ave a scrounge round the Market."

"Y'know," broke in Henry's calm voice, "I don't know

what y' all gerrin steamed up about. We've gorr'all day, we cin do the lot."

I felt relieved. The momentary threat to my leadership had passed. "Spit it out," I ordered.

"If we split inter two lots we cin do the grids up both sides of Canon Street at once," he suggested. "Then, if there's nowt there, we'll be right on the Market, an if there's nowt there we cin nip down t' the Ferry an' pinch a ride on the boats." I looked at him gratefully. "We cin always go on the rafts this afternoon," he added.

There was a chorus of approval. Fatty vanished at once to pinch some soap off his Mam whilst Dinny and I gave the poles out as though nothing had happened. Inwardly I still rankled.

For a full hour we searched the grids without result. At last, Dinny came across the road and admitted defeat.

"Bloody poverty-stricken lot round 'ere!" he said feelingly. "Nobody drops nothin' down these days. Luk, this is all we got." He held a hair slide in the palm of his hand. The Market wasn't much better. From the mounds of debris lying about, all we got were five badly bruised apples, two carrots, a battered lettuce and a penny. I split the eatables between them.

Dinny spat disgustedly on the cobbles. "With this kinda luck," he said miserably, "I'll lay six t' four we don't even gerra ride on the ferry."

He was wrong. I gave the penny to Henry as we approached the entrance hall at the Pierhead. They only collected money on the Birkenhead side, so once past the ticket office, it was possible to ride back and forth across the river until the crew caught you. Timing was essential.

We hung about until the familiar red funnel showed against the brown water at the bottom of the floating bridge about a hundred or so yards away. I winked at Henry and nodded to the collector leaning nonchalantly out of his box.

"Give 'im the gab, 'enry," I instructed.

He gave me his slow smile and returned the wink. "I'll try the old faintin' touch," he said laconically, "Keep y' eyes skinned."

"Y' got the penny for y' fare all right?" I asked. He nodded and strolled casually towards the collector. Three paces away he stopped and leaned against the kiosk.

"Get ready," I ordered, "as soon as that feller comes outa 'is box, run like 'ell."

I watched as Henry passed his hand across his forehead then sagged. All concern, the collector came out like a Jack-in-the-box.

"Now!" I hissed. One by one we slipped swiftly under the gate, and raced, chattering like monkeys, down the bridge.

"Come back 'ere, y' young sods!" he roared.

Sniffer stopped, gave him a raspberry, then stuck his tongue out, and tore after us, laughing like a maniac. Moments later Henry joined us.

Ten yards from the bottom we stopped dead, then sauntered casually on to the boat moments before the gangway went up. Henry and I left the others and made for our favourite spot, high up in the bows on top of the anchor, where the soft breeze rustled intimately through the rents in our clothing.

The world looked completely different from the gently heaving deck. Ahead, across the glistening brown water, the Liver bird on top of the Cunard buildings, seemed to soar into the clear blue sky, while astern, the tall silent cranes of Cammel Lairds, guarded the crowded river bank like sentinels. For one fleeting moment, as the wind rippled and played in my untidy hair, the harshness of the world fell away, and with feather-like touch, the magic that made Uncle Mick a wanderer, fell upon me.

For two hours, we sailed back and forth, fascinated by the ceaseless activity of the great river, hiding and re-hiding each time she tied up, but at last we were caught and chased ashore, well pleased with our pennyworth.

Despite the giggles and laughter on our way home, I felt a vague uneasiness. I sensed the growing challenge to my authority and determined to do something to re-establish myself beyond dispute without actually having to fight. But what?

Arrangements were made to meet again at two, and I

was still pondering the problem as I walked into the kitchen. There was no one in. My problem vanished in an instant. Mam rarely went out. There must be some kind of trouble. I dashed out and hammered on Mrs Taylor's door. She was all smiles as she opened it.

"Where's me Mam?" I demanded.

She laughed. "Don't worry, she 'asn't run off an' left y'. She's round at y' Uncle Matt's."

"Why, what's up?" I asked.

She shook her head. "You'll never believe it," she answered.

"Try me," I said impatiently.

"I think y' Dad's gorra job!"

I looked at her incredulously. "Y' what?" I exclaimed.

"That's why they've gone t' y' Uncle Matt's. A bloke fell sick an' they think y' Dad cin gerrit."

I felt a sudden elation, then a corresponding doubt. He hadn't worked for more than four consecutive weeks since I was three. I shot round to Uncle Matt's. I knew I was wrong the moment I stepped through the door. Aunt Sarah, then Mam, then Dad hugged me in turn. That was an event in itself. He had got it.

"What kind of a job is it, Mam?" I asked, when she had settled down a bit.

"Gardenin'," she answered.

I scratched my head in puzzlement. "*Gardenin'*?" I queried. "I didn't know Dad could garden."

" 'e can't," she answered brightly.

"Diggin'," explained Dad, clarifying the situation, "jus' diggin'."

"Where?" I asked.

"Moreton," he replied, naming a village about four miles away. It was a complete turn-up. When jobs were almost impossible to get, he, a tradesman shipwright, had landed a gardening job at a pound a week and was jubilant.

"Y'know what they cin do with their food ticket now Matt don't y'?" he said as we left to go home.

"I could give them a few suggestions," replied Uncle Matt with a grin.

"They cin stick it up their. . . ."

"*Pat!*" cried Mam, admonishingly.

The change in them was incredible. The years magically slipped away from my mother and revealed a skittish side to her nature which I had never suspected. Within fifteen minutes the whole neighbourhood knew. I was so excited that I had forgotten all about the raft, and it was half-past-two when the gang came to the door.

"I thought you were comin' to the shed after y' dinner," said Dinny accusingly. "We've bin waitin for y' . . . What's up?, aren't y' comin'?"

I looked at him startled. "I 'aven't 'ad me dinner yet. What time is it?"

" 'alf two. Are y' comin' or not?"

" 'ang on a minute while I gerra butty." I dashed in. Mam was just putting some stew on.

"What's up with you?" she asked.

"I've gorra go out, I promised the lads."

"Warrabout y' dinner?" she asked absently.

"Give us a butty, that'll do. They're waitin'."

Her mind was obviously elsewhere. Without asking questions, she put some dripping on a piece of bread and handed it to me. I didn't tempt fate.

"Tarrawell. See y'," I yelled as I dashed through the parlour and into the sunlit street.

Thirty minutes later we were afloat. Thirty-five minutes later I was facing a challenge. Henry started it quite innocently as he gazed into the oily water.

"Wouldn't it be the gear if we could swim?" he said absently. "Bet nobody's got the nerve t' try it," he added, trailing his hand over the side. I looked at the rippling water, and shuddered involuntarily.

"Li cin do it, can't y', Li?"

My neck prickled as Tommy's sarcastic voice broke quietly on the warm air. I turned and glared at him silently. He was trying to needle me.

" 'e'd drown," said Sniffer, teetering nervously. "I wouldn't go in. I'll tell y' that for nothin'."

"Ah yeh," butted in Dinny with a snigger, "but you're not cock o' the gang are y'?"

I remained silent, half angry, half terrified.

"I reckon 'e's scared!" answered Tommy with quiet venom.

The raft rocked dangerously as I whipped round on him, white-faced with anger. " 'ose scared!" I yelled at him.

He shrugged eloquently. "Words is cheap," he answered laconically. I felt numb with sudden terror. I couldn't, I just couldn't.

"I wouldn't lerr'anybody say I was scared," butted in Fatty.

"You shut y' gob before I shut it for y'!" I yelled hysterically.

Fatty slid to the bottom of the raft. But the others weren't so easily scared.

"You leave Li alone," piped up Bonk in my defence. "I wouldn't go in an' neither would you, Din."

Dinny looked across at him and cocked his head quizzically to one side. "Ah, but I'm not the cock am I?" he asked. "I don't give orders do I?"

"Shut up, Din," broke in Henry quietly. "Whaddee y' wanna go makin' daft dares like that for? 'ose gonna 'elp 'im if ..."

"I don't want nobody t' stick up for me!" I yelled ungratefully, tearing my shirt off in a frenzy. "I'll show y' 'ose scared!"

Tommy and Dinny stood watching impassively as Bonko grabbed my legs.

"Don't do it, Li," he pleaded. "Don't be a bloody idjit. They were kiddin', weren't y'?"

I looked hopefully at Tommy and Dinny as he appealed to them. They remained silent.

Terrified despite my bluster, I knew I had to go. If I didn't prove myself now it would only be something else in a day or so. It was a determined challenge to authority. I removed my trousers slowly, praying that something would happen to prevent my having to go in. It didn't.

"Y' crackers!" said Henry, as I stood on the edge trembling with fear and indecision.

"I told y' 'e was scared," said Tommy quietly.

Blind fury swept me. Then the icy water clutched fiercely at my naked body as I went beneath the surface. Terrifying, pulsating fear gripped me as my eyes opened to the dark swirling world about me. I wanted to scream, every fibre of my body struggled for air to prevent my lungs bursting. Frantic, groping fingers searched for something solid. Moments later I was on the surface, gasping and choking from the water I had swallowed and half dead from shock.

Half a dozen hands scrabbled to grasp my slippery, oil-slicked body and pull me back on board, then searing pain swept me as the rough iron edge skinned my leg from thigh to ankle.

Slowly, dazedly, a sense of triumph replaced fear. I was safe. I looked up and grinned at two crestfallen, worried faces.

"Now 'ose scared?" I asked.

"Fair enough!" they said together.

The six weeks following my unexpected dip, were among the happiest I ever spent as a child. Undisputed in the gang. Dad working. The sun shining, and peace at home. It was a rare combination. It couldn't last, and it didn't. On the last Friday in July, with the sun blazing down out of a clear blue sky, Dad came home, footsore and weary. I was drinking a cup of tea with Mam in the kitchen. One look at his face was enough.

"Don't tell me," she said simply. "Y' got the sack?"

He nodded and threw his cards on the table.

"Never mind," she said resignedly. "I knew it was too good to last, an' y' never know, things might pick up before the bad weather sets in."

They didn't. They just got worse. Moonlight flits became more popular in the district than paying the rent. A rumble of handcarts in the night, an empty house the next day, and a silent neighbourhood as to where the tenants had gone. For those behind with the rent, and not quick enough off the mark with a handcart, it was the police and bailiffs. Evictions became more and more common, and on the Tuesday after August Bank Holiday, we had the first of many in our street.

The blow fell after days of speculation on Tommy Rolf's. Tommy, at eleven, was the eldest of a family of eight. Lazarus could not have been poorer, and, until the generosity of the neighbours took over, the parents and older children had been reduced to a mixture of bread and hot water mixed to a soup, in an effort to give the youngest what they needed.

The street was packed as we turned the corner on our way home from school. Heads hung out of every window. Knots of women, stony-faced and silent, glared open hatred as the police and bailiffs forced their way through the crowd round the barricaded door.

"Come on now, make way there!" roared the sergeant, a big beefy man with hard blue eyes. "We want no trouble."

The crowd resisted silently, just giving way sufficiently for the bailiff to hammer on the door. I spotted Mam and Dad right in front and just to the left of the door. Dad glowered savagely at the thin, slight form of the bailiff as he stepped back to the edge of the pavement, cupped his hands, and shouted at the shadowy figure through the open bedroom window.

"Come on now, Mrs Rolf, be sensible. Don't make trouble for y'self. Just come out quiet."

Mr Rolf's face twisted savagely as he poked his balding head through the window.

"T' hell with y'!" he shouted hysterically. "If y' want me y' cin come an' get me."

A roar of approval crashed through the street as the bailiff shook his head helplessly at the sergeant. Suddenly Lizzie Conlon thrust her way to the front. She didn't live in our street, but there was trouble with the police, that was enough. She cupped her hands and tilted her head back.

"Take no notice of these bastards, Jimmy," she yelled. "We're with y'." She turned to the crowd. "Are yiz with 'im?"

There was a surge forward.

"You tell 'm, Liz!" shouted someone encouragingly. She did, in a string of invective. For the first time I noticed Lofty, looking harassed and uncomfortable, and bent almost double as he presented his backside to the crowd and pushed. Lizzie was yelling right down his ear. Suddenly he got irritable.

"If y' don't shut y' trap, Lizzie, you'll be right inside. Now knock it off an' mind y' own business."

She glared at him, shrugged her powerful shoulders and spat on the ground.

"You an' 'ose bloody army, Lofty?" she said challengingly. "Jus' try it."

The crowd erupted with laughter. The irate sergeant glowered at them threateningly, beads of sweat running down his face. Lofty sensed the mood and changed his tactics.

"Go on, Liz," he said amiably. "Don't push y' luck. This is none of your affair."

Lizzie picked him up in a second, as she turned to the crowd again. "Did y' ear that?" she shouted indignantly. "It's none of our affair 'e says ... *is it?*" she demanded.

Lofty and his superior eyed the restive crowd with concern as they roared support. Suddenly, unexpectedly, Dad took a hand.

"Y' oughta be bloodywell ashamed of y'self, Lofty. Y'know Jimmy as well as I do, 'e can't 'elp it if there's no work can 'e?"

Mam darted across the intervening space to shut him up before he worked himself into a flaming temper. She was too late.

"Go on, Pat!" shouted Lizzie, rallying the women into a compact band. "You tell 'im. It's about time somebody did."

Again the crowd surged into a narrow circle round the three men. Yells of encouragement came from every window in the street. Insults began to quicken. Things were getting ugly.

"It's them in the Town 'all y' wanna throw out, mate, not these poor sods," shouted someone from the back, as the bailiff hammered on the door again.

Mr Rolf popped out like a Jack-in-the-box as Lofty and the sergeant struggled.

"I told y', if y' want me, come an' get me!" he yelled.

"I'll smash the door in!" yelled back the bailiff.

"Try it!" answered Mr Rolf. "Try it an' I'll bloodywell brain y'." He waved a poker threateningly through the window.

"None o' that!" roared the sergeant. "It'll only go worse for y'." "*Worse!*" shouted Mr Rolf derisively. "You try feedin' kids on bread an' water, mate. Don't worry, it can't gerr-any worse."

Lofty ran his finger round the inside of his collar uncomfortably. He knew most of these people personally. He looked as if he wished he could sink into the ground and vanish. The crowd had a certain sympathy with him, but not much. Lizzie renewed her attack.

"Luk at 'im," she roared, pointing to Lofty, " 'elpin' t' throw eight kids out." She stuck her face close to him, "I thought you were a *man*, Lofty. Y' oughta be flamin' well ashamed of y'self."

The sergeant had had enough.

"Grab 'er!" he yelled irritably.

Lofty tried but missed.

"Leave 'er alone y' big flatfooted bastard!" shouted someone near him.

The sergeant whipped round but failed to find the culprit as the crowd screeched its support. Lizzie passed within a foot of him as she whipped the onlookers on. He grabbed her by the shoulder. Uproar broke out as she cut loose, crashed an open-handed blow against Lofty's cheek then ducked. The crowd closed in a solid wall behind her. All the while the bailiff kept hammering at the door. Suddenly he lost patience and waved to the sergeant.

"We're comin' in!" he cried above the tumult. It was the signal for a shower of missiles from above.

Cheers rang out as Mr Rolf flung everything he could find on the crouching backs.

"Why don't y' send for the troops?" shouted someone derisively. "There's only eight 'alf starved kids in there."

Lofty was turkey red with embarrassment and exertion. Twice they charged the door to the accompaniment of ribald shouts. It held. The bailiff stood back exasperated and exhausted to wipe his forehead. Suddenly there was a tremendous howl of laughter, as Mr Rolf popped his head out of the window and tipped a full 'Jerry' over the invaders.

"Pick the bones outa that lot!" he shouted gleefully.

Lofty came near laughing as it soaked his superior.

The deluge galvanised them into furious action. They charged, the door wavered, then splintered. Terrified shrieks from inside the house goaded the onlookers to fury. There was a sudden surge forward, a threatening babble of voices then the sergeant's whistle screeched its alarm. The atmosphere became electric. Both ends of the street were blocked with onlookers. Lofty stood white-faced with tension, guarding the doorway as the sergeant and bailiff went inside.

There was a sudden squeal of brakes at the top end of the street. Every head turned as reinforcements, batons drawn, shouldered their way through the angry throng. Scuffles broke out in half a dozen different places as Mr Rolf, struggling and kicking like a fiend, was dragged outside and slammed against the wall, blood running thinly from a gash in his head. Uproar renewed at the rough treatment. The reinforcements ringed the doorway.

"Shame!" cried someone.

"A free country?" howled a woman close to me. "Free t' bloodywell starve!"

"Y' didn't come an' drag us outa the trenches, did y'?" yelled a hoarse voice from across the road.

"*Trenches?*" shouted someone who obviously knew the sergeant. " 'e doesn't know what trenches are, mate. 'e was sitting on 'is arse in the police station all durin' the war."

" 'e'd pinch 'is own bloody mother for threepence, that feller," yelled a woman standing next to Mam.

A ghost of a smile flitted across Lofty's perspiring face, as the sergeant glared round, still holding Mr Rolf against the wall.

Inside the house it was bedlam. Children screamed as they tried to escape the strangers' arms. Footsteps pounded up and down the stairs as they eluded their captors, then suddenly, with a strange dignity, Mrs Rolf appeared, holding the youngest in her arms.

I felt tears trickle down my face as I watched her, red-eyed, weary and bemused, shepherd the terror-stricken children, like a mother hen, into the centre of the street. The sight spurred Lizzie to fury. Mr Rolf made a frantic effort to get to his wife and children. The sergeant rammed him back against the wall. Lizzie ducked beneath the encircling arms of the reinforcements. A roar of pain sliced through the howls of the delighted crowd as she lifted her skirts high and kicked him savagely on the thigh. He let go one arm to grab her. She ducked, rose like a rocket and slammed him hard across the cheek with closed fist.

The crowd went mad, the children screamed anew in terror.

"Grab 'er!" he roared. "Get this bitch off me." Two burly forms rushed forward and dragged her struggling and kicking up the street to the van. She fought every inch of the way, with the crowd howling her on. Outside the house Mr Rolf took advantage of the momentary diversion to try and get to his wife, but white-faced and clutching the baby in her shawl, she called to him pleadingly.

"Jimmy whisht!" she cried as the children clung to her torn skirts. "For God's sake whisht. Yiz'll only make it fifty times worse."

Her husband sagged as the sergeant slapped the bracelets on him. There was no more fight left in him. They didn't even let him speak to his wife before they dragged him away to a certain three months for assault. Only the drawn batons prevented the crowd from rioting, as the bailiff, soaked and savage, ordered the furniture to be put out. Every stick they owned was dumped unceremoniously on to the cobbles, and as quickly retrieved and taken into the care of neighbours until Jimmy came out and they could settle again.

The bemused children were split up, one to a house. Lost, terrified, and scarred for life by the laws of this green and pleasant land, this realm, this England.

"Don't worry, Jimmy!" somebody called as they dragged him to the van. "Our turn'll come." ... it did.

16

The Informer

August passed in a welter of heat and emotion. Dangerous forces began to crystallize and focus. A score of would-be leaders, most of them violent, urged and cajoled the people to take action and, unlike the Lord's words, most of the seeds fell on fertile ground.

Even moderates like Uncle Matt and Con were shocked by the violence of the Rolfs' eviction, and for the first time, the inarticulate hatred of the unemployed focused on the police as well as politicians. It boded ill for the future.

For our family, the eviction had many diverse effects. It deprived Con of his bed, and gave me a new companion in Tommy who came to live with us. It brought Mam and Bernadette together, and split Con and Dad as opinions crystallized and people took up stands. Outside, in the street and district, this division of opinion, aggravated by strident dissidents, swirled and gyrated until at last there were two distinct camps. Whole families became split on the course of action that should be taken to gain relief. Father turned against son, brother against brother, and wives against husbands. Some wanted violence, others negotiations. Only on one thing did they all agree. *Something* had to be done to release them from the bondage of destitution before the biting winds once again shrieked in from the river, and down the fireless chimneys.

The situation was dangerously fluid. Trained agitators from both sides of the river, circulated the huddled, angry groups, whispering sedition. Political extremists took this heaven-sent opportunity with both hands and promised the millenium, and in the midst of it all, sublimely unconscious of the dangers around them, the children played in the last of the summer sunshine.

For me it was a time of teetering uncertainty. Rarely a day or night passed without a meeting on the front step or in the parlour. Meals became erratic, sleep uncertain, but it was not until the third week in August, with the whole town simmering with revolt, that open division came to our house.

It was a lovely evening. A soft breeze caressed the hot flagstones. Children squealed with delight as they played in the gutters. Mothers lounged or sat on steps gossiping. Mam sat on her favourite stool in the doorway, surrounded by Aunt Min and half a dozen neighbours. I could hear the low mumur of conversation as I stood getting a wash at the sink before meeting the lads. They were discussing a problem that had plagued the district for a month: an 'Informer'.

Someone in the tight-knit ranks was slipping information to the authorities. Inspectors had pounced with uncanny accuracy a score of times. Sons and daughters had been caught at home, when officially they were living away. Shillings earned by some enterprising member of the family had to be accounted for. It couldn't be coincidence, they were too swift, too accurate.

Whoever it was, was causing havoc. More and more families had benefit stopped and were forced to exist on food tickets. Old friends began to speak warily to each other. It was a grim prospect for the coming winter.

Abruptly the conversation died. I pricked my ears up as Mam's voice percolated through the door in greeting.

"Good even' to y', Father." I heard the scrape of her stool as she got up.

"Good evenin' to yiz, sure it's bin a God given day, hasn't it?"

There was a murmur of assent for Father's sentiments.

"D'y' mind if I have a word with Mrs Sullivan?" he asked. The door thumped as Mam pushed it wide open.

"Well, goodnight an' God bless y'," I heard him say as I hurriedly dried my face. Moments later he followed Mam and Aunt Min into the kitchen. He greeted me as they sat down.

"Y' keepin' outa trouble, Liam?" he asked, bunching his fist and making a mock swipe at me.

I grinned but said nothing. Mam looked at him as he turned to her, expression changing to seriousness. "What's up, Father?" she asked abruptly.

"Trouble," he answered with equal abruptness. Mam's face paled. Aunt Min put her hand to her mouth agitatedly.

"It's not Pat is it?" asked Mam in alarm.

He shook his head. "No," he answered slowly, looking straight into her eyes. "It's Bernadette."

Mam half rose, then sat down tight-lipped and returned his gaze. Except for one or two accidental meetings, she hadn't seen Bernadette since she threw her out.

"Oh?" she said non-committally.

Father waved Aunt Min down as she rose in agitation. "Now sit y' down, Minnie," he said soothingly. "It's not that bad."

Aunt Min subsided, and Mam relaxed imperceptibly. She was bitter, but Bernadette was still her child.

"What's up?" she asked.

"There's bin a fight in the house," said Father simply, "Jimmy's brother Alfie has bin arrested."

Mam snorted, eyes lighting up triumphantly as she turned to her sister. "There!" she exclaimed gleefully. "I told y' I knew it. Troublemakers the bloo. ..." She remembered Father's presence. "All of 'em," she ended lamely.

A smile flitted across his face.

"Whisht, Mary!" snapped Aunt Min. "Would y' whisht?"

"What happened, Father?" she asked, turning away from Mam irritably.

He explained. Apparently there had been a meeting at the dock gates. Alfie, as usual put his foot in it. The police tried to grab him. He kicked one and dived for cover. Bernadette's flat on the third floor of a nearby dock tenement had been the nearest. The chase had ended in a fight during which my sister, eight months pregnant, had fallen. She couldn't come home because of the feud, so the neighbours brought Father, and here he was. Mam was still sitting tight-lipped and silent as Father finished and Uncle Matt and Dad walked in.

"They've arrested. ..." began Dad.

"I know!" snapped Mam irritably.

"Well don't snap me bloo. ... Oh 'ello, Father," he ended.

"We're just goin' round t' see Bernadette, Pat," said Father, looking at Mam. "She's had a nasty fall."

Concern crinkled Dad's face. "Is she all ri ... ?"

"I'm not goin'!" broke in Mam abruptly. They all looked at her disbelievingly.

"It's no good lukin' like that!" she snapped at Dad. "I'm not goin' an' that's that. She's made 'er bed she'll ..."

Impatience crossed Aunt Min's normally placid features as she leaned irritably across the table.

"Don't be an idjit, woman," she cried. "The girl's 'urt, she pregn. ..." She spotted me by the sink and clapped her hand over her mouth.

Uncle Matt laughed and ruffled my hair. "Ah go on, Minny," he said. "Y' can't shock kids now-a-days."

She flushed and did a little wiggle with her shoulders. "Well y'know 'ow she is," she cried.

"I don't care," cried Mam stubbornly. "It's 'er own fault. She shouldn't 'ave married a 'eathen."

Again Uncle Matt roared with laughter. "Catholics 'ave 'm too y'know," he said sarcastically.

She flushed scarlet, then glared at them all belligerently. "I don't care," she repeated. "I wouldn't be seen dead under the same roof as that feller."

Father looked pityingly and tapped his finger on her arm. "Jimmy's a good man, Mary. You should thank God Bernadette's got a good husband."

She sat rigid, lips a thin white line. She didn't agree but she wouldn't argue with the priest. Dad hovered uncertainly round the back of Father's chair. He had tried for months to make her listen. Father looked at her quizzically, then leaned forward, eyes boring into her.

"Y'know I'm surprised at you, Mary Sullivan," he said slowly. "You're arrogant." Her lips pursed in annoyance. "An' that's a sin!" She looked at him in growing alarm as he ploughed deliberately on. "But more than that, an' God forgive me for sayin' it ... y' bigoted."

There was a sibilant gasp of surprise. Her eyes flashed. For a split second I thought she was going to bite his head off. Instead she flushed and remained silent, eyes downcast.

"Now come on with y'," he said coaxingly. "It's y daughter; she's in trouble. Forget the past, it's over an done with." He gave her a gentle push on the shoulder "Come on, woman, get y' shawl and let's get."

I felt sorry for her. I could see the struggle she wa: having under the steady gaze of half a dozen pairs of eyes Her respect for the priest won. She flicked her heac defiantly as she spat the words out.

"All right then!" she snapped. "I'll come ... but i. doesn't change anythin'. *Registry Office!*" she added scornfully.

Father shook his head sorrowfully at Dad as she rose to get her shawl. "How's things in the town Pat?" he asked.

Dad shrugged his shoulders as Aunt Min clucked her way after Mam. "Rough, Father," he replied.

"An' gerrin' rougher, Father," added Uncle Matt solemnly.

The priest shook his head. "I don't like it," he said. "The Divil's havin' a helluva time of it at the moment, but please God it'll sort itself out. ... Oh hello, Con," he exclaimed as my brother came quietly through the back door.

"What's up?" asked Con. Father told him.

His eyes lit up when he heard that Mam was going round to see Bernadette. "Well, thanks be t' God for that," he said gratefully.

"It's 'is representative y' wanna thank," said Uncle Matt with a laugh as the women returned with their outdoor shawls. Father roared with laughter as he sparred up to Uncle Matt.

Mam's face looked strained. She wasn't looking forward one bit to this enforced reunion. Dad squeezed her arm encouragingly as Father turned and wagged his finger solemnly at him.

"Keep outa this lot, Pat," he said warningly. "As sure as hell there'll be trouble in the town before long, an' there's no good'll come of it. Do I have y' promise now you'll have nothin' t' do with it?"

Dad returned his gaze silently for a second or two, then he looked straight at him. "No, Father, y' don't. If I said yes I'd be tellin' a black lie."

Father sighed audibly. Uncle Matt clapped him on the shoulder.

"Y' all right, Father. I'll keep my eye on 'im don't worry."

Father shrugged. "Ah well," he said thoughtfully, as he ushered the women through the door. "I suppose we must thank God Mick's not home!"

Uncle Matt laughed. "I'd pray a bit 'arder if I were you Father. 'e's due 'ome any time now."

The priest rolled his eyes heavenwards as he made the sign of the cross over the assembled company. "That'll be nice!" he said laconically.

The door had barely closed behind them when Con voiced his opinion. "I'm right with Father there," he said. "Uncle Mick's berra where he is."

"Well he'd soon liven things up a bit, we could do wi ..."

"They're too damn lively now!" broke in Con abruptly.

Dad looked at him scornfully. "What's up with you?" he said sarcastically. "Got no stomach for a fight?" Uncle Matt looked from one to the other, sensing trouble.

"All right, Pat, knock it off," he said to Dad. " 'e's entitled t' 'is opinion the same as you are. Anyway," he added, spitting into the empty grate, "there's enough trouble outside without you two startin'."

I felt a sudden admiration for my brother, I'd never heard him answer back before in my life. He stuck to his guns and looked steadfastly at Dad.

"There's more ways than fightin' t' settle things," he said calmly.

Dad's eyes narrowed dangerously. I felt a tremor of fear run through me and edged for the door. Uncle Matt opened his mouth to speak but Dad cut him out.

"Y' frightened of a bitta rough stuff? Is that why y' don't come t' any of the meetin's?"

My brother flushed angrily as Dad sat by the grate

absently rearranging the fire-irons. The hairs on my neck bristled as he answered.

"Don't worry!" he snapped. "Just because I don't listen to them rabblerousers down there," he flicked his finger towards the docks, "doesn't mean I don't think."

Dad swivelled in his chair, and glared at him viciously.

Again Uncle Matt stepped in with a worried frown on his face. "Watch it, Con," he advised quietly. "It's y' Dad y' talkin' to y'know."

"Leave 'im alone, Matt," grated Dad irritably, " 'e's a big lad now. If 'e's gorranythin' t' say, lerr'im spit it out. Y' never know," he added, "we might learn somethin'."

Con flushed at the sarcastic tone, but he showed no fear. "I don't go to the meetin's you go to," he admitted, "an' d'y' know why?"

"Go on, I'll buy it," said Dad.

" 'Cos they're a lotta Commies that's why," snapped Con, suddenly furious. "D'y' think they give a damn about you?" he said sarcastically pointing his finger at Dad. It was my father's turn to flush angrily. He half rose from his seat.

Uncle Matt put his hand on his shoulder. "You asked him t' spit it out," he said with quiet menace, "so pin y' ears back."

Dad glared at him, but Uncle Matt was both older and bigger. He also had a vicious temper when he liked.

"What the 'ell does 'e know?" cried Dad with rising temper.

Con oozed confidence with this new-found ally. He was on to Dad's remark like a flash. "What do I know about it?" he cried angrily. "I'll tell y'. . . ."

"All right, son," interjected Uncle Matt. "Don't get y'self in a sweat, I know 'ow y' feel."

"It's all right for you, Uncle Matt," cried Con agitatedly, "burr'e thinks I'm still a kid."

"Well y' talkin' like one!" snapped Dad.

"Am I?" said Con, suddenly calm and tense. "Y' think so do y'? Y' think I know nothin'? Well, I'll tell y' warr'I know Dad. I know I'm twenny-six years old. I know I've done two months' work since I came outa my apprenticeship five years ago. I 'aven't 'ad a new shirt on me back for over two years." He held his foot up. "Luk! Even me boots are fallin' off me feet." His face went white with emotion. "What do I know?" he almost shouted. "I know four of me mates 'ave put their 'eads in the gas oven because they couldn't stick it, that's what I know. Dad gazed silently into the grate as Con shook his fist. "Don't y' think that's enough Dad? D'y' think I don't *feel*? Whaddee y' think I am? ... a bloody moron?"

I was shocked and terrified. None of the children were allowed to swear in the house however old they were, but Dad didn't seem to notice.

"All right, all right!" he shouted. "Y' dry be'ind the ears, so what? D'y' think we're gonna gerr'anywhere by talkin'? D'y' think those well fed bastards in the Town 'all'll listen to arguments?"

"Calm y'self down, Pat," said Uncle Matt quietly.

Dad shrugged his shoulders savagely. "Ah leave me alone will y'?" he snapped leaning forward towards Con near the sink. "Well come on, know all, answer me, do y'?"Con remained silent. "If y' do," added Dad scornfully, "you're a bloody idjit. Y'll get nothin' in this world without y' fight for it."

"Well, if you want t' get y' 'ead bashed in t' please the agitators, that's your business," said Con spiritedly, "but don't expect me to. Honest," he added exasperatedly, "I'm so flamin'fed up with the whole damned lot'f it, I've a good mind t' join the Army."

Dad came to his feet like a rocket, and even Uncle Matt looked disgustedly at Con.

"We want no hired assassins in this house!" Dad roared angrily. "If y' wanna join the Black an' Tans, y' cin pack y' bags an' git ... understand?"

Uncle Matt jumped in between them in alarm as Dad shook with anger. He hated soldiers and so did Uncle Matt. Their father had been shot on his own doorstep during the troubles in Ireland.

"All right, Pat, steady on," he said soothingly. " 'e didn't mean that. 'e wouldn't join the Army, would y', Con?"

Con looked shaken as he wagged his head from side to

side. "I'm sorry, Dad," he said at last, "but I still think there's other ways. You come an' listen t' Jimmy Kiernan. Now there's a bloke that talks sense.

Dad reseated himself and looked at him incredulously. "*Jimmy Kiernan!*" he cried. "Don't make me laugh, 'e's a bigger bloody trouble-maker than all the others put t'gether."

"Not now 'e isn't," answered Con emphatically. "Not since 'e got married to our Bernadette."

" 'e's right there," broke in Uncle Matt obviously relieved at the turn in the conversation.

Dad looked at him scornfully. "Don't tell me you've turned pacifist too!" he said sarcastically.

Uncle Matt flushed angrily. He was still framing a reply when Mrs Taylor came bounding up the yard. I felt a surge of relief.

"What's up?" she asked, running a practised eye round the company. "Arguin' again?"

They grinned sheepishly. "Where's Mary?" she asked. Dad told her. She clapped her hand over her mouth in delighted surprise. "Well I'll be damned!" she exclaimed. "Wonders'll never cease. I must say it's not before flamin' time is it?" They nodded agreement.

"Whaddee y' want, luv?" asked Dad.

I watched her agitated face closely. She was a great actor when she had anything to impart. She glanced round the room as though it were full of spies.

"Y'know this business about the inspectors?" she began. We all knew about it only too well. Her eyes flickered round the room and down the yard. Then she leaned forward confidentially.

"Well, I've a bloody good idea 'oo's doin' it."

They gave her a startled look. "No!" they chorused.

She nodded emphatically, raised her finger warningly and continued. "I'm not sure mind y', but I've a good idea."

" 'oo?" they asked. She went over to the parlour door, looked in, came back and leaned against the sink.

"That sanctimonious sod over there!" she said, jerking her thumb towards the entry.

"Y' don't mean *Nunny?*" cried Dad disbelievingly. She nodded.

"Never!" said Con. "She goes t' mass every day of 'er life."

"Them's sometimes the worst," broke in Uncle Matt knowingly.

Dad's temper flashed momentarily. "The bloody 'ypocrite!" he ejaculated. "I've a good mind t' go over there an' punch 'is flamin' ear'ole."

Mrs Taylor became agitated. There was alarm in her voice as she laid her hand on his arm.

"*'er!*" she cried, "not *'im.*"

"If it's 'er, 'e must know," cried Dad.

"But if it is 'er, what's she got t' gain?" asked Con in a puzzled tone. "What would *anyone* 'ave t' gain?"

"I wouldn't trust 'er as far as I could throw 'er," said Dad darkly.

Uncle Matt struck a cautious note as he shook his head dubiously. "I'd step lightly if I were you, luv," he counselled Mrs Taylor. "It's one thing thinkin', an' another accusin'."

She looked crestfallen. "I'll swear it's 'er," she said vehemently. Suddenly her face screwed with annoyance. "An' if it is," she added viciously, "I'll pull 'er flamin' 'air out."

"Pull 'ose 'air out?" Mam's voice came as a shock. No one had heard her and Aunt Min come in through the front door. I looked to see what mood she was in. She looked more relaxed than I had seen her for months. Father must have given her a good talking to. I glanced from one to the other as they began chattering about the baby, then suddenly she spotted me.

"Git!" she said, jerking her thumb at the door. "This is no place for you."

I looked at her disgustedly, but went. I felt even more disgruntled when I arrived at the shed. The lads must have got fed up waiting. After half an hour checking the odds and ends of the shed I felt irritable at their non-return and went home. The parlour was packed with neighbours, and like a squat black duck Ma Bloomfield held the floor as I walked in. She was in vicious mood.

Mrs Taylor's suspicions seemed to have been accepted unanimously, but they wanted proof.

"Don't worry," Ma was saying as I edged in and stood in the corner, between the front door and the dresser. "We'll catch the sod. Whoever it is 'as caused enough trouble without any more."

Dad, sitting alongside Mam on the far side of the room, suddenly got impatient. "Luk," he said, getting to his feet, "if it's a woman, you sort it out among y'selves, I'm goin' t' Haymarket."

"Another meetin'?" asked Uncle Matt interestedly.

Dad nodded as he crossed the room. "Comin'?" he asked.

"Why not come an' listen t' Jimmy on the Park Entrance?" suggested Con. "Then you'll see what I mean."

Dad looked across at my mother uncertainly; he didn't know quite how the land lay between her and Jimmy after her visit. His eyebrows lifted in surprise as she agreed.

"Go on," she said encouragingly, "Father agrees with 'im!"

" 'e what?" retorted Dad, disbelievingly.

"There y' are," broke in Con delightedly. "What did I tell y'? Come on, let's go'n listen."

Dad shrugged. Uncle Matt winked at Mam as he passed her. "Good on y'," he said approvingly. He stopped as they got to the door, turned and wagged his finger at the company in general. "Now don't go doin' anythin' daft!" he warned. "Don't go purrin' y' foot in it. Just make sure first ... See y'," he added as he vanished through the door. Suddenly his head popped back. "If Sarah comes, tell 'er where I am will y'? Honest she worries 'er guts out, that one." They laughed as he vanished for the second time.

For another half hour the colourful conversation ebbed and flowed in a welter of ideas to catch the culprit. At last it was Aunt Min, quietly twiddling her thumbs as she always did when she was thinking, who offered a solution.

" 'ow about if y' 'ad a lodger?" she asked Mam suddenly.

"Warree y' talkin' about?" snapped Mam impatiently at her sister. "Where the 'ell would I purra lodger? 'ang 'im be'ind the door?"

Aunt Min clucked impatiently. "Oh don't talk like an idjit. I don't mean a proper lodger. I mean one'f Maggie's." She nodded at Ma, now seated with her thick fingers folded across the acreage in front of her. The round face lit up.

"Y' mean plant one, Min?" Aunt Min nodded eagerly.

"Y' mean just let Fanny Fernackerpan see 'im?" asked Mam.

Again Aunt Min nodded. The conversation livened immediately, and I listened avidly as they laid their plans.

I was at school when Nunny came to borrow an eggcupful of sugar next day, but Mick Gaffy, our temporary lodger, wasn't. She found him sprawled comfortably on Con's bed in the parlour. I got my orders as soon as I got home from work that night.

"Foller'er," instructed Mam. "Don't lerr'er outa y' sight, understand?"

Seven o'clock Saturday morning, the chill of the paving stones struck through my bare feet as I waited at the top of the entry. Seven fifteen, the trim form came through the door, looked up and down, snugged her shawl over her head and round the narrow shoulders, then set off towards the church. As instructed, I 'follerd'. I blessed myself from the holy water font at the back of the church, leaned surreptitiously against the door while she heard Mass, then tailed her as she went by a circuitous route to the Market, down past the Haymarket, into Canon Street and passed the Assistance Office. I ducked into a nearby doorway as she stopped, turned, looked about her, then took a note from beneath her shawl and dropped it through the office letter box. That was enough. I raced home to a breathless audience and recounted my journey.

"The cross-eyed bastard!" exclaimed Ma Bloomfield.

"It's a wonder the 'and of God doesn't stiffen 'er," said Mam feelingly.

Mrs Taylor rubbed her hands together. "Don't worry, if 'e won't, I will!" she said menacingly. "Jus' wait'll I get me 'ands on 'er." She looked crestfallen as Aunt Min struck a cautious note.

"All she's done is purra note in," she said slowly. "That doesn't prove nothin'. We'll 'ave t' wait an' see what 'appens. *Then* we cin do somthin'."

They didn't have long to wait. The inspector arrived at half past eleven on Monday morning. The whole street was waiting for him. He was ushered in to the waiting women. The interview was short and to the point.

Ten minutes of close questioning, and he was on his way back to the office, red-faced and followed by sniggers from every doorway. The gang turned the corner at the top of the street just in time to meet Mam, Aunt Min, Mrs Taylor and three or four others on their way to Nunny's. We tagged on as Dad and a few of his friends came out to join them.

Word had raced ahead. By the time we had reached Nunny's house in the next street, there were a score or more women waiting. Mrs Taylor was angrier than I had ever seen her in my life. An expectant ripple ran through the crowd as she hammered on the door. Moments later a white-face Nunny appeared.

"What's up?" she began.

Mam stepped forward, face dark with anger. Mrs Taylor stuck her arm in front of her to stop her

"Leave this t' me, luv," she hissed to my mother. "I'll settle 'er." She turned to Nunny.

"Now, y' craw thumpin' 'ypocrite!" she hissed. "Warr'ave y' gorra say f' y'self?"

Sheer terror crossed Nunny Dempsey's face.

"*Albert!*" she screamed. There was a pounding of feet from inside, then another scream from Nunny as Mrs Taylor grabbed her by the hair and yanked her bodily off the doorstep. A gasp rose from the crowd as they cleared a space for the scrabbling women.

"What the 'ell's goin' on there ...?" Mr Dempsey tore out of the house and straight into a solid wall formed by

Dad, Mr Armfield, and the O'Malley. Dad stuck his fist under his startled nose.

"One peep, mate, just one," he said menacingly, "an' you'll get the same as that bloody informer's gerrin'."

Mr Dempsey, tall, thin, and with wispy hair, went grey with shock as he stared helplessly at his screaming wife. There was nothing he could do.

For five terrifying minutes we witnessed near animal ferocity. It was an eerie experience. The crowd, most of whom had suffered as a result of her activities, watched in almost total silence. Mrs Taylor fought in silence. Only Mrs Dempsey's terrified screams racketed round the close-packed houses. Her clothes were almost torn from her back, blood streamed down her thin, hawk-like face, and still Mrs Taylor pummelled her. I felt sick. Suddenly a cry swept the crowd.

"Scuffer's up!"

It was Lofty. Attracted by the screams as he paced his beat, he came racing down the street and burst through the crowd like a bomb.

"What the 'ell's goin' on?" he roared. "Separate 'em!" His helmet went flying as he executed his own order. The crowd, still rankling over his part in the Rolfs' eviction, flayed him verbally.

At last, bleeding and sobbing, Nunny escaped while Lofty held Mrs Taylor in a vice-like grip, and ran screaming for her doorway. The men let her through. Mrs Taylor, still carried away with the violence of her emotions, struggled frantically.

"Calm y'self!" roared Lofty. "F' Jesus' sake, woman, calm y'self before I slap the cuffs on y'."

Mrs Taylor, hair streaming chaotically over her normally jolly face, clothes ripped where her victim had clung on desperately, and blood oozing from a dozen scratch marks on her face, gradually quietened in the encircling arms. Dad walked over to the grunting policeman, eyes glittering as he bunched his fists. Around him a tense silence fell, and Lofty looked anxiously at the hostile crowd.

"Take y' ands off 'er, Lofty," said Dad with quiet menace.

Lofty's face twisted angrily as he tightened his grip on Mrs Taylor.

"Don't you tell me what t' do, Pat!" he snarled.

Mr Armfield and the O'Malley walked up and stood behind Dad silently. The crowd crept forward and narrowed the circle around them. Lofty's hand crept to his whistle pocket.

"Don't touch that," warned Dad venomously. His hand dropped as Mrs Taylor tried to escape. "I'm warnin' y', Lofty," continued Dad. "If y' take 'er, you'll 'ave t' take the bloody lot." He swept his hand round the crowd. A roar of approval greeted the challenge. Then Con, teetering anxiously on the edge of the crwod rushed forward.

"Dad!" he cried.

Dad's face writhed with suppressed anger as he whipped round. "Shurrup!" he shouted. "We've 'ad enough bloody cant with that 'oly bitch. She got what she deserved." Again the crowd shouted approval as my brother, silent and chastened, turned and stalked away. Dad turned to Lofty again. The policeman looked long and silently at the crowd. The whole district was ready for trouble and he knew it. I could almost see him calculating his chances of making an arrest. One wrong word or move and anything could happen; he knew then all too well to have any illusions about that. At last he shrugged his shoulders.

"That's up t' 'er," he said flicking his head towards Nunny's closed front door. "Warrabout it?" he asked Mr Dempsey, still standing dazedly on the pavement. "Are y' gonna charge 'er?"

Mr Dempsey shook his head numbly. He was still shaking with fear. The crowd waited menacingly.

"No charge, Lofty," he grunted dazedly. He pushed open the door, then turned and waved his hand limply, "Jus' forgerr'it, I don't want no more trouble." He went in and slammed the door behind him. Someone threw Lofty's helmet to him. He let Mrs Taylor go and jammed it on his head irritably.

"I could 'ave you an' 'er for disturbin' the peace, Pat," he said aggressively, as Mam and the other women led Mrs Taylor down the entry.

Dad looked at him squarely. The O'Malley and Mr Armfield stepped up close.

"I told y', Lofty," he said evenly. "Y' take one, y' take the lot ... try it."

Lofty glared at him for several tense seconds, then suddenly, abruptly, turned and shouldered his way through the crowd.

"Ah t' 'ell with y'!" he said.

17

The Volcano Erupts

As August slipped uneasily into September, and the first nip of approaching winter filled the air with a new urgency, events began to gather momentum. Opinions crystallized. Arguments grew fiercer, and the demands for militant action became more insistent. Suddenly, everyone was caught in the maelstrom of emotion. Fists pounded tables, tongues chattered interminably, and the running battle between political extremists and moderates, simmering for months past, flared into a series of open conflicts. Police walked the streets, silent, wary, ostracised.

As a result of the new found rapport between Mam and Jimmy, our house became H.Q., and life for me became a crazy round of school, work, then hawking round the petition laboriously drawn up by Jimmy and his committee. Anywhere and everywhere that men gathered, the gang and I pounced on them. In church, outside pubs, and on the pitch-and-toss schools, willing fingers scrawled their rough signatures. The demands were simple and urgent.

1. That Public Assistance should be given to all able-bodied unemployed.

2. An increase in Public Assistance of 3/- per week to be given to all able-bodied men and their dependants.

3. An immediate supply of clothes and boots for the unemployed and their dependants.

4. A cwt of coal throughout the winter months to every unemployed householder.

5. A twenty-five per cent reduction in all council house rents.

6. *No more Evictions.*

We encountered fierce opposition from the rival camp who hawked their equally simple, but infinitely more dangerous petition with as much fervour. Their demands were unequivocal.

'The immediate abolition of the Means Test as had happened in Sheffield, Wigan, and Durham, otherwise an even bigger demonstration would be forced.'

Altogether nearly 1,200 people signed for Jimmy. He was delighted and expressed his thanks to a crowded meeting in the parlour on Monday the fifth. The house bulged. Parlour, kitchen and stairs were thronged with silent listeners as Jimmy, eyes shining, faced tense with emotion, explained the drill for the presentation of the petition at the Town Hall on the following Wednesday.

For this momentous occasion, the whole family had been switched around. With Bernadette, already bed-bound, Mam and Aunt Min went to stay with her. Jimmy came to live with us, sharing the parlour with Con, and sleeping when and where they could. Dad became a human dynamo, with relations between him and Con deteriorating in proportion to the violence Dad expressed should the petition fail. Then, on Tuesday the sixth, whilst Con was cooking a few chips for a hasty meal, the telegram boy arrived. I took it and dashed through the litter of paper in the parlour. Dad's eyes lit up when he read it.

"Mick's comin'!" he shouted gleefully. I did a jig round the table.

Con went pale. "Oh my God!" he said. "That's all we need."

Dad rounded on him. "What's up with y'?" he said half jokingly. "If anyone'll liven things up it'll be Mick."

"That's warr'I'm afraid of," answered Con laconically.

Dad grabbed me as I cavorted round the kitchen. "Stop that flamin' jiggin' about," he snapped. "Go an' tell y' Mam Uncle Mick's comin'." I looked at the chip-pan hungrily.

"Oh don't worry," said Dad, giving me a push towards the door. "We won't eat your share. ... Go on, git."

I went at the double. Mam's reaction was the same as Con's. Bernadette sighed disconsolately as she leaned exhausted against the pillow in the tiny bedroom.

"God," she said, "y'd think we 'ad enough trouble wouldn't y'?"

Aunt Min put it more forcibly.

"I wish the bloody ship'd sink in mid-river!" she said feelingly.

"*Minny!*" retorted Mam in a shocked voice. "Y' own brother."

Aunt Min grinned. "Well," she said with a wink, "per'aps jus' low enough t' stop 'im gerrin' off 'til this lot's over."

The ship didn't sink. Uncle Mick arrived just as the delegation was drawing up, minus Archie.

"Where's Arch?" asked Dad after they had greeted each other enthusiastically.

Uncle Mick grinned. "Couldn't stick the pace," he said laughing. " 'e's stayin' aboard."

"Per'aps it's just as well," answered Dad. "There's gonna be some fun 'ere I cin tell y'." He explained the situation. Uncle Mick's eyes lit up with blazing enthusiasm.

"Don't start yet," he pleaded. "F'God's sake don't go without me. I just wanna slip round t' see Mary an' Bernadette an' I'll be right with y'."

Dad laughed. "All right," he answered, "but you'd berra be quick. We start at twelve sharp from the Park Entrance."

There was almost a holiday atmosphere when the gang and I arrived at the huge square outside the park gates to join the three hundred or so already there. For an hour or more before we arrived, Jimmy and his tireless colleagues had harangued them. On all sides of the square, spectators, uncertain whether to join, watched and waited as police circled the restless throng. At last all was ready. The pipe band which had volunteered its services, crashed the first defiant notes into the chill air. Children, ragged and barefoot, screamed with delight as they ran in and out among the adults. A cheer rang out from the onlookers. The column lurched drunkenly, picked up the tune, and swung, heads up, into the march and headed for the Town Hall.

They did not want the earth as they would do in three short decades. They wanted work, food for their children, but above all they wanted *justice.* They got nothing.

For three days the knocker never stopped, as people came to inquire of the progress. There was no news. Tempers rose alarmingly. On the second night, Bill Samuels, a well known agitator, and a dedicated trouble-maker, forced his way in with a body of his cronies at his back. We were all in the kitchen when they arrived, eating bread and dripping and drinking tea. Jimmy rocketed to his feet as he heard the familiar voice.

"Gerr'outa 'ere!" he roared angrily.

Uncle Mick was right behind him as they shot through the parlour and met them head on in the doorway. " 'ose this bloody feller?" he shouted, grabbing the short stocky Samuels by the scruff of the neck.

" 'e's an anti-Christ!" shouted back Dad. "A thievin' bloody lay-about 'oo couldn't work in convulsions. Throw the bastard out."

Suddenly the street was in uproar as Uncle Mick obliged. Neighbours came running from all directions to form a protective ring round the door.

" 'ose side are you on?" yelled Samuels, dusting himself down, then shaking his fist at the glowering Jimmy. "Why the 'ell don't we join forces?" His little red-rimmed eyes glinted viciously as his cronies muttered around him. "Y' gonna get nothin' pussyfootin' around mate," he shouted. "Drag 'em out string the bastards up, that's what they'll understand!"

"Go on!". roared back Jimmy, shaking his fist angrily.

"Get movin' while y' safe. We'll do things our way. We cin talk longer'n we cin fight."

"What's up?" shouted a tall thin man, towering above Samuels, his leader, "Are y' yeller?"

Jimmy went suddenly berserk. I flew upstairs and peeped through the banisters at the milling crowd in the doorway.

For a few minutes the situation looked ugly. Women screamed, men shouted, and terrified children stood silently as the two factions hurled abuse.

"Gerr'em!" shouted Jimmy. Pandemonium broke loose as Samuels' men took to their heels. An uneasy peace settled as the street emptied.

Twenty-four hours later the petition was rejected. Jimmy admitted bitter defeat. Another twelve pulsating hours and Samuels had his revenge. This time 2,000 marched, with the Communists in the lead. The terrifying roar of the 'Red Flag' bounced from the surrounding buildings as an irate crowd surged like an incoming tide round the Town Hall. They were in a dangerous mood. I looked anxiously at young Bonko Armfield standing alongside me. His Mam would have my life if anything happened to him.

"Gerr'up that post," I ordered, nodding to a lamppost a few feet to our right.

"But ..." he protested, as the last bars of the 'Red Flag' died.

"Gerrup and shut up!" I snarled. I turned to see where Dinny and the rest of the gang were. A searing pain shot up my leg as a woman trod on my bare foot. I kicked her savagely on the shin. She was too busy to notice. Dinny waved excitedly as the tune of the 'Red Flag' was replaced by thickening insults to the patrolling police. I couldn't hear what he was shouting. I cupped my mouth.

"See y' later."

My words were drowned in a welter of screaming and shouting as police reinforcements arrived and took up station in a double line across the face of the Town Hall. Then I went temporarily deaf as a voice roared down my ear.

"Are we t' starve?" it yelled.

I looked up as an answering cry came from the crowd. It was a huge docker, bristly chinned anbd drooling at the lips with emotion, towering above me. I shimmied to avoid his great feet. A thin miserable-looking woman alongside him egged him on.

"You tell'em, luv," she shouted encouragingly. I moved rapidly away as he obliged.

"Warree y' want?" he roared at the stolid building. "A town fulla corpses?"

That went down well. Suddenly a new cry arose and was taken up with fervour

"Fetch that bloody Mayor out an' string the sod up!" shouted someone above the cacophony. The cry swept the crowd like a tongue of flame. Soon they were all roaring for the Mayor. Police looked anxiously at each other, closed up and linked arms as the crowd surged, faltered, then surged again. Fear ran through me as the gap narrowed. I ducked, skidded to the right and shimmied up the lamp-post after Dinny

"It's the gear in't it?" he cried excitedly as I joined him.

I felt tense. "Shurrup!" I snapped. "An' 'ang on t' that bloody cross bar."

We looked down on the restless heads. Women in front, shawls tight wrapped against the chill air, began to spit on the encroaching police. Suddenly the situation changed dramatically. Rumours swept the assembly that the Mayor had decided to receive the dockers' delegation with Jimmy at its head. Insults changed to cheers. The police relaxed. One woman at the front of the crowd, began to jig in delight. Moments later a thunderous clapping, crackled and swelled as the rumours were confirmed. Then the wild barbaric skirl of the pipes screeched into the overwhelming noise.

For a solid hour we clung there, half frozen, but too excited to notice. As though at a signal, a deathly silence descended. I could hear my own breathing as a small knot of people appeared on the balcony. It was the Mayor with Jimmy and his committee. There was no sign of Samuels. I waited breathlessly as Jimmy waved his hand then began to shout to the crowd. Another full-throated roar shook the buildings as he announced that their demands would be put before the full Council on the following Tuesday, the thirteenth.

Spontaneous dances broke out all over the place. Cheers were called for the Mayor by people who an hour before, would have willingly slit his throat. Excitement ran at fever pitch as the town waited expectantly for Tuesday. Twice, the extremists tried to get into the house as Jimmy's speech was thrashed out, and twice, Uncle Mick, Uncle Matt, and a few chosen stalwarts threw them out. The committee wanted to avoid violence at all costs.

By Sunday night Tommy and I were exhausted from lack of sleep. Dad sent us to Dinny's, but with twelve children in the family already it was more chaotic than our house. It was like living in a railway station at Dinny's, with bugs as well as passengers for company. The Devlins didn't have meals, they snatched in transit, and in the centre of it all, placid as a mountain, sat Mrs Devlin, reading. I was amazed. Dinny straightened me out.

"Take no notice of 'er," he advised us laconically. "She's daft."

All housework was left to the children. They were no keener than she was. The results were catastrophic. Going to bed was akin; to asking where the flies go in winter. Tommy and I must have been there twenty-four hours before Mrs Devlin realised she had two extra. Dinny happened to catch her attention between chapters and introduced us.

"Fancy that," she said flatly. "Stay as long as y' like, luv."

I raised my eyebrows.

"I told y'," said Dinny, separating two of his younger brothers fighting on the bare brick floor. "She's like me Dad ... crackers." I saw his point. I was glad when Tuesday arrived.

My brother-in-law was like a hen on a hot griddle. Every time he caught sight of me, he sent me round to see how Bernadette was. When I got there, Mam was worried about Dad. Were they wrecking the house? They were, but I daren't tell her. Was Uncle Mick in trouble. He was thriving on it. At last the great day came. They got *nothing!* Three members of the Council had walked out and wouldn't even discuss the laboriously drawn up petition.

Jimmy almost wept when the news came through. He looked haggard as he put his head in his hands on the table. Dad patted him on the shoulder.

"Never mind Jim," he said consolingly. "No man could've done more to avoid trouble. Wharr'ever 'appens now, it's not your fault lad."

"An' what bloody satisfaction is that?" answered Jimmy bitterly. "If Samuels gets 'is way, there'll be murder done."

"Well, what did y' expect," shouted Uncle Mick suddenly in a flaming temper. "If y' wan' anythin', y've gorra fight for it, an' by Christ there's a few thousand 'ere that'll do it too," he added viciously.

Con looked from one to the other miserably. He hated violence. "I still don't think that's the way t' go about things," he said doggedly.

Dad rounded on him like a tiger. "Y' bloody idjit!" he shouted. "Whaddee y' suggest we do?" He pointed to Jimmy leaning disconsolately on the table. " 'e's tried everythin', they won't even listen." His face twisted with anger. "Whaddee y' wan' us t' do. Sit'n freeze t' death? Watch the kids go 'ungry . 'ow many more suicides d'y' want before y' bloodywell wake up lad? ... Go on, tell us!"

Con hung his head in silence.

"Y' Dad's right, Con," broke in Jimmy quietly. I watched him as emotion slowly took command. His jaw muscles jerked spasmodically as he fought to control his rising temper. Weary eyes glittered. "If they wanna fight," he hissed after a moment or two's silence, "they're gonna get one."

Con stared at him silently, then turned and walked to the door.

"I'm gonna see Mam," he said quietly.

For twenty-four hours the pot boiled. Reason had failed. Dad, Uncle Mick and Jimmy threw their hands in with the wilder element despite the pleas of Uncle Matt and Con who adamantly refused to join them. There was little sleep for anyone that night. Gangs roamed the streets. Police patrols in the rougher quarters were doubled then trebled, and in the grubby tenements my sister tossed and turned in an agony of suspense. I had more freedom during the next forty-eight hours than I had had all my life, and together the gang roamed the streets looking for excitement.

Minute by minute the tension built up, and on Thursday the fifteenth, a huge contingent, led by kilted pipers, paraded in front of the barricaded Town Hall. For half an hour we joined in the torrent of abuse at the silent cordon of police, then, by unspoken command, the tremendous crowd, headed by the militants, and surrounded by scores of screeching women and children, suddenly wheeled in the direction from which they came, and began to march off.

We ran alongside the band, jigging and capering like madmen, and shouting encouragement to relatives in the column.

"They're goin' back t' the Park Entrance," shouted Dinny as they headed down Canon Street.

He was wrong. Without warning the direction changed and they turned towards the residential district. Rumours swept the onlookers. The few accompanying police melted away for reinforcements as the destination became known. They were heading for the house of the chairman of the Assistance Board. The news spread quickly. People poured from houses until the street was black with them. We raced ahead of the band, wild with excitement, and over all, the pipes skirled like demented demons. Houses and shops thinned; gardens became more plentiful. Suddenly the column erupted. People cascaded over fences and trim lawns like water. The sight of the chairman's house seemed to have maddened them.

"Fetch 'im out!" they screamed. "Fetch 'im out an' string 'im up."

The first bricks began to fly.

"Scatter!" I yelled to the lads. They were already on their way. I dashed for the nearest lamp-post, always a good spot in a riot, and looked frantically for Dad. It was hopeless in that nightmare. Windows shattered like bursting bombs, garden walls were ripped up to provide ammunition. The whole world seemed to have suddenly gone mad.

My blood ran cold as the pipers scattered and screams took the place of music. Suddenly the lamp-post shuddered. I grasped the cross-bar grimly as the 'Black Marias' screeched to a halt in the centre of the milling crowd. Police poured out, batons flashing at anything that moved. I quivered with a mixture of fear and excitement as I searched the heaving mass for the lads. What had gone before now paled as the rioters tried to over-turn the vans, and the police sailed into action. The air filled with missiles. Suddenly the crowd broke. The lamp-post shuddered under the impact of crashing escaping people.

Sheer terror passed through me as my hand slipped momentarily. For one hair-raising second I scrabbled frantically as the crowd surged beneath. Palpitating, I grasped feverishly at the collar of the lamp window, then slowly hauled myself back to safety, half dead with shock.

A piercing boyish scream to my left made me turn my head, and I froze anew. It was Henry, sitting on top of a pillar box, screaming his head off in an island of cursing swaying bodies. I prayed he wouldn't slip. Again the tempo changed with dramatic suddenness. I looked down. The ranks of the rioters had thinned. Again and again the police charged, withdrew, reformed and charged again, batons swinging in vicious all-embracing arcs, then, for some inexplicable reason, the rioters, outnumbering the police ten to one, broke and swept like a millrace down any opening they could find, until only the police were left. Still I hung on. I looked round. Henry had gone. I felt suddenly isolated as I gazed at the battlefield and gasped with horror.

A score of rioters and seven police lay battered and silent.

"Come on, young'un, get down off there!" I started at the sound of the deep tired voice, and looked down at the grim, bleeding face of a sergeant. Helmetless and with tunic ripped to shreds. He looked dazed and haggard. His voice became irritable.

"Come on, y' young sod!" he snapped. "No bloody nonsense. Geddown before I pull y' down." I slipped down like a greased eel and stood quivering before him.

"What's y' name?" he demanded. I visualised myself handcuffed and on my way to the waiting van, and dreaded what Mam would do to me.

"Evans," I said without hesitation. "Jacky Evans." He nodded sombrely. "I didn't do nothin', mister, honest I didn't. I was up there all the time," I stuck my thumb at the lamp-post. I went rigid as he put his hand on my shoulder, then his face crinkled into an admonitory smile.

"This is no place f' kids," he said in a fatherly tone. "You take my advice son an' keep outa the way." He made a significant gesture towards the bodies in the roadway. "Otherwise y' liable t' gerr'urt." He gave me a final pat on the head. "Go on," he said, "skid!" I skidded straight home and right into another riot.

Mam was there in a hell of a temper. Uncle Mick sat with his head in his hands by the grate. Dad stood near the window gazing pensively at the remnants of his shirt in his hands, and Jimmy leaned over the sink bathing a swollen eye. She grabbed me by the jersey neck as I walked in and shook me violently.

"An' where the 'ell 'ave you bin?" she demanded. "I've bin worryin' me guts out about y'."

"Up a lamp-post," I replied flatly.

"Up a flamin' lamp-post!" she roared, flicking me across the ear with her free hand. "What the 'ell kind of an answer is that?"

Uncle Mick winced. "Whisht, Mary, will y' f' Christ's sake. I gorra bang on the 'ead."

"Well, I'm glad," she said unsympathetically. "Per'aps it'll knock some bloody sense inter y'." It hadn't though.

For half an hour of colourful rhetoric she lambasted them. They were adamant. They hadn't even started yet they vowed. At last, with one eye on the clock she became impatient.

"Luk," she said. "I've gorra go back an' give Minny a chance t' gerr'ome. Will y' be all right?"

Dad nodded wearily. "Warr'about some grub?" he asked.

"Sarah'll be round as soon as Matt gets 'ome," she replied. "I've left some stuff for 'er t' do for y'." She made for the door. "Now 'ave some flamin' sense," she added. "Stay where y' are an' keep outa trouble. I've enough worry round there."

It was good advice wasted. They gave her five minutes to get clear, then Dad ordered me round to Dinny's.

"An' *stay* there, understand?" he said menacingly. "If I catch y' out in this lot, I'll 'ave y' bloody liver."

I nodded. "Where y' goin'?" I asked.

"Out!" he said. "Now git goin'."

Mrs Devlin was sitting in the only chair they had when I arrived. The three youngest howled round the room playing Cowboys and Indians. She raised her liquid brown eyes from her book as I came into the room.

"Where's Din?" I shouted. She gazed at me for a second or two, then switched her gaze as a piercing scream rent the air. She raised her book admonishingly. I jumped at her startling change of tone.

"Stop that, Alfie!" she screamed. "Stop bangin' 'is 'ead, y'know 'e's not well."

Alfie, the eldest of the three there, reluctantly released his hold on his brother's throat.

"Where's Dinny?" I asked again in the sudden silence.

She shrugged. "Out seein' the fun I think," she replied without animation. "Oh 'ave y' ..." Her remarks were cut short by the crashing of the front door. Mr Devlin stumbled in amidst howls of delight from the children. He was laden like a Christmas tree with boots, shoes, clothes and food hanging all over him. William, the eldest, equally loaded, was right behind him grinning like a Cheshire cat.

"Get this lot outa sight before the Jacks come!" roared the father above the excited cries of the children. Mrs Devlin swivelled in her chair as he dumped the loot in the centre of the floor.

"Whaddee y' think I am?" she said placidly. "A bloody magician?"

Outside the street was alive with hurrying figures, most of them carrying loot. There must have been a raid on the shopping centre. I was in a fever of indecision. Should I disobey Dad or not? I couldn't bear to think of missing all that excitement. Mr Devlin cut across my thoughts.

"I've just seen y' Dad an' Uncle Mick," he said.

"Where?" I asked, side stepping to avoid the kids as they raced about in their new boots.

"Goin' down t' the Park Entrance," he replied. "There's another meetin' goin' on," he added by way of explanation. That decided me. I'd go the opposite way.

"Where's Din?" I asked him as he headed for the door.

He stopped, scratched his head, then his eyes lit up. "Round at the Co-op gerrin' some more boots I think."

I followed him out of the front door. Suddenly I heard Henry's voice yelling from the top of the street.

"Li, Li, this way!" He was waving his arms frantically for me to come.

I raced towards him. All the lads were down the entry, working like Trojans passing food and clothes from a handcart to several of the rioters. For a solid half hour we worked in frantic haste, desperately trying to find hiding places for the stuff. Out of the blue came a warning cry.

"The *Jacks!*"

There was a wild panic as three detectives came racing down the street. Loot lay scattered in wild confusion as the entry emptied like magic. We raced up the narrow passageway, shot out at the top and straight into a milling crowd making its way to the meeting. There wasn't a uniformed policeman in sight. Seconds later we were part of a mad gyrating throng pushing and shoving its way towards the Park Entrance. *Then* we saw the police. Scores of them. Chin straps tight, batons drawn, anxiously watching the speakers as they whipped the crowd into a frenzy. I spotted a familiar face.

"There's that bloke who evicted Mr Rolf," I yelled to the lads.

Heads turned as I pointed at the red-faced, irate-looking sergeant. At once a yell went up from those nearest.

"Get the sod! Gerr'im!"

I went white with shock as the crowd surged about me. Henry glared at me reproachfully.

"Y' mighta waited 'til we got somewhere safe," he yelled. There was no time to answer him as tempers flared.

"Over t' the lavatory!" yelled Dinny from a few feet away. I looked round desperately to see how far away we were from the public convenience to the left of the park entrance.

"See y'!" I screeched back, crashing my way out of the press, then racing round the fringe to safety. We just made it. Gasping for breath we helped each other up the side and on to the flat roof.

It was a fantastic sight. Amid tremendous noise, Jimmy and half a dozen other speakers harangued the crowd.

"Y' wanna see it round Ermine Street," gasped Dinny, rubbing his knee where he had scraped it on the wall. " 'alf the winders is broke, an' people's pinchin' stuff all over the place."

"You're kiddin'," I said shortly as another roar swelled from the crowd. "I saw y' Dad with a load of stuff round your 'ouse."

Dinny grinned broadly. "There's no flies on me Dad when it comes t' gerrin' somethin' f' nothin'," he answered.

I felt a tug at my shoulder. It was Tommy Rolf. "There's y' Dad, Li," he shouted in my ear. I looked and spotted Dad. His dark, hawk-like face was alive with anger. Alongside him, Uncle Mick shook his fist high in the air.

"Are we gonna starve?" he yelled.

"*No!*," roared back the crowd.

I don't know what Uncle Mick was talking about. He had a good job aboard ship. I hid behind Dinny in case Dad saw me. I needn't have bothered. Sniffer suddenly screeched in delight.

"Luk at that!" he screamed pointing to a huge car showroom on the far side of the square. "Jus' luk at that."

We turned in a body and caught a fleeting glimpse of the

sergeant, held high in the air by a dozen pairs of hands, his mouth opening and shutting silently. Seconds later there was a tremendous crash as they hurled him bodily through the window. For a split second there was a strange hushed silence.

"Jesus!" gasped Tommy, white-faced. His words had scarcely formed when the police charged. The noise redoubled. Hate filled the air. I looked frantically for Dad. There was no sign of him in the milling crowd. An exultant mixture of terror and excitement gripped me. I found myself dancing like a dervish, yelling until the cords of my throat were raw.

Years of frustration and humiliation had erupted in a wild orgy of fighting. Missiles thickened as the crowd went berserk. Reinforcements appeared like magic from side streets to face the maddened crowd.

"Christ!" yelled Sniffer with a note of panic in his voice. "What a bloody place t' pick, Li." I agreed with him and cursed myself. It was like a treeless island in a storm lashed sea. Suddenly the railings on either side of the convenience began to sway. I looked down. A score of rioters were tugging frantically at them. I thought they had gone mad, but they hadn't. They were after ammunition. We stood rooted with shock as the spear-like railings came out of the ground and went hurtling into the ranks of the police. A constable went down as though he had been pole-axed. The crowd hacked at the inert form with their feet. His comrades circled him like blue devils, scything the air with their batons.

Then there was a new diversion. A great roar hit the street like a solid wall.

"The Queen's is gone!"

We looked across at the public house across the square. Every window on the ground floor had gone. Scores of men struggled in the doorways, others clambered through the broken windows to get at the stock.

I felt a vice-like grip on my shoulder. A wild scream left my lips as I teetered on the edge of the roof, then another hand grasped and steadied me. It was Tommy, blood pouring down on to his bare foot from a wound in the leg.

I bent to look at it, then straightened with shock as another scream blasted down my ear. Sniffer had caught a brick right in the small of his back and rolled in agony on the concrete roof.

"Let's get t' 'ell outa 'ere!" I yelled.

The fighting had shifted over to the pub. It was now or never. Between us we got Tommy and Sniffer to the ground, and edged along the fringe of the fighting to a quiet back street.

"Cor bloody Norah!" exclaimed Henry in one of his rare outbursts. "This is a day an' a 'alf this is. Let's git." We got, to our house. It was locked. I daren't go to Bernadette's until I had cleaned up. We all went to Dinny's instead.

It was like Christmas when we arrived, except that there was more food about. They had more groceries than the grocer's. Bread, sausages, meat, black puddings, sweets, boots and clothes lay in wild confusion, and in the centre, drunk as a lord, Mr Devlin played his accordion. I stayed with them, through a very restless night. Nobody slept, and about one a.m. the door knocker rattled harshly.

"The Jacks!" yelled Mr Devlin drunkenly. The whole house became a kaleidoscope of frantic activity as we tried to hide the loot. Footsteps raced up and down the stairs, kids squealed in a mixture of fear and excitement, advice flew like hail as we sought hiding places, in the cock loft, behind the Sacred Heart picture, in the lavatory. Everywhere bulged with ill-gotten gains. It wasn't the Jacks. Devlin swore like a maniac while Mrs Devlin held her sides with laughter on their solitary chair.

Well before dawn the kids were out swanking with their new boots. I staggered out, bleary-eyed. The whole street had a cock-eyed look, nearly every window had been smashed where the police had swept through in a series of baton charges. Con was in when I got home. He took one look at me and stuck me under the tap.

"Y' bloody idiot!" he yelled as he scrubbed me. "Why the 'ell didn't y' come 'ome. I've searched the town for y'."

"I was in Dinny's," I protested, spitting soap from my mouth. "Me Mam said I could stay with 'em."

He shook me like a rat. "Well, she didn't tell me," he snarled as he threw a towel at me. " 'ere, dry y' face," he snapped as he slammed the kettle on the stove. I watched him furtively as I dried my face. He looked worried sick.

"Where's me Dad an' Uncle Mick?" he asked suddenly.

"Last time I saw 'em they were with Jimmy fightin' on the Park Entrance ... 'ave you bin in the fightin'?"

He gave me a disgusted look. "Don't be so damned daft," he snapped.

"Well," I said proudly, lifting my boot up to show him, "I gorra new pair'f boots outa it anyway."

His eyes popped. "Gerr'em off!" he roared. "If me Mam catches y' with them on, she'll kill y'." I protested vigorously. "Gerr'em off!" he shouted again. "The Jacks'll be round lukin' f' loot as soon as it's light. Take 'em off an' throw 'em in the entry."

Reluctantly I took them off and gazed at them longingly.

"Go on," he said menacingly. "Stolen things is no good to anybody." I flung them over the wall from the back door. He grunted in satisfaction and thrust a piece of bread and dripping into my hand. "Now get that down y', then get round t' Bernadette's before y' go t' school. Tell Mam I'm stayin' at Uncle Tom's 'til this lot's over."

I went to see Mam, but I didn't go to school, neither did the gang. There was far too much excitement about. She was livid when I told her about Dad and Uncle Mick.

"The idjits," she shouted. "If their brains were made'f gun powder, it wouldn't blow their bloody 'ats off." I remained silent. Aunt Min fussed round the tiny apartment.

"Honest," said Mam as she smoothed the blankets round my sister, "it's like livin' in a flamin' mad'ouse. Go on," she said turning to me, "get t' school, an' if y' see any of 'em tell 'em t' come 'ere." I nodded, raced along the landing of the tenement, down the stairs, and out into the unquiet streets near the Town Hall. Sporadic fighting took place all the way as police chased looters.

Behind the barricades at the Town Hall, busloads of police waited for the next major flare-up.

The day passed quickly. Twice the gang was ordered off

the streets by the police, and twice we slipped round the nearest entry and back again. By six o'clock I was back at the tenement according to Mam's instructions. Bernadette was very close to her time. At ten past six I was dozing fitfully on the floor just inside the door. Mam was pacing impatiently up and down and Aunt Min had just come out of my sister's room when Mrs Taylor burst into the room. For a moment or two she leaned against the settee, gasping after her rapid climb up the stairs. I was wide awake in an instant.

"Mother'f God what's up?" cried Mam.

Mrs Taylor waved her away as she steadied her breath. "Your Con's gorrit!" she gasped.

Mam clutched her breast in alarm. Aunt Min made the sign of the cross, opened her mouth to speak, then turned as Bernadette shouted in pain. Mam was suddenly dead calm.

"Is 'e 'urt bad?" she asked in a flat voice.

" 'e's unconscious," replied Mrs Taylor laconically as she sank on to the settee.

Tears sprang to my eyes. It was sheer irony. Con, the quietest in the family, batoned.

"Where is 'e?" asked Mam, in a business-like tone as she reached for her shawl. Mrs Taylor put her hand on her arm.

"I wouldn't go out there if I were you, Mary. 'e'll be all right, 'e's in the priest's 'ouse."

Mam let her shawl drag on the ground. " 'ow did it 'appen?"

Mrs Taylor shook her head. "Dunno," she answered. "They found 'im lyin' outside the church. There'd bin lootin'. The police were 'ittin' anybody in sight."

"The bastards!" grunted Mam as Aunt Min popped her head round the door. "What's up *now*," snapped her sister irritably.

Aunt Min flicked her head towards the room. "She's worried. She wants t' know what's goin' on. She wants Jimmy."

"Well, she'll 'ave t' bloodywell want, won't she? ... She

knows damn well 'e's a marked man, if 'e comes 'ere, they'll 'ave 'im. Jus' shut 'er up, I'm gonna see Con."

She turned her drawn anxious face to me.

"Go an' find y' Dad an' tell 'im what's 'appened," she snapped. I felt dog tired. I wanted to sleep.

"Where will I find 'im?" I protested.

"Go'n luk!" she cried. "An' make sure y' back before dark. There's gonna be trouble."

I had a stroke of luck. All three were at home, bruised and battered, but defiant. Uncle Mick's eyes were shining as I walked in.

"Jus' wait 'til t'night," he was saying to Dad. "Jus' you wait, if they ... Oh, hello Li, where've you bin?" I told him then turned to Dad.

" 'ow's Bernadette?" asked Jimmy.

"Me Mam an' Aunt Min's with 'er," I answered. "Mam says she's gerr'in close, wharrever that means."

They grinned at each other. Dad patted Jimmy on the shoulder. "Don't worry, lad," he said encouragingly. "Mary knows what she's doin'; she'll be all right."

"Me Mam told me t' tell y' that our Con's been batoned," I broke in flatly. Dad straightened as though I had slapped him. He stared at me disbelievingly as the others shot to their feet.

"Y' what!?" he cried, white-faced. I repeated the message. He went off like a bomb. Uncle Mick calmed him. "When?" he hissed viciously, taking me by the shoulders. "Where? ... is 'e badly 'urt?"

I felt bemused by the battery of questions, and stammered out the story as far as I knew it. Uncle Mick went purple with anger. For two full minutes Dad raged round the room swearing, threatening and punching his fist into the palm of his hand. Suddenly he stopped dead, picked up his torn shirt from the back of a chair, and slung it on.

"Come on, Mick," he said in icy tones. "Let's go'n see 'im, then some bastard's gonna pay for it."

All three were gone before I could say a word. I went back to Mam and hoped I'd get something to eat.

By eight o'clock Bernadette was in labour. Outside the

district rocked. Mam and Aunt Min cast worried glances at each other.

"I wish Mrs Taylor was 'ere," said Mam at last. "We can't leave 'er, an' as sure as 'ell the baby'll be 'ere t'night."

" 'ow the divil are we gonna get the midwife with this lot goin' on?" asked Aunt Min.

"She'll 'ave t' come," snapped Mam. "It's gonna be an awkward one." I looked at them uncomprehendingly. I didn't understand what they were talking about, but I knew they were very worried.

Outside the noise mounted steadily, running feet, shouts, bangs, and the sound of breaking glass blasted through the open window. Mam suddenly got irritable.

"Shut that flamin' winder, Minny, will y', it's enough t' damn well deafen y'."

Aunt Min waddled to the window and shut it. She flicked a finger at me. "D'y' think it's safe t' send 'im?"

I pricked my ears up. I knew where the nurse lived but I didn't relish going out. I sighed with relief as Mam shook her head.

"Can't send 'im out in that," she said emphatically. "Not after Con."

For another uneasy hour I alternated between sleep and wakefulness. The noise outside worsened rather than eased. Suddenly Bernadette shrieked. My hair stood on end as Mam and Aunt Min dashed into the bedroom. Seconds later Mam returned.

"Get the nurse, quick!" she ordered. I felt a shiver of fear. "You'll '*ave* t' go," she cried as I hesitated. "Go down the entries. Be careful, but 'urry up. Tell 'er it's urgent. Go on, now git!"

I slipped my jersey on and dashed out of the room, every sense alert to danger. Broken glass lay everywhere. I wished Con hadn't made me throw the boots away. The night was full of flashing lights, furtive figures and the shrill blare of police whistles. Grids had been opened to trap unwary police as they charged and twice I nearly fell down one. It took a full half hour to cover the quarter of a mile. My greeting was frigid as Nurse McKay opened the door the merest fraction.

" 'oo are y'?" she snapped irately.

"Liam Sullivan. Me Mam says you've gorra come. Our Bernadette's close she says."

Nurse McKay had hardened considerably since the night they dragged her from a dance to deliver me. I heard her snort disgustedly.

"Sullivan! I mighta bloodywell known she'd pick a time like this," she rasped. "All right, 'ang on a minute," she added irritably.

The journey back was almost as bad. When we arrived a solid mass of jeering people blocked one end of the street.

"It's Nurse McKay!" she roared. "Let me through." The locals recognised her voice immediately. On all side voices urged one another to let her through. We slipped along the wall in the full glare of the headlights of a Black Maria drawn up at the other end of the street, and all the while, the crowd taunted the police, goading them to charge.

Moments later we were tearing up the stone steps, past the piles of bricks, bottles and bits of old iron stacked ready for a siege. Mam almost dragged us inside as the whistles shrieked below.

Nurse McKay looked at Mam solemnly.

"Peaceful sort of a night isn't it?" she said sarcastically.

"Aye," answered Mam, as I dashed to the window. "An' it's gonna get a helluva lot more peaceful by the sound of it."

Below was a blaze of light. I gasped in surprise. The police had turned the tables completely. Now I knew why they hadn't charged. They had been waiting for the reinforcements now at the other end of the street and now hemming the crowd between them. I watched breathlessly as the helmeted silhouettes advanced in line, dodging every kind of missile from the windows above.

The whole scene was etched in the stark shafts of light from the vans. The mob was trapped. Suddenly a familiar, threatening figure darted out of the crowd, waving his fists and shouting defiance.

"There's Uncle Mick!" I yelled.

There was a concerted rush for the window. It was him all right. Shirt in ribbons, hair tangled, throwing bricks as fast as he could go. Dad and Jimmy joined him as we watched. We opened the window as the vans crashed into gear and slowly advanced, squeezing the mob tighter and tighter. There was an impatient snort above me.

"I can't stand 'ere all bloody night watching those silly sods," snapped Nurse McKay, "I've got work t' do."

Suddenly Aunt Min screamed. "Luk, luk!" she shouted, pointing downwards.

We were a fraction too late. Whistles shrieked a signal. The blue lines charged and the rioters broke and spilled into a dozen different openings. Feet pounded on the steps. Harsh grating voices cursed as people raced along the landing outside. Nurse McKay dashed into Bernadette's room.

"Don't lerr'anyone in!" she roared above the tumult. "Bar the door, I think she's started."

"Cin y' see Mick?" shouted Aunt Min, quivering with excitement as the door shuddered with crashing bodies.

"T' 'ell with Mick!" yelled Mam. "Bernadette's started. Bar the door." Aunt Min didn't hear her. Mam strode across the room, grasped her by the shoulder and yanked. "*Minny!*" she roared down her ear. "Come away from there. Bar the bloody door, quick."

I had a fleeting glimpse of police battling their way into the tenement before Mam flung me to one side.

"Stay there," she snarled. "One move an' I'll slit y' flamin' throat."

I crouched near the bedroom door, Bernadette's sharp cries punctuating my racing thoughts. Mam and Aunt Min began dragging the settee across the door. Aunt Min gasped from her exertions. Suddenly there was a piercing cry from Bernadette's room. Mam dropped her end of the settee and dashed in. Aunt Min sank gratefully on to it.

"T' 'ell with it," she gasped. "If they wanna break in lerr'em." She had barely settled when there was a tremendous crash behind her. She left her seat like a rocket as the door burst open and Uncle Mick, Dad and Jimmy tumbled into the room in a heap. Mam and Nurse McKay hurtled out, hair awry, eyes popping.

"Jesus, Mary an' Joseph," yelled Mam. "What a bloody time t' come 'ome."

"Shut the door!" yelled Uncle Mick, as I danced round in a fever of excitement. "F' Christ's sake, shut the door, they're right be'ind us."

" 'oo? " shouted Aunt Min hysterically.

"The police!" yelled Dad, "we've gorra 'ide."

"Where the 'ell cin we 'ide y' 'ere?" shouted Mam irritably. "There's nowhere t' 'ide ... Go on, gerrout. Bernadette's started."

Jimmy made a dash for the bedroom. Nurse McKay stood in the doorway, square and determined.

"Gerrout," she shouted above the appalling noise. "If she survives this lot it'll be a bloody miracle, go on, gerrout."

"They're after them two," cried Uncle Mick agitatedly. " 'ide 'em or they'll be inside."

"*Thoughtless* all of y'!" roared Mam. "Thou...."

"Oh shurrup," shouted Dad gazing frantically around the room. "Jus' 'ide. ..."

There was a thunderous knocking at the door. Uncle Mick gazed wildly around for a place to hide them.

"Come on, Sullivan! We know you're in there," shouted an angry voice.

Sheer frenzy took over and everything seemed to happen at once.

"In there!" hissed Uncle Mick in a strangled whisper. He pointed to the bedroom. Dad and Jimmy swept the nurse out of the way and dived under the bed. Mam threw a shirt to Uncle Mick.

"Get that on y," she cried. He grinned as the door shuddered.

"Come on, Sullivan, or we'll come in an' fetch y'."

Aunt Min subsided on the settee and began to titter. Mam looked daggers at her as she swept the nurse before her into Bernadette's bedroom. My sister screamed in pain as the baby started its journey. I sat in petrified silence on the far side of the room. Uncle Mick glanced round quickly. Everybody that mattered was out of sight. He winked at Aunt Min.

" 'ave y' no souls out there?" he shouted suddenly. She gazed at him in astonishment, then held her face in her hands laughing. "Me wife's 'avin' a baby. Why the 'ell don't y' go 'way an' give us a bitta peace?" There was an ironic laugh from the other side of the door.

"Come off it. We've 'eard that one before ... open up."

Mam poked a worried face round the door.

"Bloody 'eathens!" he roared back. "I'm tellin' y' the truth. If anythin' 'appens to 'er it'll be your fault, I'm warnin' y'."

"Shut up an' open up," came the peremptory reply.

"All right," cried Uncle Mick, smoothing his ruffled hair into place, "but I'll 'ave y' for this night's work me buckos." He slipped the bolt. A constable and a sergeant shouldered their way in. They were part of the reinforcements from Liverpool. Uncle Mick barred their path. "Y' ought t' be bloodywell ashamed of y'selves," he snapped indignantly.

"We're after Sullivan an' Kiernan," retorted the sergeant. "We were told they were 'ere." He moved to push his way further into the room. Uncle Mick stepped in front of him.

"Y' comin' no further," he snapped. "Me wife's 'avin' a baby. The nurse is in there with 'er now."

They looked at him cynically. "All right, mate," continued Uncle Mick, "if y' don't believe me, 'ave a luk f' y'selves."

They did. Seconds later, I heard Nurse McKay's voice yelling at them. They turned, red-faced and crestfallen. The sergeant began to stammer an apology. Uncle Mick drew himself up impressively.

"Away with yiz, an' leave peaceful people t' their business. Believe me," he added as a parting shot, "the Chief Constable will 'ear about this!"

The door closed behind them, and into the uproar came a new cry. Mam dashed from the bedroom in delight.

"Thanks be t' God, it's arrived," she said. Instantly the room was filled with laughter as the fugitives came from beneath the bed. Nurse McKay came out and leaned against the door exhausted.

"Next time she 'as one, Mary," she said sarcastically, "try an' arrange it more peaceful will y' ... I'm gerrin too old f' this game!"

Epilogue

For three more days the poorer quarters of the town rocked to insurrection. The unemployed got their three shillings, but oh at what cost in mutual hatred. The fruits of the seeds then sown, are being reaped as I write, but the true cost is as yet unknown.

For us, the children, it was not only the end of the riots, but the end of a turbulent childhood. In less than eighteen months, we would, with no skills, litte learning, and no prospects be part of the adult destitution around us. Already we were debris for the economic scrap heap. ... God help us!

* * *

Statement by the Mayor of Birkenhead, September 1932:

'The only thing that can be said, is that one is pleased to see wisdom has prevailed, and the public are now settling down. I feel confident that members of the council will do everything in their power to do right by the unemployed and put into operation as many work schemes as possible during the coming winter.'

* * *

P.S. What a tragedy that men should have been brought

almost to the level of animals before such wisdom prevailed.

The Author.